THE
BLINDSPOT

Praise for *She and I*

'Not only beautifully written but gripping and full of soul'
Sarah Pearse, author of *The Sanatorium*

'A nifty fusion of psychological thriller and police procedural'
Sunday Times

'A taut and unrelenting mystery, expertly woven with the
bruising drama of girlhood'
Anna Bailey, author of *Tall Bones*

'Gripping. Thoughtful. Lyrical… It's got all the right shades of
Tana French. This writer is going places'
Imran Mahmood, author of *You Don't Know Me*

'King really understands suspense'
Holly Watt, author of *To the Lions*

'A heart-racing, addictive read'
Woman's Own

'*She and I* is a stunning portrait of claustrophobic teenage friendship
that races to a haunting conclusion. A powerful and moving
debut – King is one to watch'
Heather Critchlow, author of *Unspoken*

'*She and I* is a stunning debut from Hannah King. [With] complicated
and deep characters and a strong sense of place, this is a rich,
atmospheric and highly addictive suspense novel'
S V Leonard, author of *The Islanders and The Influencers*

———————

ALSO BY HANNAH KING

She and I

THE
BLINDSPOT

HANNAH KING

NO EXIT PRESS

First published in the UK in 2025 by No Exit Press,
an imprint of Bedford Square Publishers Ltd,
London, UK

noexit.co.uk
@noexitpress
info@bedfordsquarepublishers.co.uk

ISBN
978-1-83501-169-0 (Hardback)
978-1-83501-170-6 (Trade Paperback)
978-1-83501-171-3 (eBook)

2 4 6 8 10 9 7 5 3 1

Typeset in 12 on 15.8pt Garamond MT Pro
by Avocet Typeset, Bideford, Devon, EX39 2BP
Printed and bound in Great Britain by
CPI Group (UK) Ltd, Croydon CR0 4YY

MIX
Paper | Supporting
responsible forestry
FSC
www.fsc.org   FSC® C171272

The manufacturer's authorised representative in the EU for product safety is
Easy Access System Europe, Mustamäe tee 50, 10621 Tallinn, Estonia
gpsr.requests@easproject.com

Upon this beach the falling wall of the sea,
Explodes its drunken marble
Amid gulls' gaiety.

Which ever-crumbling masonry, cancelling sum,
No one by any device can represent
In any medium.

Turn therefore inland, tripper, foot on the sea-holly,
Forget those waves' monstrous fatuity
And boarding bus be jolly.

Louis MacNeice, *Upon This Beach*

PROLOGUE

There is sand in his shoes – so much fucking sand. Even though he's running, quickly, quickly, not pausing for breath, he can feel every grain. His trainers are new: tonight is the first night he has worn them. Bright white with the very thick soles he knows his family hates. That hadn't stopped them buying them for him, handing the shoebox over with five beams and a card. Well, four beams. Ciarán was at work, but he'd texted to say Happy Birthday all the same. He knew his sister had picked the shoes. And probably wrapped them. And he knew from the handwriting that she'd written the card too, even though she'd given him another card, just from her. And now the shoes are scuffed and covered in sand a week later.

So what? he thinks. He hopes they're ruined; he doesn't deserve nice things.

Vetobridge is quiet at this time of night, and he passes nobody as he runs. His T-shirt is sticking to him in the residual warmth of the June night and his long shorts – shorts the others had laughed at, actually *pointed* and laughed at – have some sort of stain below the pocket. Good, that's a reason to throw them in the bin. He'd thought they were all right, really, but apparently not. Apparently, they were literally laughable. He'll tell his sister they got stained and had to go.

It helps to think of these things, of these little unimportances.

When he's been running for ten, fifteen, maybe even thirty minutes, he stops. He doesn't have his inhaler – he wouldn't dream of bringing that on a night out, not in a million years. He'd rather die of an asthma attack. He puts a hand on the brick wall to his left and doubles over, panting. He read somewhere that it helps to bend at the waist when you're out of puff. They tell footballers to stand straight with their hands on their heads but apparently that's bollocks. They did research into it. He loves reading research.

He wishes he wore a watch. He has a sudden, itching desire to know what time it is. When did he leave the housewarming party? When did he start running? The bit in between those bits, the bit that changed everything, he'll think about later. Not now.

He looks around him. His eyes, which had focused only on the roads and pavements in front of him on his run, blink to adjust. The streetlights are still on, and there's no hint of a sunrise. It's rising earlier and earlier, lately. Sometimes on a Saturday night, after her shift, his sister tells him she is driving home to the most gorgeous sunrises. She takes photos and shows him on Sunday afternoons when she gets out of bed. Really, he only gets out of bed then too. He waits until he hears her up, hears the whir of the extractor fan in the bathroom, the smell of her shampoo wafting next door to his bedroom, and then he throws something on him and goes downstairs to make her a coffee. Their Sunday morning routine, lately. Or it was, until last week. Beautiful sunrises. Early sunrises.

In fact… He thinks carefully for a moment.

Yes, today is the longest day of the year. Or it will be, once it gets started. So the sun will rise, when? Before five, he thinks. So it's definitely not five yet.

He's lived in Vetobridge, County Down, his entire life. Eighteen years and one week, to be exact. But he's not sure he recognises where exactly he is. Every doorway is a shadow, and every corner looks like a black hole. He's a bit dizzy, now that he thinks about it. Maybe the inhaler wouldn't have been the worst idea in the world. He steadies his breathing and tries to focus on where he is.

He lives at the bottom of the town, in a tiny terrace, and you have to walk down one mini main street, as his dad calls it, to get to the bottom of the hill that you then have to walk up if you want to visit the *main* main street. The roads are all cobbled and old-fashioned, and it's shit on his new car. He gets that little frisson of joy again when he thinks of it. *His* new car. A car all for himself. A ticket to – well, to anywhere.

The Blindspot

This isn't the bottom of the town. What does that sign over there say? He squints. He isn't wearing his glasses because he doesn't wear them on nights out. Or in any classes he's in with the other boys. Or, really, at any time, unless he's at home. They just don't suit him. He knows that. No matter what anyone says, he knows they don't suit him. So usually he just squints.

He goes closer.

The sign reads: *Wits End*

Ah! He knows where he is now. He's covered more ground than he thought. He's far enough away from his house, from his sister's new house, from the beach… This will do.

Someone got murdered here a few years back. Some influencer or something? He can't remember the details, doesn't like social media. Doesn't understand it, really, which is rare because he understands most things.

He takes the phone from the pocket of his ugly, awful shorts. He turned it off before he started running properly. He's seen on TV the police can ping you off phone towers, that nothing that gets deleted off a phone is ever *really* deleted. That's why he decided, without thinking about it properly, without pausing to consider, that he should probably just get rid of it entirely.

Thinking about sunrises, about his glasses, about the taunts of his classmates, he has managed to forget. For about two minutes. He's distracted himself well.

Now, he thinks of nothing else.

There's a drain grate just up ahead, the worn metal glinting under a streetlight, a pool of shine on the otherwise pitch-black island of road.

He pushes the phone between two bars and waits until he hears the *plop* when it hits the bottom. Then he takes the other phone and does the same thing, for good measure. It doesn't make the sound – or at least, if it does, he missed it.

He leans down further, willing his eyes to focus, to adjust to the darkness inside the grate. Did it drop? He definitely didn't hear it hit the bottom. Could it be stuck?

He leans so his nose is almost touching the dirty bars of the drain grate… Yes, he thinks maybe he can see the phone. A slightly lighter shape against the darkness. Only a few inches below him, the screen facing down, the phone has landed on a tiny ledge of sorts.

Fuck, fuck, fuck, fuck, fuck.

Come to think of it… he doesn't even know which phone this is. They're the same model, the same colour. Which phone is it? Which one dropped and which hit the bottom?

Does it matter? Is this a foolproof hiding place?

Then he looks around again.

The housing estate is completely in darkness. Too early even for the Dublin commuters. There's a Spar garage up ahead – not the one he works at, a different one – but it'll be closed. It'll be safe to pass it. If he goes this way, it'll take a bit longer as he'll be coming right around the outskirts of the town, over country roads, only to go down the hill to home, but that's fine. It gives him another half hour to sort himself out, just in case anyone is awake when he gets back. He is just about to take a look for a stick, something he can push into the drain to move the phone off its ledge, when an engine roars around the corner. It's one of those huge lorries, the driver high up and invisible behind its powerful lights.

He stands and moves quickly away from the drain, keen not to be spotted crouching over it. He turns his face to the side as if interested in something in the trees.

The driver dims his beam as he passes him, and is gone in a whir of sound.

For some reason, he finds he is panting again, his mouth a little bit open.

The driver dimmed his lights so he didn't blind him… so the driver *saw* him. It's too late, too impossible, to get either of the phones back out of the drain and put them somewhere else. He has no choice but to go on.

It'll be someone transporting milk or Guinness or potatoes from one side of the country to the other, he thinks. It's not as though it was a Vetobridgian who would be able to recognise him.

The Blindspot

The thought steadies him somewhat, and he starts to head towards home, walking this time, the sand in his shoes and the pain in his heart making him feel heavy, heavy, heavy.

He passes the garage.

The glaring price of diesel lights up the night.

1

The Accused

The front door of my dad's house is almost never locked and this morning is no exception. It used to bother me, when I was younger and full of outward worries about burglaries and masked men. Now that all of my worries are closer, internalised and more realistic, I don't really think about it. Besides, my brother Ciarán reasoned with me after he moved out, there's usually at least one person in the house.

I'm not sure how that was supposed to make me feel better, the thought of my dad or one of my brothers or me having to *deal* with said masked men, but in a strange way it worked.

I use one elbow to push the handle, keeping the little tray of coffees straight in my hands.

'Morning?' I call softly to announce my presence.

My guess is that Dad and Jordan will be up, Dad cooking himself a fry and Jordan weighing his oats and cutting up fruit to go with it. Decky will still be in bed at this time – ten o'clock on a day off – and Jack... Well, I'm not sure about Jack.

'Hi, love!' Dad calls from the kitchen. 'Come on through. How'dya get on? Last night good?'

I have to gently kick some trainers – Decky's – out of my way to go through the tiny hall to the kitchen. The carpet needs hoovering, I notice. Jordan must have been working long hours not to have noticed that.

The kitchen smells like burnt bacon and tobacco. As revolting a combination as ever, but if I don't think about it I can almost tell myself I don't notice it.

There they are, one third of my family, exactly as I'd known they would be.

Jordan looks up at me and beams before his perfect white teeth clamp around a spoon of oats and raspberries. He is dressed for work, in a tracksuit bearing the logo of the local leisure centre. None of the dominant smells in the room come from him. Indeed, when I sweep past his usual place at the tiny table to get to Dad, I catch a whiff of his expensive aftershave. It's the one I first bought for him about ten Christmases ago, that I now associate with my second brother and his obsessive need to be clean and presentable. He's learned now, by the ripe old age of thirty-one, not to put so much hair gel in, so he looks better than he ever has.

Dad is pushing two rashers of bacon around in a very greasy pan. I just hope it was clean when he started. The splashback is covered with droplets of oil or fat, and I have to hold my breath as I go near him. He is holding a cigarette in his free hand, but is dutifully blowing smoke towards the open window from the side of his mouth. He used to just let the kitchen fill with smoke when we were younger, until I told him the other children would make fun of us for coming to school smelling like five little ashtrays, so this is his gracious solution to that problem.

'I brought coffees,' I say, holding them out in front of me. I take another breath and lean in to kiss Dad's cheek. 'And yeah, last night went well!'

'Do you know what coffee does to your insides?' Jordan asks with pursed lips, even while he lifts one from the tray.

'No, but I'm sure you'll tell me if I ask.'

Dad laughs and takes his coffee too. 'Thanks, lovely. I'm surprised you're up so early; I wouldda thought you'd be nursin' a wee hangover. Was it not a late one?'

'No, Daddy.'

I have to lift a heap of post, a water bottle – that Jordan promptly snatches – and three mobile phones, each with their back covers taken off, and place them on the floor so I can set the tray on the table. Decky takes apart and repairs phones for fun. Really.

'I sent them all home about one,' I continue, taking the lid from my own coffee and blowing on it. 'I was all partied out. You should have come down, both of you.'

'Work this morning,' Jordan murmurs. 'And a weigh-in tomorrow. Alcohol stays in your system for three full days after consumption, bloats you.'

Dad angles his body so he can roll his eyes at me, as if Jordan is ridiculous. 'Your sister works hard,' he tells Jordan. He switches the oven off at the wall, which makes me happy as he has been known to forget. He plates up his bacon, grabs a loaf of bread and comes to sit next to me. 'She deserves a wee treat now and then.' Then, to me, 'I didn't want to *cramp your style*, my love, otherwise I'd have been down like a shot. Did Ciarán make it?'

Apparently, Dad spent the first years of my eldest brother's life correcting people on the pronunciation of his son's name. He'd emphasise the fada, insisting his son was *Keeer-awwwwn*. By the time Ciarán got to primary school, though, he was introducing himself as Keer-in, and it stuck because it was easier. Dad's the worst for shortening it now, to him he's just Keern.

'He didn't bother,' I say.

'How did you manage to continue the night without him?' Jordan asks sarcastically.

We smile at each other, and Jordan goes to clean his bowl in the sink.

'Decky came after work,' I say.

'Get himself a bird?' Dad asks, mouth full.

'*Women* are not something you *get*,' I say, only half-seriously, pushing him. 'He was there until the end, I think. Had a good enough time and a good few drinks.'

'That'll be why he's still in his pit on such a gorgeous morning,' Dad says.

'Aye, that's why.'

'What about Jack?'

I nod my head and sip at my coffee. It's from the new place up the road, exactly halfway between my new flat and Dad's house. It's seriously good; I can see myself becoming a regular.

'Jack came after Paul's party, just for a wee while at the end. I can't really remember. He said his last exam went well, though. It was maths yesterday.'

Dad nods enthusiastically, a sliver of bacon fat hanging out over his hairy chin. His eyes are dull, and if I'm not mistaken his skin looks greyer than it did when I saw him on Saturday. His checked shirt has a wee stain in the middle and I try to meet Jordan's eye so I can motion to him to wash it.

But Jordan is standing by the sink with his back to us, on his phone.

'Aye, maths!' Dad says. He swallows, continues to nod. 'Yes, he was saying. He said it went well.'

I can't imagine Dad would have known to ask about Jack's last A-Level, but he likes to pretend he's as interested in his education as I am.

'That's the main thing,' I say. 'That's him all done. No more school. Mad, isn't it? I just called up to get my last couple of boxes, thought I could use my day off to work on the flat. It's looking really well, Dad. Will you come up and see it now, after your breakfast, and help me put a shelf up?'

'Of course I will, love. Here, it was good of Aul Norm to swap shifts with you yesterday. He was tellin' me last time I was in that he's not cut out for any evenings at all now. Says he's for bed at nine this weather. Just covered you last night as a wee favour.'

'Sure, I'm good to him too. We're the dream team.'

'What age would Norman Waltz be now?' Jordan asks.

Dad thinks hard, one hand rubbing his cheek. 'Now let me see… We had his fortieth the year Ciarán was born. No, Jordan. No, it was Decky. I remember now. So that wouldda been…'

'Twenty-eight years ago,' I offer.

'Right! Must be near seventy now, then. He'll be for retiring soon. Looks well, though.'

My boss absolutely does not look well for nearly seventy, bless him. He looks like a corpse somebody pulled out of a river, and he has done since I was a child, but he has a heart of gold and he's one of my favourite people in the world.

Dad and I sip our coffees.

Jordan taps quickly on his phone.

'You on until seven tonight, Jordy?' I ask, to make conversation.

He turns towards me but continues to tap on his phone. 'Aye. Think I might head out after though.'

'Thought alcohol stayed in your system for three days?'

He glares at me. 'Going out doesn't have to mean drinking *alcohol*, my dear, deluded sister.'

'All right,' says Dad. 'Don't get your knickers in a twist.'

Jordan's eyes dart to Dad who innocently butters another piece of bread for himself. Since telling us all two years ago via the family WhatsApp chat that he was gay, Jordan sees slurs and insults where there aren't any. And sometimes he misses ones from Ciarán that are *definitely* there.

'Jack not up yet?' I ask. I look up towards the ceiling as though I'll be able to see him through it.

'I didn't even hear him come in,' Jordan says. 'I heard Decky and got up to tell him to be quiet. He was stomping about, pissed as anything. Some of us have work this morning, it's not all revelry and no responsibilities.'

'It is for a wee while if you've just done your last exam or you've moved into a new flat,' Dad says, in the most scolding voice he can manage. He was never a scolder. 'You went a wee bit mad when you were finished your exams, Jordy, or do you not remember?'

'Wait,' I say. 'You heard Decky come in? I assumed they would have left together. Did they not? Jack was with him, surely?'

Jordan shrugs. 'Nah. Just Deck. About… quarter past one or so?'

'So where was Jack?'

Jordan makes a point of throwing the last of his coffee into the sink. 'I am not my brother's keeper,' he says. He plucks his gym bag from the floor under his chair and swings it over his head. 'I think that's you.' He laughs at his own joke as he goes into the hall.

Confused, I stand and follow him, though I'm not sure where my interrogation is going.

There's no point asking Dad, who frequently forgets how many children he has, never mind knowing their whereabouts. It's not out of badness, he just loses track.

Jordan opens the front door and jumps back.

There is a woman standing there, her hand poised as though she was about to knock.

Jordan laughs, startled. 'Hi, sorry.'

'Jack Campbell?' The woman's voice is loud, clipped. She shows no sign of reciprocating Jordan's good-natured awkwardness.

I come closer so I'm standing next to Jordan, and I hear Dad's kitchen chair scrape back.

I will remember these things.

All these tiny details that I register before I allow my brain to see that she is holding up a formal-looking badge.

'No,' Jordan says slowly. 'No, I'm not Jack.'

'Is this Jack Campbell's residence?'

She's police. The police are at the door, asking for Jack.

The fact is drifting slowly, slowly, slowly, from my brain and through my body like sand in an egg timer.

Something's happened.

Jack never came home.

He's been in a car accident.

No, he would have had no need to get into a car after he left my housewarming party; I live ten minutes away.

Drugs.

Fucking drugs, I knew it would be drugs for one of them.

Just – it's awful but I think it anyway – not Jack. Not Jack.

Someone else.

Anyone else.

Even – no, it's too awful, I can't think it – a different brother.

'Yeah?' Jordan says in answer to the woman's question.

It's only now that I register the second officer behind her. This one is in uniform, hesitating on the road, not quite leaning on the car – the police car, unmarked but still obvious – that is parked right by the front door, but not making any attempt to come forward.

The terrace is quiet at this time on a Tuesday. The men have all gone out to work (and they are all men), and the women will be in town by now, getting the shopping. The terrace was a bit left behind when women were excelling in business and families were swapping around gender roles however they liked, and nobody ever thought to tell them. The families that live here are all almost exactly the same age as my dad, so any kids they had have all grown up and either moved away – though not far, never far – or stayed in their childhood bedrooms.

The policewoman doesn't look much older than me.

Maybe it's an end-of-year joke? I think hopefully. Organised by the school. Sending a police officer to the home of the Head Boy. That's funny.

'Has something happened?' I demand, finding my voice finally. It's stronger, louder than I thought it would be. 'Is Jack okay?'

She lets her brown eyes rest on me for only a second before she looks back to Jordan. She seems to think he's in charge. She's wrong.

'We need to chat with Mr Campbell about an incident that's been reported.'

Mr Campbell.

I nearly laugh.

My *dad* isn't even 'Mr Campbell'. Dad is just Pat, or Paddy or even sometimes Patrick if we're feeling affectionate. Jack, my baby brother, is not a Mr anything. He's just a child.

Though, technically, we did celebrate his eighteenth birthday last week.

19

There is a moment, as I glance away from the front door and up the stairs, that my eye falls on Jack's primary school photograph, framed and hung inexpertly by me when I was fifteen. He is missing a front tooth, but beams at the camera all the same. In my head, this is what he looks like still: a blond child, with hair that he didn't ever want cut, that grew curly and grew *up* instead of growing longer; grey-blue eyes that always looked like they were glinting; and a cheeky expression that never wavered. Beautiful, happy, serious only if he wanted to be, only if he wanted to get his own way. Perfect.

I look further up the stairs and see that a pair of bare feet have appeared at the top. Then some bare, muscular legs, then a pair of purple boxer shorts, and then my brother, Jack.

The same face, really, though he has all his teeth. The same perfect hair.

He is safe, is all I can think.

There's been a mistake at the door. They've come to the wrong address, or they've asked about the wrong brother.

At least Jack is here, in front of me and whole.

I try to smile at him, but something doesn't feel right.

Something in the air between us all is buzzing with something awful.

'What's going on?' His voice is a little hoarse. His eyes move from me to the strangers at the door and back. He clears his throat.

'Nothing to worry about,' I say. 'Just some mistake.'

He ambles down, rubbing at his eyes in an almost comically childlike way. His bare chest is on display. Not huge like Jordan's, because he doesn't put the same efforts in, and there's no hint of a beer belly like there is with Ciarán and Decky and Dad, but Jack is still big and taut. The few stray hairs on his chest you could count on one hand, the only thing tying him to the child I know he is. He isn't a Mr, I reason. He doesn't even have a hairy chest.

'Mr Jack Campbell?' the woman asks again. She sounds fed up, as though we're being deliberately awkward.

'Abi?' Jack asks, his eyes only on me. 'What's going on?' He is scared.

20

The Blindspot

Jordan and Dad are both talking, and the hallway is suddenly loud.

Dad is asking the woman why she's there, as loudly as he can, and making some comments about his land and his property. It's unlike him to get so agitated so quickly. Jordan is, unhelpfully, saying *what have you done?* over and over again to Jack. The woman is holding both her hands up and insisting that everyone listen to her, and the policeman has come forward and is trying to calm everyone down.

Jack and I stare at one another, and I can only see him.

What have you done?

Just need to speak to Jack—

... Come back with a warrant, I suggest

An incident, just to chat—

Tell us what it is and maybe

What have you done?

It's all white noise.

I stare at Jack and he stares at me. Again, he says, 'Abi?' as though I'll take him by the hand and lead him back to bed and pull the covers up to his chin and make it all go away. Maybe I will.

I go to him where he still stands on the stairs and I put one arm around him, ready to steer him away from the chaos that has nothing to do with us.

Then the policewoman's voice rises above everyone else's. 'Mr Jack Campbell, you're under arrest on suspicion of rape. You don't—'

My hand, which must have been sweating, slips away from Jack's skin in surprise.

Everyone else stops talking, but the policewoman carries on, saying words we've heard only on TV.

I wait for someone to laugh first so I can join in.

It's rising in my throat and then it comes out. A shrill, ridiculous laugh. Loud and echoey in the stuffy hall.

Jordan stares at me.

So does Dad.

And then the only person not looking at me is Jack.

21

2

The Baby

When my brother Jack was born, our mother died. Almost immediately, it seemed, and with a great sigh of relief. We all assumed, though we were young, that she'd been holding on for Jack and, once he was safely pushed through and in the hands of the midwives, she lay back on her pillow and slipped away quietly, not wanting to bother anyone. Never one for fuss.

That's the way we told it to each other, anyway. In reality I think there were about three days between Jack's birth and her official passing, but we've told the story to one another so much that it seems true. Besides, once Jack was here, she wasn't really properly alive ever again.

Ciarán, Jordan, Decky and me. The three boys had an almost perfect three-year age gap between each of them. All intended, all prayed for and waited for with crossed fingers and the odd hastily murmured Rosary. Thirteen months after Decky, though, they got their first and only daughter, me, and their family was accidentally but happily complete. Or so they thought.

We ambled on for nine years, the six of us, happy and poor in equal measure. Mum and Dad had bought the little terraced house in Pine Street when they only had Ciarán and when houses cost less than twenty grand. Dad worked for a landscaping company, and since he'd never learned to drive, his boss swung by to pick him up at eight o'clock every morning and dropped him off home again at six. Mum had worked in the corner shop part-time but gave it up when Ciarán was born. She decorated the Pine Street house just as she liked it, with a cream leather sofa and furry cushions that I remember from photographs, and they lived on the tiny wage Dad got from the landscapers and they were happy. They made the money stretch when Jordan was born, and Dad was proud as punch to have two sons.

When Declan was born (and he was born Declan, Decky only really came when he was in school), they stopped getting takeaways on Friday nights because the pennies wouldn't stretch, and when I showed up on his coattails soon after, Mum decided she'd have to stay in on a Saturday night to look after us all while Dad went to the pub. There wasn't enough money for the both of them to have their pints of beer and (if you believed Dad), she felt Dad deserved his more than she did, since he worked so hard cutting grass and trimming trees in the sun every day.

Two little ones running rings around the pool table in The Rooster, hyped up on Coke and crisps, raised no eyebrows. Everybody did it. What else were you supposed to do with your kids on a Saturday night? But with having to bring the double buggy in, with me and Decky, that was pushing it. So in actual fact *that* was why they put a stop to it, and instead of spending their Saturday evenings lining the pockets of Norman Waltz, the landlord, Dad nipped in for a few pints before dinner and was never home later than seven.

The first nine years of my life have a certain scent. Gravy and floor cleaner and a sweetness like you get from a bakery, though nobody in my house has ever baked.

Ciarán and I had new things, when we could, but poor Jordan and Decky spent their entire lives in hand-me-downs. We qualified for free milk at break time and free school lunches, and Mum would never have seen us without our dinner, but there was nothing spare, never anything extra, never seconds. We couldn't really attend birthday parties unless Mum was able to speak to the other parents and explain that we couldn't buy their child a present, and most of the time that was fine. People were kind, they understood. We could never have birthday parties of our own either, not big fancy ones like some of the girls in school did. They had horse riding parties, cinema parties, trips to the zoo and everything, but we couldn't afford that for the six of us, never mind a whole class-full.

That was fine with me. There was never anyone else I wanted to be with apart from my parents and my brothers.

Instead, on each of our birthdays Mum would buy a cake from the Windsor bakery, and she would inexpertly ice our names onto it. She liked to say if she iced it herself, it was homemade. One year she forgot Ciarán's 'n' and we all called him Ciara for weeks. Dad would bring home fish and chips that day, as a treat, and we would get one present each and a card that promised it was from the whole family. Usually the present was something we really needed, something useful that they would need to get us anyway. A new coat for me, quite a few years, as my birthday is in December. Ciarán had rollerblades that he'd got one year before I was born, and they were cleaned and shined and repaired three times, and given to each of us in turn as a present. Just as Jordan got bored of them, they were made as good as new for Decky's birthday, and then for my eighth birthday they were passed on to me. We didn't mind, and we didn't mention it. We were just happy.

When I was nine, Mum fell pregnant again. It was a surprise to them and it was a surprise to us, apparently. I think I just acted surprised even though I'd secretly hoped for a little sibling my entire life.

Ciarán was sixteen and was happy, Jordan was thirteen and seemed disgusted about it, and kept tutting and saying 'gross'. Decky and I, still not totally sure how babies were made, pressed our hands to Mum's belly and pretended we could feel the baby moving from the moment she told us. I wanted it to be a girl. I think I even prayed for it, even though I'd only ever prayed in school and never at home. If I had a little sister, I thought, I could dress her up and take her out in her buggy. I wouldn't be the youngest any more, I could take care of her and teach her to read and she'd be my best friend forever.

Mum hadn't been to the hospital since she'd had me. None of us had ever spent time in hospital – we were lucky and careful. No broken bones, no stupid accidents, no illnesses. Dad had a constant cough, but that was his smoking, and he seemed healthy enough apart from that.

They did tests on her, confirmed the pregnancy, and then discovered a lump on her breast that the doctors were baffled had not been noticed before.

Those last months of her life were unusual.

Ciarán was old enough to look after us, but he spent a lot of time outside the house with the love-of-his-life-forever girlfriend Claire, or smoking on street corners when he was supposed to be at home with us, while Mum and Dad were at the hospital. It seemed to my young mind that they lived at the hospital, then, and I can barely remember seeing Mum's belly grow. We still had to go to school, which was unfair because I was going to have a little sister soon *and* my mum was poorly on top of it, but nobody seemed to think those were good enough reasons reasons to stay at home.

Decky and I got excited over baby names and made cards for Mum suggesting our favourites and telling her what we were doing at school and all the things we would do when she was feeling better and we were a family of seven. Dad said he'd pass our cards on, but I remember finding one in his coat pocket a month after we'd made it, so I don't think he ever did.

Ciarán walked us to the primary school every morning, and though he said he'd meet us at the end of the day, he was often late or forgot entirely, so Decky and I would skip the mile back to our house, enjoying the lengthening days and the rise in temperature. We would pick flowers from one of the pensioners' gardens, and tie handmade bouquets together with string, intending to give them to Mum when we saw her, but the flowers always died before we got the chance. At one point, there were seven dead and rotting bouquets in my tiny box room, all lined up on my windowsill in a row of increasing decay and disappointment.

Finally, on the brightest day of the summer so far, when there were only two more weeks of school until the summer holidays, Dad came into my bedroom to wake me up.

The Blindspot

His eyes were red and watery, and he looked like he'd been sweating. He said it was time, and we were all going to the hospital that morning. We could forget about school, just for that day.

I wasn't sure why nobody spoke on the bus. We were getting a new baby sister, why was nobody excited? I looked at Decky, my first point of contact for most things, and even he was looking down at his trainers. Ciarán sat slouched in his seat, his arms folded, and Jordan was resting his forehead on the window. I glanced back at Dad and he tried to smile. When the bus paused at a traffic light, I got up and went to him and sat on his knee even though I was too big.

'Is the baby coming today?' I asked.

'Yes, love.' He took a look at his wristwatch. 'They'll be bringing Mummy in shortly. You'll need to wait in the wee family room for a while, and then I'll come and get you when he's here.'

'Who?' I asked, confused.

'The baby,' Dad said.

'The baby is a boy?'

'Yes, love.'

I was so disappointed that I slid off Dad's knee without another word and went back to Decky.

'The baby is a boy,' I muttered to him.

'Ha ha,' he taunted, sticking his tongue out. 'I told you.'

I decided I wouldn't like the baby. And I didn't really like Decky.

We waited for what felt like a week in the family room in the hospital.

At one point, driven to misbehaviour by boredom, the boys decided to take it in turns to throw the hospital-provided toys at the ceiling, to see who could rip one of the spongy tiles first. I sat with my head buried in an Enid Blyton book I'd borrowed from the school library, tutting at them. Twice, different nurses came in and shouted at us to be quiet, there were patients sleeping, recovering, trying to heal themselves, and they didn't need to listen to our nonsense.

The third time the door opened, it was Dad.

His eyes were even more watery, but he was smiling.

'The doctor says you've to take it in turns; but come and meet your new wee brother.'

Ciarán went first and took ages. He took so long that I took his place in the toy-throwing competition and won. Jordan went next and came back within two minutes, shrugging. Decky went and came back smiling, hand-in-hand with Dad.

'Your turn, Abi,' Dad said. 'Mum can't wait to see you.'

It was generally accepted that I was Dad's favourite and Ciarán was Mum's favourite, but I had felt something of a shift in Mum's affections towards me in the last few years. Ciarán was spending less and less time in the house, was shaking his head at everything and seemed to want to get away from us all the time. Mum had taken me under her wing a little bit, and had showed me how to clean the house at the weekends (something I, strangely, loved to do). She'd even let me help her prepare dinner a few times, though she didn't want me going near anything hot.

She didn't look like Mum, sitting up in the hospital bed.

In fact, she still looked pregnant, if the bump under the sheets was anything to go by.

I hesitated at the door, thinking she had fallen asleep, but she rolled her head slowly towards me and smiled.

'Hello, best girl.'

'Hello, best Mum.'

The baby wasn't on her chest, like it usually was on TV, but was lying in a tiny, clear box at the end of the bed. I tiptoed over to it and peered inside.

I'd expected a pink, nothing-y blob in a hat, but instead I saw a tiny version of my own face looking straight back at me. He only looked at me for a few seconds before he closed his eyes again. He had hair. Quite a lot of it, pale and fluffy, like a real person, and he was wearing a little nappy and had a white wristband on his wrist. I reached my little finger in and stroked his cheek. It felt like air.

'You take a seat and I'll let you hold him,' Dad whispered behind me. 'Go on.'

I did as I was told, and Dad carefully lifted the baby and set him on my knee. He showed me how to hold him behind his head. He was surprisingly heavy. A warm, comforting, heavy weight.

The baby opened his eyes and looked at me again, and I looked back, feeling myself smiling against my will.

Okay, maybe I would like him. Maybe he would be okay.

We looked at each other, and I matched my breathing to his. He wriggled a little, and his eyes closed.

'He likes you,' Dad said. He seemed unable to get his voice above a whisper, but I liked it. The room was humming with machines, and though I could hear the clatter of steps and voices outside the room, the door muffled it so well that it was like we were in our own little bubble inside. I wondered if Mum would let me feed him sometimes. I wondered if I could push him in the buggy to the park at the weekend. Maybe even that weekend.

'You'll look after him, won't you, my girl?' Mum murmured. She was smiling weakly, and even though her skin looked papery, she was beautiful. Her eyes, too, were starting to close. I wondered if this was due to some unseen baby/mother connection.

'I will,' I said, nodding at her. 'I will, Mum. What's his name?'

'Yes,' she said, already on the cusp of a smiling sleep. She hadn't heard me properly.

'What about...' I thought for a moment. Thought of the battered copy of *Secret Seven Mystery* tucked into my school bag in the family room. My favourite character in that was— My heart beat faster. 'Jack?'

Mum and Dad ignored me. Mum was nodding vaguely at Dad who was patting at the blankets around her, as though afraid to touch her directly.

'Jack,' I repeated, testing it out. I liked the sound. Crisp and sharp. Nobody would mess with someone called Jack. Nobody would ever hurt him. Not if I had anything to do with it. 'Jack,' I said again. 'This is my brother, Jack.'

I looked up at Mum, hoping for some sort of praise over how well I was holding him. Supporting the neck, not clinging too tightly. But she was fast asleep, her forehead creased, now, in a way that looked painful.

'We'll leave her,' Dad whispered. 'No, no, take the baby with you,' he added, for I had looked towards the clear box. 'You keep hold of him. We'll go and put him in the wee nursery so she can sleep.'

I wasn't sure how to stand with such a weight in my arms, but I managed it clumsily and followed Dad out of the room.

I was more mature than my other brothers and their silly games, I thought; I didn't have time for children's things any more.

I was so intent on staring at my new brother that I don't think I even looked back.

And shortly after she was gone.

We'd been a family of seven. Lucky number seven. Secret Seven.

Then we were back to six.

I didn't even care if I was still Dad's favourite, because Jack was mine.

3

The Suspect

I stand at the foot of the stairs, trembling as we all wait for Jack to get dressed. The male police officer has gone up with him, and Decky has come down instead as though Jack's tagged him in. His face flushed with sleep, Decky just looks between us, asking over and over again 'But, why? What happened?'

Dad's mouth has set in a single, immovable line and he leans against the living room door, gripping the handle behind him as though he's ready to dart inside.

Jordan is in the kitchen, calling the gym to let them know he's had a family emergency and won't be in work today.

Decky, unable to get any answers from anyone else, holds my elbow tight and looks into my face. 'Abi, why are they arresting Jack? What the fuck's happened?'

'It's a mistake,' I say, my voice no more than a whisper. Then, more loudly, making sure the police officer can hear me. 'It's a mistake.'

She ignores me, and stands straight, looking at the top of the stairs, waiting for her colleague and Jack to reappear.

'They've got the wrong person or something,' I say to Decky. 'Something about a – about a rape.' The word feels dirty and animal in my mouth and I want to be sick.

I think I really might be sick, so I dash to the kitchen and lean over the sink. The smell of tobacco and bacon makes my stomach clench and I retch. Jordan is standing with his phone in his hand, tapping it against his palm in a nervous jiggle, his call finished, but he still manages to look disgusted at the idea of me throwing up.

'Oh, fuck,' Decky says. He has followed me. 'Did you say a – a rape? Is that what you said? Oh, fuck.' When nobody responds he says, 'It's just a fuck up, somebody's given the wrong name or got confused. Yeah?'

'Did something happen at the party?' Jordan asks me. 'At his mate's house?'

I shake my head quickly.

After their last exam, a boy in Jack's physics class, Paul, had thrown a party at his house for the whole year group. Jack had shown his face for a few hours, then made his way across town to enjoy the last wee while of my housewarming party, telling me Paul's house in Springhill Manor was too big and too old and that a load of *posh twats* from the other grammar school had been invited, so it was no fun.

'Nothing happened,' I say. 'I saw him, sure. I spoke to him, he was fine.' I look at Decky, hopefully, and say, 'And then you left together.' Why wouldn't they leave together? They live together.

Decky frowns, pulls his pyjama top up to scratch his stomach thoughtfully. 'Nah. Nah, he didn't come home with me, sure. I don't know where he went after yours, but he definitely didn't leave with me.'

I blink at him. My heart is starting to thud again.

We hear footsteps on the stairs and go as one to the hallway.

Jack has put on a crumpled blue T-shirt that I know has been on the floor of his room and I want to shake him for being so stupid. He's going to a police station to be interviewed, he could at least put on a clean top.

It is me he makes a dart for.

'Why are they saying this?' he moans as quietly as he can. His eyes are full of tears and his voice is thick with the effort of holding them in. 'It's all bollocks, Abi. You know it is. What should I do? What do I do?'

'I'll go with you,' I say immediately. 'It'll be fine, Jack, it's just a wee mistake.'

'There's no need for you to accompany Mr Campbell. Are you

32

his… girlfriend?' The policewoman lets an expression show for the first time, a slight curiosity at the age difference. She told us her name but I can't remember what she said.

'I'm his sister,' I snap. 'Of course I'm going with him, he's only—' I stop.

'Eighteen?' The policewoman guesses. 'We're just going to have a quick chat, get the facts sorted out. You understand how serious this allegation is, I'm sure, Miss Campbell. We can give him a lift back when we're done if… if that's required.'

I open my mouth and I know I want to say something, but words won't come. I look to Dad, to Jordan, to Decky, but they're all as dumbfounded as I am. Nobody says anything. Why is nobody saying anything?

'Ready, Mr Campbell?'

Why do they keep calling him that?

Jack looks at me, panic in his features, shaking his head.

'It'll be fine,' I hear myself saying. 'Just go and tell the truth and be honest. Get it sorted and I'll see you when you get back. It'll be fine. I promise.'

I want to call after him to take a coat, just as an excuse to call something, but it's too warm outside. Too warm inside, too. Muggy and clammy and awful. So I don't call anything, and just let the three of them leave. The door swings shut behind them.

We listen as the police car starts up and pulls away.

The whole thing has taken less than ten minutes.

'Do you want to phone Ciarán?' Decky asks me.

They are all looking at me.

They're always all looking at me, but it irritates me now.

'You've a phone and two hands,' I say. 'You do it.'

'Aye. Okay.' Decky goes upstairs.

Jordan lets out a long breath that he has been holding. 'I might… I might just go into work, actually. I don't know if there's much point hanging around here. Like you said, it'll be a wee mistake. No point missing a day's pay, is there?'

Money has always been Jordan's thing. Now that he has his own, he pretends we were never living hand to mouth. He actually seems to shrink back into himself if anyone mentions it, like that happened to someone else's family and he doesn't want to think about it.

'Off you go, son,' Dad says. 'Like you say, no point losing a day's pay.'

If Dad is thinking about Jordan's rent money, I swear I'll crack up.

Jordan leaves, and Dad and I are alone in the hall.

I hear Decky on the phone upstairs.

Dad is still leaning against the living room door. 'Shall we… Did you want to go and put those shelves up?'

I look at him. Dad is about five foot nine – I'm the only one of his children who hasn't overtaken him in height and weight. While he has a beer belly now, he has skinny wrists and thin legs and a hollowed-out looking face that I know from photographs was once ruggedly handsome. His hair is white now, where it had been blond, and I could take a pencil and fill in the lines on his face. Or, Jack could. He's the artistic one. He's the everything one.

'I might actually go,' I say, finally. 'I'm gonna go to the police station and wait on him.'

'Wait on him,' Dad repeats. 'Yes, you go and wait on him love, at the police station.'

My dad has a habit of repeating everything I've ever said since I was a child and passing off my words as his own ideas.

'I'll go now. You wait on Ciarán and… and maybe you should call Francie? Just in case.'

Francie is an older man who used to drink in The Rooster with Dad, but who moved back to Belfast. He does something in law, but I'm not entirely sure what that something is. Either way, he's the person anyone from Vetobridge calls if they need a hand dealing with the police.

'Phone me when you know something,' Dad says, relieved. 'And I'll wait on Ciarán and I'll phone Fr—'

I am out the front door and into the street before he can finish.

The Blindspot

My sprint home to get my car is quite different from the leisurely stroll I took in the early morning sun less than an hour ago. Past the corner shop, past the coffee shop, my trainers pounding the pavement – I have no idea why I'm rushing. All I know is I have to be there, wherever Jack is.

My tiny white Hyundai is parked behind the building, in one of only two spaces. The RESIDENTS ONLY parking sign doesn't stop cheeky shoppers from leaving their cars there all day, so I always consider myself lucky when I get a space. I open the car and tumble inside.

OLDRY POLICE STATION ELECTRONIC AUDIO TRANSCRIPTION FILE

CASE NUMBER: 210623XZ

[FOR ACCOMPANYING VIDEO RECORDING PLEASE CLICK <u>HERE</u>. FOR CONTACT DETAILS OF OFFICERS PRESENT PLEASE CLICK <u>HERE</u>. PLEASE CONTACT OLDRY IT DEPARTMENT WITH ANY PROBLEMS.]

21 June 2022 – 11.45am – Initial Interview with Jack Campbell – Verbatim

JC – Jack Campbell

PM – DC Paula Mathers, PPB

ZA – DS Zachary Andrews

[ZA]: For the benefit of the tape, DS Zachary Andrews and DC Paula Mathers interviewing Jack Campbell as a suspect under caution. Mr Campbell has been offered legal representation and has refused, he has been made aware of his rights and is happy to proceed with interview. It is… quarter to twelve, Tuesday afternoon, 21st of June 2022. Can you just confirm you are Jack Campbell, of 11 Pine Street, Vetobridge, County Down?

[JC]: *[Inaudible]*

[ZA]: Can you speak up, please?

[JC]: Yeah. I am.

[ZA]: … When's your birthday?

[JC]: Thirteenth of June. 2004.

[ZA]: Where were you last night, Mr Campbell?

[JC]: I was… at a party. At two parties, actually.

[ZA]: Where were these parties?

[JC]: One of them was up in Springhill Manor… You know, up at the top of the town, past the primary school. The other one was at my sister's new flat, on the mini main street.

[ZA]: Where, sorry?

[JC]: The Old Droless Road. Sorry.

[ZA]: Okay. And did you make a detour to the rockpools at some point after one or both of these parties?

[ZA]: Mr Campbell? Do you need me to repeat that?

[PM]: Jack? Are you listening? It will be easier for us to get this matter sorted if you co-operate with us. We just want you to put your side across.

[ZA]: What time did you get to the rockpools?

[ZA]: What time did you get home?

[ZA]: You didn't have your phone on you when you came to the station. Where is it? The phone with the number that ends in 656.

--

[ZA]: Our team will locate your mobile phone, they're doing a search of your home at the minute. Do you know where it is now?

[JC]: I lost it.

[ZA]: When was that?

[JC]: Last night. On the beach.

[ZA]: Okay... We can still check your phone records without the actual handset. Mathers, will you make a note and we can ask the Techs to do that ASAP?

[Inaudible]

[ZA]: *[shuffling, inaudible]* ... alleges that she was sexually assaulted last night, up by the rockpools. She says you raped her.

[ZA]: This is a friend of yours. Why would she say that if it isn't true?

[JC]: I don't know. I don't know.

[ZA]: She didn't come home last night when she was supposed to. Her curfew was one a.m. Her mum woke up in the middle of the night and she still wasn't home. She called and called her, worried sick. And rightly so. Luckily she uses Track My iPhone with her daughter so she was able to use that and drove up to the rockpools herself. She knew something was wrong right away, even if her daughter was confused and being sick. She drove her straight here. And at seven o'clock this morning she made a statement… saying she'd been sexually assaulted. By you, Jack Campbell.

[ZA]: What do you have to say about that?

[PM]: Jack?

[JC]: No comment.

4

The Toddler

When my brother Jack was two, he escaped from nursery by climbing out of a low window. It was a week before my twelfth birthday, and it was freezing cold in the mobile classrooms of Seaview High where I'd started the previous September. Decky was in the year above, Jordan was doing his GCSEs and Ciarán had left a few years before, tried to become a joiner, hated it and got a job working in a call centre. He was living at home still, but was hoping to move in with his love-of-his-life-forever girlfriend, Molly, soon.

The nursery was in the grounds of the primary school at the other side of town, and for a whole glorious six months, the last of my primary school years, I'd been able to sneak over at lunch time to see Jack and give him a cuddle. Some of the girls in my class watched enviously as I walked him up and down outside the front of the nursery, picked him up and showed him the birds and the insects. The assistants who worked there complimented me and told me I was a natural, so they never said anything about me coming to visit, even though technically it wasn't allowed. Sometimes I would take him into the empty primary school classrooms, show him where I sat, show him my work on the wall, tell him he would soon be sitting at one of the little tables, having his own work up there.

Now, every morning we dropped Jack off at half-past eight and didn't get to see him again until after school. I felt my heart break a little bit more with each step we took towards our own school, but the weight lightened as the day went on and blossomed into excitement that I'd get to see him again after three.

The day he escaped, I came bounding into the nursery bang on time as usual. Decky and Jordan came with me sometimes, but mostly they went off with their mates or, in Jordan's case, to the gym after school.

I gave my perfunctory knock and opened the door, poking my smiling face around first like I always did, mouth open ready to exclaim my happiness at my little brother. That day was different – there were no semi-circles of children sitting on the floor, no colourful television show on, no aprons on to protect the kids from paint. The kids were sitting in the corner, being read a story by one assistant, but two of the others were huddled together, speaking seriously, one with a phone pressed to her ear. She exclaimed when she saw me and hung up.

'There she is!' she cried to her colleague. 'Abi, please, please tell me he's with you?'

'Who?' I asked blankly, wondering why she would need to speak to Decky or Jordan.

'Jack?' the other girl sobbed. I hadn't realised she was crying and I blinked at her. 'Please, is he?' she continued. 'Did he come home?'

I froze, staring at them. 'Jack? I – I dropped Jack off,' I stammered. 'This morning. I dropped him off with you at half-eight. You were here. What do you mean? Where is he?'

The girl holding the phone dialled a number again, mumbling *fuck fuck fuck* over and over again.

'We can't get your dad,' the sobbing girl explained. 'We thought maybe Jack would go home—'

'What do you mean?' I shouted, surprising myself. 'Where did he go?'

'He escaped. Does he know his way home?'

I turned to see a third girl, donned in the same pink polo shirt as the others, out of breath. I didn't recognise her.

She addressed her colleagues. 'Not behind the bins, not in the senior playground, not in the car park, still no sign of him anywhere.'

My heart beat fast. They were talking about Jack, about my Jack. These people that were supposed to mind him for just a few hours a day. Why couldn't I trust anyone but myself? Not even these people who got paid to look after him? On some level I acknowledged that I was angry, but the cold fear was overpowering.

'Can you nip home and see if he went there, Abi?'

I'm not even sure if I replied. I know I didn't look at them again.

I turned on my heel and flew off across the courtyard, my school bag swinging behind me, hair flying out of its plait.

A group of P7 girls had stayed behind after school for football practice, and they were kicking the ball about the playground as I zoomed past. One of them called a hello to me, that started off bright and excited and ended up sounding more like a confused, 'Hell-Oh?'

I was home in ten minutes, my heart nearly popping out of my chest, a stitch in my side and no breath left for anything except to call 'JACK?'

Ciarán's head appeared out of the living room door, mouth full of sandwich. 'Huh?'

'Did Jack come home?' I panted, running upstairs.

I heard Ciarán swallow and come into the hall. 'Nah, what you on about? Sure he's at Lilypad Lane today, is he not? Are you not meant to be collecting him?'

I had already poked my head into my own tiny box room, into Dad's room where Jack slept, and into the boys' room, and I was running back down the stairs.

'He escaped,' I said, distracted. I was looking around the house for I knew not what. Evidence Jack had taken his keys and phone? How does it work when the missing person is a two-year-old?

'Escaped?' Ciarán paused with his sandwich raised halfway to his mouth. 'What the fuck?'

'Where would he go?' I demanded of him. 'If you were Jack, where would you wander off to?'

'If he didn't get hit by a car outside the school grounds, you mean.'

Ciarán seemed to realise what he'd said, for his face fell. 'I'll get my coat and come help. You go back to the school and I'll phone Dad and go the opposite way. Hey, Abi.' He pulled my arm towards him and looked at me seriously. I was trembling. 'He'll be fine. He's a good wee boy, he's just wandered off. Some nice aul doll will have brought him in and offered him sweets and she's trying to get his address out of him. Yeah?'

More running. Chest pounding. Stitch. Sore ribs.

Sore heart.

Once I was back at the school, I allowed myself to slow down and think.

Think, Abi. Think.

I hadn't even asked them when. How long had they been trying to phone Dad? Ten minutes, an hour? How fast did a little boy's legs move if he was determined?

I'd stopped by the huge green wire fence that surrounded the primary school and nursery. From there, I could see the redbrick mobile classrooms and the green football pitch that, even now, just three months into my high school life, seemed so much smaller than it ever had when I went here. I walked slowly in a circle around the school buildings. The primary one class, the reception. Inside the main building, I could see one of the nursery assistants running about like a blue-arsed fly. She was shouting Jack's name, though I couldn't hear her. I could just tell by the way her mouth moved. I knew what it was like to say *Jack*. I knew better than anyone.

I didn't realise I was crying until I got to the primary five classroom and my vision blurred.

Primary six. You hear about children going missing all the time. Paedophiles, I knew that word. I wasn't sure exactly what they were, but they were nothing good. Some kids don't come back from paedophiles. Jack's face would be on the news. Why had I trusted those stupid – I thought of one of Ciarán's favourite words – those stupid *fucking*—

Primary seven, my old classroom.

The Blindspot

Automatically I pushed myself through the swinging door and went into the cloakroom, the same way I had for a whole year. Thirty identical, yellow pegs all in a neat row. Two coats that had been left behind that day, one scarf. One lunch box lying open that smelled like something spicy and healthy. And then—

'Babby!'

A tiny blond beach ball, it seemed, came rolling towards me. I crouched automatically and stopped his headfirst charge before he picked up too much speed. Life slowed down again, and I breathed. He was wearing his dinosaur jumper – brand new that week, no hand-me-downs for Jack – and the tiny chinos I'd found and begged Dad for, but no coat, no scarf. It must have been two degrees outside, if even. He felt freezing to the touch.

'Hello, Jack Attack,' I said, trying not to show how relieved and upset I was. 'Where have you been?' I answered my own question immediately. 'Were you waiting for me by my cubby?'

I'd taken Jack into the cloakroom on my lunch breaks so many times, as he loved seeing all the brightly coloured school bags and adored more than anything taking my colouring pencils and arranging them on the floor.

We'd spent hours last term picking up and putting away coloured pencils. Such a stupid, wonderful thing.

Jack grinned at me, showing me his tiny white teeth. There was jam either side of his mouth, but I let him burrow his head into my school jumper anyway.

'Are you cold, little man?'

He pulled away to nod solemnly at me, then giggled and grinned again.

'Home time, I think,' I said. I took off my own scarf and tied it around his neck. Round and round we went, both giggling at how much material there was to fit around such a tiny human. 'You going to walk?' I asked.

Of course he was. He walked and talked early, and never stopped. He strutted proudly to the door and out of sight, leaving me rushing to pick up my bag and go after him.

The assistants were relieved. Two of them cried.

Ciarán was delighted, in an eye-rolling, cursing under his breath kind of way.

We never did find Dad. He'd told us he was on a job in Droless that week, but when Ciarán called his boss to ask, he said he'd never heard of the job. Said he hadn't had any work on for nearly three weeks. I had a sneaking suspicion that if either of us had dared venture into The Rooster, we might have found him propped up against the fruit machine, dressed in his work overalls. The polished surface of the bar was the only landscape he seemed to decorate, then. We ended up never telling Dad about what had happened, and even though I was visibly upset for days, I don't think he noticed.

As Jack and I walked away from the playground, I felt the need to turn him to face me.

'Jack,' I said, as seriously as I could while his pink cheeks poked out from the top of the scarf. 'You can't go running off like that. Miss Byrne and Miss Pinner were really worried about you, they didn't know where you were. Nobody could find you.'

He looked confused, but then he smiled. 'You find me,' Jack said simply. He blinked his huge eyes once, then he took my hand and continued to pull me along home.

OLDRY POLICE STATION ELECTRONIC AUDIO TRANSCRIPTION FILE

CASE NUMBER: 210623XZ

[FOR ACCOMPANYING VIDEO RECORDING PLEASE CLICK <u>HERE</u>. FOR CONTACT DETAILS OF OFFICERS PRESENT PLEASE CLICK <u>HERE</u>. PLEASE CONTACT OLDRY IT DEPARTMENT WITH ANY PROBLEMS.]

21 June 2022 – 12.30PM – Initial Interview with
Jack Campbell – Verbatim
JC – Jack Campbell
PM – DC Paula Mathers, PPB
ZA – DS Zachary Andrews

[PM]: Would you like another cup of tea, Jack?

[JC]: No, thank you.

[PM]: Did you get enough of a comfort break? Are you sure you don't want something to eat?

[JC]: No, thank you.

[ZA]: Resuming interview. Mathers and Andrews still present with Jack Campbell, suspect. Mr Campbell, what we want to understand is why this woman has made these allegations. Did you… have a row with her last night? At the party?

[JC]: No.

[PM]: You two were good friends, in school. Is that right? That's what she and her mum told us.

[PM]: Had you seen much of her, lately?

[JC]: *[Inaudible]*

[PM]: Sorry?

[JC]: Just Snapchat.

[PM]: Ah! Yes. I know it. My son has it as well, he's never done taking selfies and sending them to his friends. Was last night a

47

celebration? You must be finished your A-Levels by now?

[JC]: Yeah. Last exam was yesterday.

[PM]: What a relief, I bet?

[JC]: Yeah.

[PM]: Where are you hoping to go in September?

[JC]: I have a conditional for MUSE.

[PM]: For what, sorry?

[JC]: Sorry. Sorry. It's Mingle University of Science and Engineering.

[PM]: Wow. Prestigious! What are you hoping to study?

[JC]: I've got a scholarship to do Astrophysics with a research year. Just need the grades.

[PM]: That's amazing. You must be so clever.

[JC]: *[Inaudible]*

[PM]: Ha! Sisters always champion their younger brothers, don't they?

[ZA]: Did you and Katie talk much at the party in Springhill Manor?

[JC]: A bit.

[ZA]: What about?

[JC]: This and that. College and uni. Exams.

[PM]: Did you walk home together?

[JC]: I… I can't remember. I was really drunk.

[ZA]: You can't remember?

[JC]: What I mean is… No. We didn't.

[ZA]: What time did you leave the party in Springhill Manor to go to the party on Old Droless Road?

[JC]: … Eleven? Maybe? I can't be sure. My… my friends would know. They might know.

[PM]: Which friends are these, Jack?

[JC]: I… No comment.

[PM]: You can tell us your friends' names? Surely?

[JC]: No. No comment.

[PM]: Jack, we'll be speaking to everyone who was at the party, so we will find them. It'll be easier for you just to tell us which friends you were with last night. Especially if, as you say, they can shed some light.

[JC]: No.

[PM]: Okay. That's fine. Well, maybe you could tell us a bit about your relationship with Katie. Were you good friends? Close?

[JC]: Not any more, really. We used to be mates.

[PM]: Hard to keep in touch when one of you doesn't stay on at school, isn't it?

[JC]: *[Inaudible]*

[PM]: Did you know she was going to be at the party in Springhill Manor?

[JC]: No.

[PM]: When did you last see her? Before last night, I mean.

[JC]: Maybe... Maybe on a night out a few weeks ago. I can't really—

[ZA]: You chat to her on social media much, Jack?

[JC]: What?

[ZA]: Snapchat, you've said, but anything else? You've kindly provided your computer password, so we'll know soon enough.

[JC]: What do you mean?

[ZA]: Were you a bit obsessed with Katie?

[JC]: What? No.

[ZA]: Her mum thinks you were, a bit.

[ZA]: Says you were always messaging her. Is that true?

[JC]: No comment.

[Inaudible]

[shuffling]

[tape unable to decipher. Please click here to listen to original recording]

[ZA]: For the benefit of the tape, DS Mathers has just stepped out to—

[Inaudible]

[PM]: Jack's solicitor is here. Jack, Francis Finn is here to see you, he says your dad sent him. Are you happy for him to be your representation?

[JC]: ... What?

[ZA]: Interview suspended. Twelve-forty.

5

The Released

For nearly five hours, I sit in the visitors' car park of Oldry Police Station. I drove Max here once when his phone got stolen, about four years ago now. The wait then was quite different – my heart hammering in anticipation of him coming back to the car, trying to work out where we would park up that night, how many times we could have sex in the back before one of us (him, always) had to go.

I feel a nagging part of me wishing I had a book, but I know in my heart I wouldn't be able to concentrate. I have a vague memory of my mum telling me that you should always have a book with you, no matter what you're doing or where you're going. Which is funny because I don't think I ever saw her reading in my life.

There are two doors in my sight, and my eyes flick between them even when I try to relax. One seems to be for staff to come in and out. Indeed, one man has already had three smokes leaning against it before stubbing his cigarettes out on the wall and heading back inside. The other I'm not sure. I imagine Jack in an interview room just inside it, explaining in his best, charming way that they have the wrong boy.

I pull out my phone. I have a text from Max from this morning that I've missed, just him checking in, asking how the party went.

It's now after three. On Tuesdays, his timetable is full. He will be teaching for another half hour, but there's no reason I can't text.

I type out, *Can you call me when you get a chance? X*

He does, at half-past three on the dot.

He's been more reliable than usual, lately. Has even slept over in my new flat twice in one week.

I think of it, my tiny little space above the Vape Shop, and I'm filled with a longing for it that I never felt about my family home in Pine Street. I've only been there a week tomorrow, and it already feels like home. The only place that's ever been just mine.

'Hi, what's up?' Max sounds breathless. I can hear the chatter of children for a few seconds before he closes a door. Try to imagine Jack as one of them only a few weeks ago, before he got off on study leave. 'You sound serious.'

'I'm at the police station,' I blurt. 'Jack's been arrested.'

'What?' Max sounds as though he genuinely hasn't heard me.

'I don't know why. I'm not sure. I – I don't know. The police came to Dad's house this morning and took Jack away in a cop car. He's been arrested for…'

I can't say the word rape to Max, can't say it out loud ever again.

'Jack? Your Jack? Oh, Jesus. What happened?'

'I'm not sure. I think it's all a mistake. Oh, shit, Max, somebody else is phoning me here, I have to go. Come over later?' I hang up before he can respond and click into the other call. An unknown number. 'Hello?'

'Abi?'

My breath catches. It's Jack, though not calling on his own mobile phone, the one I bought for him on the day he got his GCSE results. I have never been so grateful in my life that I made him memorise my number. Good boy, Jack.

'Hi, yes. Are you okay? What's happening?'

'I can leave,' Jack mumbles. 'They say they'll bring me home, but if I start walking can you lift me instead?'

'I'm here,' I say, delighted that I can say this. I knew it was a good idea to come. My heart soars.

It's over.

If we could call something so brief, so stupid, a nightmare, then it's over. We've woken up. 'I'm just outside. I'm in the visitors' car park, I'll drive round to the reception bit. Meet me there?'

The Blindspot

Jack and his crumpled T-shirt have already arrived at the reception building by the time I swing my little car around. The automatic door opens behind him and a woman rushes to his side. She is older than Jack, maybe even older than me, dressed in a short skirt and a strappy top. I pull up next to them and watch as she hands Jack something. He nods his thanks and tries to smile at her, but he's making for the car all the while.

Her gaze and her smile linger on him for longer than is strictly necessary, even as he closes the passenger side door behind him and does up his seatbelt, and then she turns and goes back inside.

'What was that all about?' I ask, grateful beyond words that I can ask about this tiny, innocuous thing instead of asking about everything else.

'I dropped my tenner,' Jack mumbles. 'She was giving it back.'

My tenner. This is a running joke between us. Jack insists that nobody carries cash now, and I think he might be right, but I don't feel happy that he's relying on his phone battery to pay for things, especially on nights out. What if he can't get home some night? I gave him a ten-pound note nearly two years ago, and he carries the same one with him in his pocket constantly.

'Giving it back and giving you the eye,' I can't help saying. 'My God, she was staring. Do you know her?'

'Nah. We were just both in the reception making phone calls.'

He doesn't say anything else, just looks straight ahead. I can't tell if he's been crying or not, and usually I'm pretty good at that sort of thing. When he was a child, any time he cried his whole body would rack with sobs, his chest heaving, but the two or three times I've seen him cry as a teenager, his complexion clears in an instant as if it never happened. His face is pale, and he looks exhausted – that's the only thing I'm sure of. It must have gone okay.

I indicate out onto the main road and we make our way back towards Vetobridge. Once we're on the A1, it's a straight eleven minutes on the carriageway until we can pull into the town. We'll be able to smell the sea in no time.

'How was it?' I wait until we're out of Oldry to ask. The aircon is up full but somehow my palms still feel sweaty. Having sat in the car park for hours, I only now realise that I badly need to pee.

'Awful,' Jack says quietly. He doesn't offer any more.

As soon as we pull into Vetobridge, I make a right at the roundabout.

I feel Jack looking at me in confusion. 'Bathroom,' I explain. 'Sorry. Been sitting there ages. Just going to nip into work.'

'No!' Jack almost shouts it. The car has been quiet for so long that this makes me physically jump. 'No, don't do that! Here, go into Tesco and go there.'

He reaches over and puts my indicator on for me. He always does this, says I'm the reason women drivers get such a bad rap, because I don't always bother with my indicator.

He's so careful. Always. He's a better driver than I am and he only passed his test in January.

We have to drive past The Rooster, where I work full-time as a barmaid, to get to Tesco, but I don't say anything.

I park and we both get out, blinking in the sun. I realise I'm starving and look at my phone. It's not even four o'clock. It feels like years ago I bought those coffees.

'I've an ever-so-slight hangover,' I say, as we dander towards the entrance. 'I was pretty sensible last night, I stopped drinking at one, but I just don't feel right. Ropey, you know?'

Jack nods for a little bit too long – he must not be listening.

'How are you feeling today?' I ask.

'Mm. Yeah, same. Ropey. You know?'

'Shall we get Kinder Buenos and Fanta?' I ask, my eyes on the side of his face.

Kinder Buenos and Fanta have always been our thing. Back in the days when I was going out and Jack was still a child, he'd nip to the corner shop on a Sunday morning and get some for the pair of us, and we'd spend all day in our pyjamas watching TV and planning the nights out we'd have when Jack was old enough.

'I'm not hungry,' he murmurs, and suddenly I'm not either.

The doors slide open to let us in and the powerful air-conditioning blasts us both in the face.

'Be two minutes,' I say as I make for the bathrooms.

I stand and look into the mirror for most of my two minutes. I wonder if Jack and I will still look alike when he's my age. My hair darkened to dirty fair as I got older, but Jack's is still pale as anything. I used to say he was like a golden retriever puppy.

I think of the woman staring and smiling at him at the police station.

Was she actually coming on to him, this older woman? Was the police station a popular place to pick up someone, really?

He is attractive. Of course he is, even I can see that.

But he's a boy, a child.

Though not in the eyes of the law, I hear myself think.

I shake my head. I'll have to ask him exactly what happened, just to put my mind at rest. I can't not know.

I wash my hands and head back into the store.

Jack is standing by the plastic-wrapped bunches of flowers – but he is not alone.

One of his friends from school – Reggie or Budgie or Freddie or something, I can never differentiate them now that they're older and they all look exactly the same – is standing next to him. They are talking seriously, in low tones, both their faces set. Surely... surely they aren't talking about where Jack has been?

I don't want Jack telling *anyone* about what happened this morning. Why would he tell someone about it? Rumours can spread so easily.

I make more noise than is necessary as I stride over to meet them, clearing my throat and making sure my trainers slap off the floor.

'Hiya,' I say to Jack's friend. Yes, I definitely know him from primary school, maybe from a birthday of Jack's a few years ago, but I couldn't swear which one he is. 'How are you?'

The boy blinks at me, but doesn't smile. Instead he looks at Jack as he responds. 'Hiya. Grand. Just in with my brother... I'll have to go back to him. Bye, Jack. Bye... *Abi.*' He stalks off towards the travel magazines. I look after him, not sure why he put the emphasis on my name.

'Let's go,' I say to Jack as brightly as I can. Then, 'Which one was that?'

'That was Ben.'

'Oh, him.'

We go back to the car, not looking at one another. When we are both belted up, I turn the car on and put it in gear. Then I turn it off and put both hands on the steering wheel and say, lightly, 'Will you tell me what happened?'

He has always done anything I asked. This is no exception.

'Yeah,' he says. Then he is silent so long I think he isn't actually going to. Finally he says, 'It was horrible. They're saying... *She's* saying...' Silence again. Then, quietly '... That she was raped.'

That word again.

Five letters, one syllable. So why is it echoing through the car?

I don't speak, afraid I'll break the spell. I keep looking forwards, watching a dad pushing twins in one of those huge double-seat trollies, not really seeing them, feeling my heart beating in my throat.

'I didn't,' Jack whispers.

I have to look at him to make sure I'm hearing him properly. He is looking at the dashboard as though it's a ghost. It's only now that I register it: instead of David Beckham aftershave, sugar, the smell of *clean* that I associate with my brother, I can smell beer, and smoke and something else. The fingers of his left hand run themselves over those on the right. Jack has a scar over his palm, wrist and fingers. Has had it, the spidery, raised bumps, since he was a toddler.

My fault. My heart clenches as it does every time I look at his hands.

'Didn't... didn't do it? Didn't have anything to do with it?' I say, hope breaking through the tension in the car.

'It wasn't me,' Jack says. 'I didn't do it. Why would she say that?'

I shake my head, feeling my ponytail swinging and tickling the back of my neck.

'Francie was really good. He shut them down… said it was one person's word against another's until there's… evidence. But there won't be, obviously. They kept asking the same questions over and over. Once I'd answered them all once, Francie told me just to say no comment, and it… worked.' He flinches at the word. 'I haven't even… I've never even had sex.'

Any other time, talking about sex with Jack would be the most embarrassing, awful thing I could think of. We both want so desperately to cling to us both being virgins. It's the one thing we've never talked about.

Now, though, in the car, in the sun, after the police, it's comforting to hear those words. This is an awful, terrible misunderstanding. Maybe there is a test they can do to prove it can't have been Jack. To prove that this has all just been a silly mistake, made by some poor…

'Who?' I ask. Suddenly, it is the only important question in the world. Why haven't I asked this before? Why didn't I ask the policewoman this morning? The only thing that matters here is which girl has made this terrible mistake.

He glances towards me, an unmistakeable blush climbing up his face.

'Katie Waltz,' Jack whispers, and I feel my grip on the world slacken.

OLDRY POLICE STATION DIGITAL EVIDENCE FILE

CASE NUMBER: 210623XZ

[PHYSICAL PRINT OUTS SHOULD BE PLACED IN THE CORRESPONDING CASE FILE, IN NUMERICAL ORDER. PLEASE CONTACT OLDRY POLICE STATION ADMIN DEPARTMENT WITH ANY PROBLEMS.]

Technical Evidence #01 – Excerpt from the Facebook Messenger™ App

Messages from account registered to Jack Campbell to account registered to Katherine Waltz.

Note from OPS Admin Dept: Messages have been digitised for ease. Emoticons or 'emojis' have been removed from digital files but can be viewed on physical copies.

[18.10.2015]

Jack Campbell 1731: Hey! Wtc? Have u done homework for Murray?

Katie Waltz 1750: Heyyyy Jack, hows u? Not yet, finishing art first and then doing it, is it hard??

Jack Campbell 1750: Am good. No it's ok, if u need any help you know where I am

Katie Waltz 1801: Awwww ty!!!

Jack Campbell 1801: NP

[25.12.2015]

Jack Campbell 1217: Happy Christmas KT!!! Hope u r havin a brilliant day

Katie Waltz 1450: Merry Christmas Jack, you too!

Jack Campbell 1500: Tell your granda I said the same :)

Katie Waltz 1501: He says it back! lol

Jack Campbell 1515: Is it just yous and ur mum today?

Katie Waltz 1516: Yh :)

Jack Campbell 1520: Happy xmas to her too!

Katie Waltz 1520: Awww thanx. Same to your fam, see you soon

Jack Campbell 1520: bye x

[01.01.2016]

Jack Campbell 0001: HNY KT!

Katie Waltz 0004: Same!!! Hope it's a gd 1 x

Jack Campbell 0004: xxx

[14.02.2016]

Jack Campbell 1314: Your still life was abs brilliant on Friday btw, I meant to say

Katie Waltz 1507: It wasn't, I totally mucked up the orange lol

Jack Campbell 1508: Nah I thought it was original, a yellow orange lmaooo

Katie Waltz 1508: Stopppp

Jack Campbell 1510: It was brill. Happy v day

Katie Waltz 1511: And you x

[30.06.2016]

Katie Waltz 1630: Hey! I couldn't find you today to say bye, have a lovely summer!!! Xx

Jack Campbell 1750: Hey, sorry, Ben wanted us all to join in on his prank. Pathetic tbh

Katie Waltz 1800: Omg it was you guys who covered Miss Devon's car in post-its!?!?!

Jack Campbell 1800: Not me! But I was there

Katie Waltz 1800: Mmmm I don't think that would stand up!!!

Jack Campbell 1801: Prob not lol.

Katie Waltz 1805: Just wanted to invite you to my 13th birthday party, it's next Saturday, we're just gonna go bowling and cinema :)

Jack Campbell 1806: Aw brill thank you so much. Yes please, what time?

Katie Waltz 1810: Meet at SuperbBowl about 2? Do u need a lift?

Jack Campbell 1812: My sis can hopefully leave me off :) who alls goin?

Katie Waltz 1813: All the girls in our form class, you, Harry and Phil!

Jack Campbell 1815: Thanks KT... I'll get u something nice :)

[10.07.2016]

Katie Waltz 1001: Thank you so much again for the beautiful watercolours Jack, you are so sweet x

Jack Campbell 1030: My pleasure :) Thanks for a fun day, u r really good at bowling lol

Katie Waltz 1031: I know! It's one sport I can still do even tho am fat

Jack Campbell 1031: Omg what? U r not fat

Katie Waltz 1035: Chubby then

Jack Campbell 1036: U r beautiful x

Jack Campbell 1830: U really are

6

The Hurt

When my brother Jack was four, I realised I'd have to get a job if I wanted his childhood to be as good as mine had been. Thirteen, about to turn fourteen, was young, I knew, for such a big realisation, for sure a mature decision, but I'd felt like an adult from the moment I first held Jack in my arms, so applying for jobs didn't feel as ridiculous to me as it probably looked to the shop-owners and landlords upon whom I thrust my hand-written CV.

They all asked about a National Insurance Number, something I'd never heard of and had to ask Ciarán about.

And when I couldn't produce one, they all refused, of course.

I was tall for thirteen, but unable to pass for a sixteen-year-old.

Ciarán had just moved out, was renting a two-bed semi in Oldry with the love-of-his-life-forever girlfriend Amelia, and working as a manager in the call centre. Jordan had stayed at school to do his A-Levels, and had scraped all three, but was currently unemployed, panic-cleaning the house twice a day and doing the food shopping with Dad's money. The manager of the leisure centre he frequented had taken a shine to Jordy over the years, and had offered to put him through a personal training course in the new year, but Jordan was liable to panic, and hated the thought of doing nothing for the next two months. Quite the opposite of Decky who, if he was any more laid back, would have been lying prone twenty-four/seven. Decky was in the first year of his GCSEs, but often managed to sleep through his own alarm, as well as mine and Jordan's. He would get up out of bed, blearily go for a pee and get back into bed 'for just five minutes' before dozing off again. Most days I had to leave the house without him and make my own way to Seaview High, dropping Jack off at his school along the way. Decky was smart, though. Super smart, in a different way from my elder brothers. He had a head for numbers and computers, technical things. He had told me, privately, he'd even joined a coding club in school, so he couldn't meet me in the canteen on Tuesday lunch times. He was going to make our family its fortune, I thought. He'd invent a new game, he'd invent a new way of paying for stuff online – I couldn't hint at him to get a job, his brain needed all that sleep to keep growing.

So it was up to me.

It was a Saturday afternoon, ten days before my birthday. The cobbled streets of Vetobridge were frozen solid, and I was inching forwards slowly in my wellies, trying not to fall at the same time as trying to look older, sophisticated, helpful. I had tried four shops that day, and everyone had said no. One person had even laughed. I was going to try one more place and then give up for the day. I had to get back to Jack, it was nearly dinner time.

I stood outside the closed door of The Rooster for a moment, bracing myself. I could hear music coming from inside, loud folky stuff, and lots of voices and laughing and swearing. The undeniable swell of Christmas parties. I looked up and down the street. It was getting dark, even though it wasn't even four yet. I could go home now and make some hot chocolate and get warm again. I didn't have to enter the noise and the chaos. I hated noise, hated shouting. I liked things to be ordered and neat and quiet. I liked to be in control. Maybe a job in a bar wasn't for me.

I still went with Dad during the week sometimes, if Decky and Jordan were at home to take care of Jack. I liked sitting with Dad as he watched the horse racing. I usually brought a book, and Dad would buy me a Coke and tell me stories about Mum and tell Norman Waltz how proud he was of me. Maybe I could ask just to work during the week, I thought.

And with the money, I could get Jack a brand new school uniform next year. He'd had to have a plain red jumper and second-hand, rolled up trousers this year, and though it hardly bothered him, it bothered me.

With that thought, I pushed on the metal door.

From the outside, The Rooster just looked like a dank doorway. No windows, a hairdressers on one side and a Chinese takeaway on the other. But once you got inside…

Noise flooded towards me, and even though it was at the far side of the bar, I felt the heat from the fire warming my face almost immediately. I closed the door behind me and wiped ice and mud off my wellies, taking my gloves off as I did so.

I craned my neck, trying to see over the singing and dancing figures gathered in the tiny space, their arms around each other, pints of beer swinging dangerously in their hands. The song had changed. It was the Christmassy one with the swearword in it that always made me flinch.

I bit my lip, feeling suddenly very out of place.

The crowd started to sway and sing along with the lyrics of the song, and I took advantage of the slight dip in volume to approach the bar. I had to stand on the skirting of the bar to lean my body over it, and I stared at Norman Waltz, content to stare until he saw me.

He was running around, a tray in his hand, his hair a frizzy mass of grey curls flying behind him. Decky had shown me a picture of Albert Einstein the week before and said, 'Look, it's Norm!' and I was sure I wouldn't be able to think of anything else again.

He ducked out from behind the bar and dashed back in a moment later, the tray empty. He tried to type something into the till, paused, shook his head and tried again.

A broad man elbowed me out of the way and shouted, 'Another three Guinness on!' He smelled of booze and tobacco and I slid further away from him.

I knew how to pour Guinness. It was my dad's drink of choice. You had to pour it at an angle, he said. Norm had even let me pour one once. I loved drawing faces on top of them at the end, but I decided I probably couldn't do that if I worked here.

'Gimme ten minutes, mate!' Norm called, ducking out from behind the bar again, change in his hand.

The man next to me sighed and swore.

Norm was back, pouring a pint in each hand, blowing his long fringe out of his face.

He was an old man, I thought, but he was quite… bendy and quick, in a way that made him seem younger than my dad. Maybe bar work kept you fit.

'Three!' the man shouted.

'Aye, I heard ye. These aren't for you. Gimme ten.'

'Fuck me,' the man clicked his tongue.

I hesitated, my eyes flicking between the men. Then I slipped behind the bar without lifting the hatch and picked up a Guinness glass.

Norm did a double take, set down one of his pint glasses to turn off the tap.

'Abigail? Is that you? What are you doing, pet?'

'Can I have a job, Norm?' I asked. I pulled the Guinness tap down and held the glass in both hands, just as he'd showed me. Tongue between my teeth, I watched it rise, carefully, carefully, and I pulled the tap up just as it hit the harp symbol. I repeated this for two more pints, my heart beating in my ears.

Norm hadn't answered me. He'd slipped out twice, three times more by the time my pints were ready. The black body and white head looked beautiful, like a freshly printed newspaper. I set each one carefully in front of the big man and blinked at him expectantly.

Dad's pint was one pound ninety. So these were—

'Five seventy, please,' I said, holding out my hand.

The big man didn't bat an eyelid at the child serving him. He handed over a crisp ten-pound note, scooped up the three glasses in a triangle in his big hands and stumbled away, back into the crowd.

'Wait! Your change!' I called after him.

I felt Norm's hand on my shoulder. 'That's for you, love, you keep that.'

Side by side we continued to work for the next two hours, Norm shouting the prices across and shaking his head, laughing, any time he saw the pathetic heads on my lager pints. The customers didn't seem to care. They smiled and took them away, keen to keep dancing and drinking.

Finally, in the lull between parties, he took me aside.

'Does your daddy know you're here?' he asked, eyes narrowed.

I nodded eagerly. 'Oh, aye. He thought I'd be good at bar work.'

Norm laughed, showing me his yellow teeth. Only then did I realise one on the bottom was missing, and another one was gold. It was funny how much you could miss, being on the other side of a wooden bar. He wasn't ugly or scary looking, though. He was just… Norm.

'I bet he did,' he said. 'Paddy's a right chancer. Okay, I can let you help me out on Saturdays, if you really are sure? But if anyone, *anyone* asks –'

'I'm eighteen years old?' I guessed. 'Yes, that's fine. Thank you, Norm.'

So that was that. I worked every Saturday, helping Norm with the rushes, memorising the prices, doing the maths in my head and getting better and better at it. I could feel my confidence growing and even – though I wouldn't have admitted it – loved getting out of the house, being somewhere that felt like it was just for me.

Not that Dad and Ciarán never visited – they did, and they thought it was brilliant.

I'd been working in The Rooster for six months when there came a Saturday when everyone else was occupied.

Dad was on a contract for a new housing estate in Droless, and he was working twelve-hour shifts every day until the gardens were finished. Jordan was covering a shift for his friend in the gym, as well as working his own hours, and Decky was getting the bus to Belfast to go to a comic book convention with his friends. Ciarán rarely visited unless it was an occasion, and when I'd called him during the week and asked him to look after Jack, he'd said he was working, and sounded genuinely sorry.

I didn't want to let Norm down. It was the final of the Premier League that day – I had taken on the role of checking sporting fixtures so Norm could, for the first time in his landlordship, know in advance when we were likely to be busy – and we were expecting to be especially busy. He was even trialling food for the first time, a burger, chips and a pint for a fiver, all prepared by him in the tiny kitchen, so he couldn't do the shift alone.

I fretted about it all week, and on Saturday morning I got Jack dressed and packed his school bag with books and colouring pencils. Jack was a reader – he loved anything sciency, anything with dinosaurs or space – and I knew if I could just pop him in the storeroom for a few hours, he'd be happy as Larry until Decky got home from Belfast.

I pulled the round plastic footstool from beside the shelves stocking the spirits and placed it by the ice machine. Jack sat himself down, looking around with interest at the place he'd only ever heard about in stories – I didn't let Dad or anyone else take him to the pub, so it felt a little hypocritical bringing him here on a day like today.

'You be a good boy,' I said, kissing the top of his head. 'Read your book, and I'll bring you some food in an hour or so. Okay? Shout me if you need anything, and if Norm asks—'

'I'm waiting for a lift,' Jack finished, and he beamed, delighted to have remembered.

I grinned at him and went into the bar which was already starting to fill up, greeted Norm and went about my shift, making sure to volunteer to be the one to nip into the back storeroom if we ran out of anything.

I was quite proud of the way I'd handled my dilemma.

We were busy for hours, but Jack sat happily in the back, looking up with interest if I stuck my head in, even learning some of the different names of the bottles so he could hand me whatever I asked for from the shelves.

It went well. I got nearly fifty pounds in tips.

The Blindspot

'Abigail?' Norm called, his eyes on the till, typing in a particularly long order from a piece of paper in his hand. 'Would you be a love and make tea for the lunatics at table eight?' Norm hated it when anyone ordered anything except alcohol. 'Fucking *tea* on a Saturday afternoon in a pub. Sorry, love. Excuse my French. I've a full tray load of them bloody dack-ree things to do here.'

I nodded, waited until Norm was busy in the cocktail corner making strawberry daiquiris, then fetched Jack from the back store and ushered him down to the kitchen with me.

He looked around with wide eyes and a grin.

'This is your kitchen!' he said with glee.

I smiled at him. It wasn't much bigger than the kitchen we had in Pine Street, but with its singularly white surfaces and humming fridge freezer, I supposed it was a little bit impressive.

'Yes,' I said. I lifted a teapot and bags from above the coffee machine and filled it. 'You wait there for a few minutes – I'm gonna give this to a table and then I'll be back. It's quiet, so I'll make you a wee sandwich, okay?'

'Give it to a table?' Jack asked. 'What will a table do with tea?'

I gave his shoulder a playful tap with my free hand and lifted a milk jug and two cups.

'You'll be really quiet?'

'Really quiet,' Jack repeated.

'Like a wee ghost?'

'Like a ghost.'

Jack happily leant his side against the fridge, playing with the two magnets we used to pin the delivery notices.

I dashed my tray of tea into the restaurant and was promptly called over by two women who wanted to ask if the football in the bar could please be turned down. I explained about the importance of the match and offered to get them another drink each to apologise for the noise, feeling irritated in a way I wouldn't have six months before.

I was gone longer than I had intended. Maybe seven or eight minutes.

69

When I got back to the kitchen I knew immediately that something was wrong.

Jack was no longer leaning against the fridge, no longer reaching up to the magnets.

Instead, he was crouched on the floor, almost bent double, whimpering.

'Jack?' I shouted, immediately on high alert.

He looked up, his face stricken, and he held his hand out to me.

'I'm sorry,' he wheezed. 'I'm – I'm sorry I touched it. But – it hurts. Abi!'

His whole arm was shaking violently, and I couldn't tell what was wrong. Had touched... what? He was racking with sobs, though he seemed unable to properly cry.

'What?' I demanded, sounding crosser than I intended.

'I'm sorry!' Jack shouted. 'I touched it!'

'TOUCHED WHAT?' I grabbed his arm and pulled it towards me. And then I saw it.

His arm was shaking – vibrating, nearly – so badly that it was a blur across my eyes. All I was able to register was the deep red colour of Jack's hand. There was a split second when I thought it was a piece of fabric. A funny tea cosy.

But it wasn't, it was his skin.

He was screaming now, incoherently crying and shouting with the pain.

I stared at him, my heart beating quickly underneath my black shirt, and then I screamed too. I had absolutely no idea what to do.

I was aware of my pulse in my ears, the sound of Jack's screams and the fact that I had to do something.

And then Norm, alerted by my absence and my screams, was next to me.

Questions, questions. Demanding.

He swore, and I was certain then that I would lose my job.

I don't care if I lose my job, just make Jack okay, just make Jack okay, just make Jack okay

Norm picked him up and practically threw him onto the counter, turning the tap on above the huge, deep sink. He was still asking questions, glancing down at me between feeling with his own fingers under the tap. When he was satisfied, he pushed Jack's entire arm under the water and pushed his sleeve up.

Jack's screams stopped abruptly.

He whimpered, and used his left hand to cling to Norm so he didn't fall off the high counter.

'Oil,' Norm panted. He looked as though he'd just ran a marathon. His hair was standing on end like it always did, but I'd never seen his face so stricken. Had those lines on his forehead always been quite so pronounced? 'Abi, why did you let him touch that? What's he doing here anyway? Why didn't you call me or put water on it?'

Quite the opposite of most nicknames, Norm only ever called me Abi if he was feeling serious, which was rare.

So it was a burn.

Of course it was, I understood now.

Jack had burnt his hand.

I glanced at the deep fat fryer, a new addition to the tiny kitchen. A silver net full of oil, hot and waiting for the next portion of potatoes to be tipped in. The shape of the counter, Jack could have climbed up onto the shelf below and stuck his hand in. I hadn't thought of it.

And instead of telling him not to touch anything, I'd been more concerned about him being quiet. So he didn't call for me. How long had he been in unspeakable pain? The whole eight minutes?

'With burns,' Norm said, his hand steadily holding Jack's under the tap. 'It's lukewarm water. Not cold. No ice. Now, if you go back behind the bar and into the storeroom, there's a little green zipped bag. It's a First Aid kit. Get me that, there should be burn cream in it.'

I stumbled over my own feet trying to get to the bar.

Just as I entered, a team scored and the punters stood up and roared with an almighty cheer that made me jump.

'Any chance of getting served?' called one of our regulars, an older man who smelled like pee.

I ignored him, dived into the back for the First Aid kit.

'Can I get a pint?' the same man called. He caught sight of my face and winced. 'Sorry, pet. You all right? Where's Norm?'

I was crying too.

'What's he doing here?' Norm asked when I returned. He used his free hand to unzip the bag and took out a small tube. 'He shouldn't be here. Why didn't you call me? Why didn't you help him?'

Norm was doing that thing where adults ask you something but they don't really want an answer.

'Are you all right, wee man?' Norm asked.

'It hurts,' Jack whispered. He was whiter than the fridge behind him.

'Let me see…' Norm pulled Jack's hand away from under the tap and Jack's cries started up again. He hastily pushed it back under the tap. Norm shushed him, gently and kindly, then pulled the cap off the tube with his teeth.

'I'm sorry,' Jack said again, to both of us it seemed.

'It's not your fault,' Norm said immediately. 'Just want to make your hand better, wee man. Your daddy will be cross with me if I've let something happen to you in here.'

I nearly laughed.

Dad wouldn't even notice there was anything wrong with Jack's hand if we didn't tell him. And Norm knew that.

And so did Jack.

The guilt was immediate. A horrible, sickening feeling that started in my stomach and made its way up my chest. I'd left him alone and he'd been hurt. The one thing I actually wanted to do with my life was take care of Jack, save him from harm. I'd told my mum that's what I would do, hadn't I? Some job I was doing.

'I'm so sorry,' I whispered. 'I'm so sorry, Jack. I'm sorry, Norm.'

Norm nodded, swallowed. 'It's okay, love. No point worrying about it now. The day and hour you turn sixteen, I'm going to put you on a health and safety course. I'll run you through all the basics next week when we're a bit less busy. It's my own fault. You weren't to know.'

The Blindspot

I wasn't sacked?

I could hardly believe it.

And Jack had stopped crying, so he must be okay. I could use this as a learning experience.

No lasting harm.

I'd do better, next time.

I'd do more, do anything, to make sure Jack was never hurt again.

7

The Golden Boy

'The only thing any of us needs to focus on is the fact that it's not even eight o'clock and Jack is back home where he belongs. Do you know what that implies to me? Do you, Pat? Do you know what it implies? Is that they have sweet fuck all evidence against him. This is a very, very minor thing. It's a *hesaidshesaid*, and do you know what the statistics are on cases like that? Do you? Well no, me neither, specifically, but cases like this almost never stand up in court. I'm nearly positive. Don't waste your time worrying about it, any of you.'

I'm not quite sure who Francie is trying to reassure with his constant stream of nonsensical enthusiastic patter, but I notice that it works very well on Dad and not at all on me, Jack or Ciarán.

I can't feel too badly towards Francie, even if the things he's saying are making me angry and uncomfortable in equal measure. He's done exactly what he was supposed to do. He got Jack out of the police station, unharmed though shaken, and he seems to think that everything that happened this morning was a misunderstanding. I haven't asked about his fees yet. Yes, he's a family friend, and yes, he likes my dad, but I'm afraid that if we admit that we have about two hundred pounds between us all in total, he'll drive Jack back to Oldry Police Station and leave him there.

Nobody's brought up money yet. God forbid Dad should take charge on that one.

'Can't thank you enough,' Dad says again. 'Honestly, Francie. You're one in a million. Did I disturb you this morning?'

'You did, Pat, but never worry. I nipped back to the office once young Mr Campbell was released. Sorry I couldn't see you home myself, son.'

'It's fine,' Jack murmurs.

After Jack and I stopped off at Tesco and Jack revealed the identity of his accuser, neither of us could think of anything to do except go home and sit there. We've both had three cups of tea, and I haven't moved from the kitchen table. Jack stands behind me, leaning against the kitchen counter.

Ciarán came after work, asked a few inane questions and nodded thoughtfully as we – well, mostly I – answered him. He's had two cups, and keeps slapping his thighs as if he's about to announce his departure, but something always gets in the way.

Last time he had slapped his thighs and even got as far as saying, 'Well—' when the front door banged open. The booming Belfast accent that could only belong to Francis Finn hurtled through the house, followed by the man himself appearing in our kitchen doorway, his tie loosened, his trousers badly fitting and his hairpiece – yes, an actual bloody hairpiece – askew, and looking ridiculous.

Was this really the best we could afford for my baby brother?

'Francie, I didn't even offer you a beer!' Dad says now.

The height of bad manners in Vetobridge, not offering your son's solicitor a beer the second he steps over the threshold.

'What'll you have? Tennents or Harp? Or I'm having a wee Guinness?'

'Just a wee one?' Francie waggles his eyebrows. 'Go on then, I'll join you. Anything at all, Pat. Anything. No, not that shite! Yes, that'll do.'

Dad busies himself with taking two bottles from the fridge and – bizarrely – finding clean glasses for them both.

I shake my head impatiently, keen to get back to Jack. 'So, honestly, Francie, you think that's it? It's over?'

Francie accepts his Guinness with a nod to Dad that shuffles his hairpiece worryingly close to his eyes.

'Yes, love. I think so.' He takes a sip and grins at me. 'The thing is – if the police thought the wee girl had a case, Jack would still be there. They couldda held him for a full twenty-four hours. Thirty-six, if they were super serious. But they didn't. They obviously couldn't. Unless they get some DNA results back that show Jack was…' He has the grace to blush, aware that he is in front of Jack's family and the boy himself '… intimate, with her,' he continues. 'That's him home and hosed. And Jack says he didn't touch her, so they won't. Case closed.'

Dad and Francie have both been referring to Katie Waltz as *the wee girl*, and so has Ciarán. As a young woman in a predominantly male environment most of the time, I can relate to being called this and resent it, but I don't say anything. How can I stick up for the *wee girl* who has made these accusations?

'Really appreciate this, Francie,' Dad says, as if Francie has dropped off a bag of shopping, not defended his youngest son against a rape charge.

'It was nothing,' Francie says, and they clink glasses. They both take a long sup, then he adds, 'I didn't do much, only told Jack to keep no commenting, didn't I, son?'

I glance at Jack, who has told me just as much, but who seems unhappy about it.

'Was that wise?' I ask. 'Sorry, I know you're the expert but… it seems like Jack should have tried to help as much as possible. Loads of "no comment" answers might make him look as if he's…' I don't say the word, they all know what I mean.

'Nah,' Francie says, a deep noise in the back of his throat. 'He'd already denied it when I got there, and that's all he had to do. After that, no comment was fine. Here, it worked, didn't it?' He nods at me and reaches up to scratch his fake hair, pulling it unsubtly back into place.

I have an awful feeling that Francie doesn't get too many wins, so I let him have it.

'Well.' Ciarán slaps his thighs and stands up before he can be pulled back into his family drama yet again. 'I'm away. Work in the morning and haven't seen Bex all day so… Right, Da.' He slaps Dad on the back. 'Abi.' He nods at me. 'Francie.' He shakes Francie's hand. 'Jack.'

The boys nod at one another without making eye contact, and Ciarán is gone without another word. He practically sprints to the door.

That leaves a vacant seat at the table again, but Jack doesn't move to fill it. I have a feeling Jack wants to go to bed, but he doesn't want to seem ungrateful by not staying to talk to Francie. If I can think of a way to get him—

'Sure, you're a cracking boy, Jack,' Francie announces, and he salutes Jack with his glass. 'You're a good egg. Clever clogs, good looking lad, family round you. It was never going to go any other way, was it?'

What he's saying is true, of course, but it makes me feel cold inside to hear it said so blatantly, so casually.

'So, what if they do find whoever hurt Katie, and he's a good looking, smart, family boy too?'

I'm not sure what made me say it. I just… couldn't not.

Francie narrows his eyes and gives a little snort. 'What do you mean? Don't worry about that. The police will find the real culprit… if there is one.'

It's not what I meant, and everyone in the room knows that, but nobody says anything. I run my hand over my face and then pull my hair back into a ponytail.

'Besides,' Francie says, accepting another beer that Dad is offering, 'Jack's no record. He's squeaky clean, aren't you Jack? Nothing with the police, nothing with the school. He's golden.'

I look behind me at Jack under the guise of fixing my hair, and we meet each other's eye for a split second.

Max comes over late.

I've donned my shorts and T-shirt pyjama top and pulled a bottle of white wine out of the fridge. It sits on the counter, condensation dribbling down the neck, making a pool underneath. I watch it from the high stool at what I've decided to call the breakfast bar. It's just a tiny part of the counter that doesn't have a cupboard under it, but it's big enough to sit at and eat my breakfast if I push my legs to the side. Normally I'm all about coasters and cleanliness, but I can't bring myself to move the bottle or get a coaster, or do anything ever again, really.

Twice this evening I've genuinely wondered if it was all a dream. Dad calling Francie, Jack needing a solicitor, a grown woman giving him the eye at the station... That doesn't seem like something that could have happened in real life.

Max presses the buzzer twice in quick succession – the little code we've established. I can reach the button from here, and I let him in, confirming the coast is clear.

He is humming an awkward, stilted tune as he comes up the stairs, and I hear him fuss with the key I gave him before he lets himself inside the flat.

The door opens straight into the kitchen cum living room, and he closes it behind him.

He has a plastic Tesco bag clutched in a fist and pulled up towards himself. He never carries shopping bags by their handles; I have no idea why, but I used to find it endearing. He is wearing his white shirt with the pinstripes that we can't agree the colour of. I think grey, but he says blue, so he's wearing a pair of pale blue chinos too. He hasn't changed after work. I love him most like this. The faintest smell of his aftershave accompanies him, almost washed away by the busy day he's had. I've read somewhere that fresh sweat doesn't have a smell, but his has the slightest, slightest smell and usually I find it intoxicating.

He is looking at me with his head on one side, and I look back, mustering my first smile of the day for him.

'I got you a bottle of wine,' he says. His voice is soft – I've never heard it go too far above sotto, even when he's teaching. He cops the bottle already on the counter and pretends to click his fingers in a *drat!* 'But I see you beat me to it. Shall I get glasses?'

He doesn't wait for a response, but sets his bag down and busies himself pouring us a glass each.

'How was work?' I manage, taking the glass from him and following him over to the sofa. His presence has spurred me into action, into movement. Like I've been one of those motionless street-performers whose shift is now over.

I don't have a TV yet, and there is a suspicious stain on one of the cushions on this sofa that came with the flat, but it's comfortable in here, and there's a huge semi-circular window opposite us that lets in a lot of light. If I stand and crane my neck at one side, it lets me see the Mournes beyond. If I open the window during the day, the smells of strawberry and bubble gum and lemon from the Vape Shop below are almost overpowering. That exact spot by the window is an imperfect, tiny stamp of unusual paradise.

'Oh, the usual. Nice quiet timetable now everybody's off on study leave *except* for Tuesdays. I'll be glad to see the summer. Children are wonderful, but my God they're exhausting.'

'Yes,' I murmur, thinking of the one I raised.

'So.' Max takes a sip of wine, then sets it carefully on the carpet. As soon as I can afford it, I want to get the carpet stripped out and redone. I think the person who lived here before me had dogs, and sometimes, judging by the smell, I think he forgot to take one with him when he left. I should also buy a coffee table. I will do all of this when everything feels less ridiculous and awful. I'll have to write it down. Plan.

Max does that thing with his hands, where he makes a triangle of them, as if he's about to pray, and then puts them to his side and looks at me seriously. His way of telling me I have his full attention.

He doesn't need to say any more.

'Jack's been accused of forcing himself on Katie Waltz last night.'

If Max is surprised, he hides it well. Maybe a slight slump of his shoulders, but that's all I register before I continue.

'He left my house and went to meet his mates at the other side of the town, that's what happened. But this girl, Katie, do you know her? She'd have had to take your class until fifth year, do you remember her?'

Max is nodding. 'Of course. Isn't she Norm's granddaughter?'

I feel my teeth clench. How on earth am I going to face my boss after the awful lies his granddaughter has told? I'll deal with that tomorrow evening when I go in for my shift.

'Yeah. That's her.'

'Okay. What does she say happened?'

I recount to Max the story that Jack told me in the car. I think of the trail and want to scream at how ridiculous it is. How fucking childlike this very adult thing is. *Jack told me that the police said that Katie said*

I try and do a better job of the story than Jack did. His account leapt backwards and forwards. He says his own memories about last night are hazy; that he was very drunk from early on and he can't be sure of timelines himself.

'She said she was hanging out with a few boys on the beach after the party and that Jack met them there. Late, but she has no idea what time. After one in the morning... Jack agrees that bit is true. They were all smoking weed, I think,' I say this bit quickly, even though it's ridiculous to be ashamed or embarrassed about your brother's smoking when he's been in the police station that same day accused of rape. 'And Katie says, she *admits*, her memory is really groggy and confused.' I want to make sure Max knows that bit. 'She says they ended up by the rockpools. Next thing she can be *sure* of...' I put emphasis on the word sure and raise my own eyebrows so Max knows not to pay heed to what I am about to say next, 'is that Jack was... was on top of her. Forced himself on her. She can't remember if the others were still there or not.'

Max stares at me for a minute, then turns away and looks at the spot on the opposite wall where the TV might go. He looks at it as if the TV is already there, as if some interesting show is on. Then he blows his cheeks out and makes the triangle with his hands again.

'That's really serious,' is all he says.

'Yes,' I say. 'It is really serious. She's either got it in for Jack or her memory of last night is completely warped. Either way, she needs help.'

Max blinks at his triangled hands. 'I meant it's really serious for Jack.'

'I know,' I say, a creep of irritation in my voice. 'But they let him go. Jack gave his version of the events as best he could and it's over. For now, I think. My Dad's mate is a solicitor and he got him out in just a few hours.'

'What does Jack say happened?'

I take a sip of wine. 'He says he left here, went to meet his friends on the beach… chatted for a bit and then went home. Says he isn't sure of times and can't really remember the route he took, but he says nothing happened. To Katie. Not while he was there.'

'And his mates?'

I sigh and swirl the wine around in my glass. 'Don't know. The police will be talking to them, obviously. They maybe already have. Jack lost his phone last night so he hasn't been speaking to any of them.'

Max looks at me.

'What?' I ask.

'He lost his phone?'

'Yeah.'

'Last night?'

'…Yeah?'

'That's a bit—'

'A bit what?' I snap, feeling my eyes widen.

Max and I don't fight. We don't even bicker, we're not that kind of couple. Things are easy, enjoyable, happy, with Max. That's why my heart pounds as I stare at him, daring him to say something more.

'Nothing,' he says finally.

'He was a teenage boy out for a drink,' I say lightly, concentrating on my fingertips on the thin stem of my glass. 'He lost his phone.'

He reaches to the floor for his own wine and motions at me to put my feet on his lap. I wait a moment before doing so, letting my heart return to normal.

The Norah Jones album I put on my phone before Max arrived still plays quietly from the kitchen area. We listen to it for a few minutes and Max rubs my bare feet, both of us thinking carefully.

'They took his laptop,' I say. 'I'm not sure why. Looking for communication between him and her, maybe. Thank God his exams are finished, can you imagine trying to revise without a laptop these days?'

'These days,' Max smiles. 'As if you did your own exams forty years ago.'

'Nine years ago,' I say. 'That's ages. How long ago did you do yours?'

Max rolls his eyes, but he's grinning. 'Must be… Jesus. Twenty-four years ago I did my A-Levels. Is that right? That can't be right. Is it twenty-three? That's a whole generation ago. My sixth formers weren't even born.'

Jack is – was – one of Max's sixth formers until, I suppose, yesterday. Max would agree, Jack was probably his best ever student. If he gets into MUSE in September – and he will, he must – he'll be the first student from Seaview High ever to go there on a scholarship. He met with the tutors last year and they want him to come and research… something to do with a piece for a microscope. Or a telescope; I really have no idea. I must ask Jack to explain it again. Either way, I'm delighted for him and it sounds exciting.

And the city of Mingle, nestled just south of Dublin, is not so far away that he won't be able to come home the odd weekend.

'So how was it left?' Max asks. 'It sounds like a … a bit of a "he said, she said", thing, so what do they do next?'

'He's…' I swallow. This is the part I don't understand all that well, the part Francie explained for the third time just before he left Dad's house earlier. Jack understands it better than I do, like most things. 'He's released under caution, it's called. So… I don't think the investigation is over, or anything, but for now he's fine. He's home. At Dad's.' It still feels strange to call the house in Pine Street 'Dad's' and not 'mine'. 'He has to be there and be contactable, and they're going to bring him in again if they need to ask him more questions. He's not allowed to contact Katie or go near her, which is obviously fine. I can't see them salvaging much of a friendship after this, can you?' I try to snort my disgust, but it comes out as a half-sob. Max squeezes the sole of my foot and nods slowly.

'It's a pity,' he says lightly. 'They've been friends a long time.' When I don't reply he adds, 'Eighteen-year-olds are obsessed with sex.'

I think back to being eighteen. I stayed in school for my A-Levels, but I'd picked up so many shifts in The Rooster that I only passed one. It hardly mattered, I wasn't going anywhere or doing anything.

'I wasn't,' I say softly. 'I was just obsessed with you.'

Max blushes, as he always does when I talk about the fact that actually, he was my teacher too for a few years.

With my eye bags and my second-hand uniform and charity-shop shoes, I thought he probably didn't even know my name.

But he did.

'And now the tables have turned,' Max says. 'And I'm obsessed with you.'

He leans in and kisses me once, softly. He pulls away and we smile at one another.

'Will you do me a favour?' he asks.

'Mm?'

'Will you let me put up that shelf?' He nods his head to the side. A single white shelf, delivered by Amazon early this morning, when the world was recognisable, sits neatly on the carpet, a tiny plastic bag of screws and a hammer beside it.

I grin. 'I've no spirit level, I was going to get my dad to do it with me. He's good at all that.'

'So am I, and it's doing my head in. I can eyeball it?'

'I'll allow it,' I say.

I lie back on the sofa and stretch out, sipping my wine, as Max gets to work with the shelf. He puts the first nail in the wrong place and makes me wince, but he fixes it in a few minutes and taps the shelf proudly. 'There you go. What's going up here, pride of place then?'

'Not sure,' I say, thinking of the degree certificate Jack will get in three years' time. As long as things blow over. Which, of course, they have to.

'You're a homeowner now,' Max says, stretching his back. His shirt is sticking to him after this brief exertion. 'You get to decide what goes where. How does it feel, a week in?'

'Great,' I say automatically. 'Never had anywhere that was mine before.'

'You'll not know yourself. It's the best thing ever. Strangely rewarding, doing laundry and cleaning and tidying and being able to sit down after it and look about you and think, I did all that.'

I think sometimes Max's head is so full of formulae and facts that he forgets who he's speaking to. Who does he think cleaned and did laundry at my dad's house? I hate it when he says things like that, hate when he patronises me without even realising it. I'm never sure if it's an age thing or… No, it's not a man/woman thing. I wouldn't be with him if it were that.

Then he turns to grin at me, and he looks tired and happy, and that's my favourite way for Max to be and I feel myself melt a little bit.

'Thanks,' I say. 'Shelf looks great.'

'Best shelf I've ever seen. Maybe we could print a photo of us to put on it.'

It's just words, it isn't an actual suggestion. Just a game we play, something to think about and smile about.

He comes over to the sofa and kisses me again.

And then again.

And then some more.

The thing with an extramarital affair is that you spend so little time with one another that the passion never goes away. In a relationship, there's passion and then over time that becomes comfort – or so I'm told. With Max and me, there's passion and more passion, and more and more and…

An image of his wife comes into my head as he kisses my neck.

I wonder what she's doing right now. It's Tuesday, so no Pilates or Judo for Caroline tonight. She's probably at home, lying in bed, watching TV. Maybe she's already asleep. I wonder what excuse he gave her tonight.

Does he even bother with excuses any more?

Max moves our wine glasses out of the way and presses me down onto the sofa, his mouth finding mine with more urgency this time.

And then an image of Katie Waltz pops into my head and I feel my breath catch. Max misunderstands my reaction and kisses me deeper, and my mind races off in a direction over which I have no control, a direction I don't want to travel in. I can see rockpools, and moonlight glinting on water...

And then I am staring at the white shelf glowing in the dark, willing myself not to think at all.

8

The Scapegoat

When my brother Jack was six, Dad got a phone call from the school and had to go and pick him up after lunch. He wasn't working that day – had 'cut his hours' from four days a week to two because he just 'didn't feel as young as he used to be'. Nobody questioned it. We had money coming in from Jordan's personal training and Decky had taken to repairing phone screens in his bedroom and had quite a few customers, so he was nearly better off than any of us. I had enough for myself and treats for Jack as I'd started doing Fridays and Mondays for Norm in the bar as well as my Saturdays, to give him a bit of a break. Ciarán had broken up with Amelia and moved in with his love-of-his-life-forever girlfriend Charlene on the same day. He still came over two or three times a week to take food out of the cupboards and collect his post.

When I got home from school, I found Jack perched in front of the TV, his mouth wide open, swinging his legs.

'Hi,' I said breathlessly, unwinding my school scarf. 'How are you? Did you have to come home sick? Dad texted to say he was lifting you.'

Jack looked at me, then looked away again.

I glanced at the TV. It was his favourite show, in which two wacky-haired presenters did science experiments and made awful jokes together.

'Did you have a bad tummy?' I asked, leaning over to feel his forehead.

He squirmed out of reach, right to the far side of the sofa, and pulled his legs up to his chest.

'Okay…' I said, backing out of the room.

Dad was in the kitchen, smoking.

'Hiya, love. How was today? Did you have your…?'

'Science mock,' I said, filling in the blank because I knew Dad couldn't actually remember what exam I'd had that day. 'Yeah. It was okay! Don't think I'll be discovering a new element any time soon, don't get me wrong.'

I was average at science. I was average at basically everything, maybe a little bit better at English than some of the others. But basically in the middle. At everything.

'What's wrong with Jack?' I asked. 'Is he sick?'

'Hm?' Dad blew smoke away from me. 'Oh, no. He was misbehaving. He's suspended for a day. A single day, isn't that a joke?'

My stomach dropped. I stared at Dad. 'What?' I asked. 'What are you talking about? How's he been suspended? He's in P3! What do they say he did?'

Dad rolled his eyes. 'He pulled a wee girl's skirt off her or something. Nothing serious. I've had a word with him, don't you worry.'

'He – what?' I shook my head, feeling my eyes burning. 'Jack wouldn't do that. Are you sure? Who was it you spoke to? Was it Mrs Myers herself?'

Dad stubbed his cigarette out in the ashtray and shrugged. 'Can't remember her name. Older woman. Glasses.'

'Mrs Ross, the head?' I demanded. 'Dad, why didn't you phone me? I could have come down. What *exactly* did they say?'

Dad pushed his seat back from the kitchen table and came towards me, arms outstretched. 'Abi, it's fine. It's taken care of. Come here—'

I pushed him away and darted back into the living room. I reached for the remote control and switched off the TV.

'OI!' Jack protested, but at the look on my face he closed his mouth and looked ashen.

'What did you do today?' I asked calmly. 'Tell me. Now.'

He looked at my school scarf, draped over the sofa arm. He reached for it, playing with the ends.

'Jack,' I said. 'This is serious. Tell me.'

'They told me to,' he said in a small voice, his eyes on the scarf and not on me. 'They made me do it. It wasn't me.'

'Who? Jack, look at me.'

He looked up at me, then back down at his hands. I followed his gaze, saw the scaly, raw burn across his fingers, felt my anger dissolving into something else.

'Darling,' I whispered. I knelt down so we were face to face. 'Who told you to do what?'

'The boys,' he said. His eyes over time had deepened to the exact blue of the copper flame I'd been writing about just an hour ago. 'They told me to pull down Jodie's skirt. I had to. They said I had to...'

'Where was this?'

'... Playground.'

'Did people see?'

'Yeah. It wasn't funny. I thought it would be funny. They said it would be. Her pants came down too.'

I closed my eyes. 'Oh, Jack.'

'I didn't mean to,' he said desperately. 'They made me do it. I thought if I did that they'd...'

I waited, watching him carefully. The single dimple on the left side of his mouth, the way his nose had the slightest upturn at the end, just like mine but much more beautiful. That one especially long blond curl over his ear that we could just never tame. The face I knew better than my own, that I had watched and kissed since the day he was born.

'What?' I whispered, glancing over my shoulder to make sure Dad was still in the kitchen.

'They'd stop being mean to me,' Jack whispered back, leaning close to me. His breath was like sugar. Like it always was. He picked at the thread on my scarf and pulled it so it started to unravel. I didn't stop him.

'What have they been doing?' I asked, keeping my voice low and calm, even though inside I was suddenly seething. I knew who he meant by 'the boys', a group of lads in his class who acted older than their six or seven years. Picking up Jack from the afterschool club, I'd heard them saying curse words as loudly as they dared, glancing over at the assistants and giggling. 'What have they been saying?'

'Nothing bad!' Jack said hastily. 'They're my friends. They're just joking. But it's a bit... A bit mean. They say I'm...'

I waited, feeling that Jack was on a roll. He'd tell me, he always told me. He was a great speaker, a really good communicator. Good at talking about feelings and good at thinking. Much better than most six- or seven-year-olds, I thought proudly.

'They say I'm Lizard Boy.'

I blinked, moved my head away a little. 'Lizard Boy?' I repeated. 'I don't understand. Is that... Is that a nickname? Is it bad?'

'Because of this,' Jack said, trying to roll his eyes as if it was obvious, but they were full of tears now, and this only made them leak out. He held up his right hand, showing me his scar as if I hadn't looked at it every single day for the last eighteen months.

I got it now.

Lizard Boy, because of his scaly hand.

The scars he'd been left with after the hot oil incident in The Rooster healed well in the first year. A trip to A&E for some more burn cream and painkillers, a hastily given lie when the kind doctor asked what happened, and a week off school. That was all that was required. What began as huge, red and pink liquid-filled blisters gradually burst, leaving behind wrinkled, twisted skin that still gave Jack bother when he tried to use his colouring pencils. He never talked about it after that first week, and I never asked, being too afraid to hear he was in pain, being too ashamed to look him in the eye and acknowledge that it was all my fault. His thumb and index finger had survived intact, untouched. His third finger was covered in the scaly scar, but the fourth and little fingers were the worst affected. They were dark red, nearly purple, and when I did let myself think back to the incident in the kitchen at The Rooster, I imagined those fingers plunging into the hot oil first. All it would take was a split second of not realising what he had done. The palm of his hand had healed better than the digits, fading to a pale red that he could pass off as a birthmark, were it not for the accompanying fingers and the fact that the back of his hand had somehow suffered the worst. It really was scaly. It was awful. I could understand why a group of little boys might liken his skin to scales. I hated that I could understand it.

'That's not a nice thing to say,' I said finally. 'Your hand looks fine.'

'No, it doesn't!' Jack said, suddenly shouting. 'You're lying, you always lie to me! You're not supposed to *lie* but you are! You tell me things that aren't true. You tell me – you—' Jack had to stop shouting to take a few deep breaths. Without hesitating I grabbed his school backpack from the armchair and fished around inside, pulling out his pale blue inhaler and giving it a shake. I held it up to his mouth and he took a few deep gasps. The doctor had given this to Jack the year before, telling us he was sure Jack's asthma wasn't bad enough that he'd ever have to use it. Precautionary, he said. Still, I made him carry it everywhere he went.

He pushed the inhaler away and looked up at me, defiant now he'd got his breath back. 'You're a liar,' he repeated. 'I'm not the best at maths. I'm not special. I'm Lizard Boy! They're right. It's ugly, it's… It's FUCK!'

I blinked at the swear word as it filled the air between us. Of course, his brothers were under strict instructions from me not to swear in front of him, but Jack was observant and clever, so it was no surprise he'd picked it up somewhere and used it out of context. Probably he'd heard it from his idiotic classmates too. But he was a smart boy. He knew there was a time and a place for things. He was trying to hurt me.

'FUCK!' he shouted again, in my face. 'FUCK. FUCK. FUCK. FUCK.'

I just stood there, crying, until Dad came in and looked at me with more concern than I'd ever seen on his face before. He shouted at Jack to stop shouting, and then they were both shouting. Dad probably didn't care much about the cursing, just that Jack was making me cry, and he'd never let anyone do that.

Later, when Jack was asleep in his bottom bunk bed, I crept inside. One side of his face was lit by the Star Wars nightlight that had once belonged to Decky. Jack slept with both arms above his head, making a halo of sorts around him. His scar shone in the light.

'Jack,' I whispered, crouching beside his bed. 'Jack, are you awake?'

He wrinkled his nose and turned around. 'Hm?' he asked, sleepily. 'Is it time to get up?'

'No, darling. It's only eight. At night-time.'

He let out a sigh and reached his scarred fingers towards me to take my hand. 'Are we still best friends?' he said.

I smiled. 'Of course we are,' I said, because we were. 'I just wanted to talk to you about today.'

Jack blinked and sat up, his head not touching the bunk above that Decky would creep into later.

'What you did to that girl,' I said slowly. 'It's really not okay. It's really serious, Jack – no, don't get upset, I'm not cross with you! I just need you to understand… You can't do that again. You can't touch people like that, can't hurt them like that. That girl is probably really embarrassed by what happened. You wouldn't like to feel like that, would you?' He shook his head solemnly. 'I know you were only doing it because the other boys told you to,' I continued, imagining for one glorious moment a world in which it was fine to wring the necks of children who hurt perfect angels like Jack. 'But that doesn't make it okay. I'm going to speak to Mrs Myers about it tomorrow, explain about the nickname and how they've been making you feel. Okay?'

'No,' Jack moaned, gripping my hand tighter. He looked at me seriously. More seriously than any adult ever had. 'No, Abi. They'll hate me. They won't be my friends any more if I tell on them.'

'I don't know if they are your friends, darling,' I said, reaching out to stroke his curls. 'Why don't you play with some of the others tomorrow, instead?'

'They are my friends,' Jack says quickly. 'They are. You're lying again—'

'Shhh,' I whispered, shaking my head. 'Okay. Let's not get into it now. You understand what I'm saying to you, don't you, Jack?'

He nodded slowly and lay down again.

I stroked his curls behind his ears for a moment and then said, 'I never lie to you, you know.'

His eyes blinked slowly. He was already being pulled back into the encompassing warmth of childhood dreams.

'I just try to protect you,' I murmured. 'It's not lies if it's well-intentioned.'

I left his bedroom feeling that, even if it had been an awful day, an awful incident, I'd handled it well. I was even a little bit proud of my closing statement, felt I could write it down and use it again some time.

9

The Houseguest

I t is hot when I wake up, and I think that's what's woken me.
I blink a few times in the murky half-light – the room is dark, and
the sky outside is dark, but there's a glowing orange streetlamp right
outside my bedroom window that lights up my chest of drawers in a
weird sepia. I throw the covers off and pull my T-shirt away from my
sweating skin.

Max isn't here, he must have snuck off after I fell asleep. The bed is
still warm, still a little damp, where he lay. Back to Caroline. Always
back to Caroline.

The intercom buzzes and I realise that's the second time – that's
what woke me. I thought it had been part of my dream.

Delirious, I stumble to the kitchen.

'Hello?' I croak into the intercom, my mouth dry from the bottle-
and-a-half of wine.

'It's Jack.' His voice sounds thick with emotion, like he's crying or
he's got a bad cold.

Immediately I am awake, completely sober and in control. 'Come
up!' I say, and buzz him in. I switch on the lamp that sits on the floor
– another thing I have to find a place for. I hear Jack opening, then
closing the door downstairs and I tap the screen of my phone that I've
left on the counter. It's three in the morning. What on earth is Jack
doing here at three in the morning?

Something else must have happened.

In the bathroom, the toilet flushes and my stomach lurches in tandem.

Fuck fuck fuck fuck fuck fuck

'Did someone buzz?' Max calls. I hear the tap turning on, the sounds of him washing his hands. 'It's the middle of the night. Was it kids messing?'

Fuck fuck fuck

Jack's footsteps reach the top of the stairs and he taps lightly on the door.

Max's face appears from the bathroom, pale and confused. 'Who is that?'

'It's Jack,' I hiss.

'Why?'

'I don't know why! Fuck.'

'Why did you let him in?'

'I didn't know you were still – just go into my bedroom, be—'

But it's too late. The door to the flat, the door we forgot to lock before we fell into bed, opens and Jack stands in the doorway, two inches taller than his physics teacher.

It's the most bizarre situation I have ever been in, and I can't think of anything at all to say.

The men blink at one another. Max topless, wearing only a pair of loose grey boxers. Cotton, as well, and old. I'm suddenly ridiculously embarrassed by this stark reminder of his age. Which is entirely the wrong thing to be worried about. Jack, in jeans and a purple hoodie, hesitates where he stands, and looks—

'Fuck!' I say, going to my brother. 'What happened to your face?'

Jack's lip is cut, and one of his eyes is half-closed and looks sore. It hasn't bruised yet, but I can tell, even in the lamplight, that it will.

He looks away from Max, finally, to me, and his lips tremble. I can tell he's about to cry, so I throw Max a hasty look and he obediently retreats into my bedroom and closes the door. I hope to God he's getting dressed.

'Come and sit down,' I murmur. I realise with a stab of horror that a torn condom wrapper is lying on the floor next to the sofa, and I hastily grab it and scrunch it up in my fist as Jack sits down.

'Can I stay here?' he mumbles, sniffing. 'Or is it not a good time? Can I stay for a while? Just a while?'

'Of course you can,' I say, bewildered. 'But why, Jack, what happened?'

The door to my room opens and we both look up. Max is dressed, has his glasses on again and looks more like himself. More like Jack's teacher. Which makes his presence in my flat at three in the morning no easier to digest.

'Hi, Jack,' he says softly.

'Hi, Mr Murray,' Jack says, not looking at him.

Max pushes his glasses up his nose and does an awkward little shrug and grin. 'I think Max is okay, given the circumstances and the fact you're technically no longer a pupil. I'll leave you two to it.'

He goes to the door and I follow him onto the tiny square of carpet outside the door that acts as a landing.

'I'm sorry,' he whispers. 'Is he okay?'

'I'm sorry,' I say. 'I'm not sure yet. I'll phone you later.'

'Yeah, course. Be good.' He kisses me on the cheek and pads downstairs.

I go back to Jack.

His eyes are wet and his shoulders are shaking now.

On some base level I realise I'm the tiniest bit glad he's upset. At least now I don't have to explain why Jack's form tutor and physics teacher was half-naked in my flat in the middle of the night. Maybe I'll have enough time to think of something plausible.

Sure, Abi

'J-Jordan,' he sobs. 'He said horrible – horrible – he said—'

'Jordan?'

'It was so s-stupid. It was so dumb. I told him – t-told him to switch the light off—'

I fish a packet of tissues out of my bag and bring them to Jack. He takes a few steadying breaths, mops at his eyes and tries again.

'He got up to… I dunno, go to the bathroom. And he turned the light on. I'd just – *literally* just fallen asleep. I haven't slept for – I'm so tired, Abi. I told him to turn it off and he swore at me. He said something like, you don't get to call the shots, and I told him to fuck off, but not serious, you know what I mean? And I tried to go back to sleep, and he said… Something. I didn't hear him, I had my duvet over my head but he… He said something about… About her. About Katie. He said her name.'

Jack blinks at me, his eyes wide, not understanding. As if he's six years old again, as if things are new to him. As if he needs me to explain things in a way that fits into his world. Only… How can I, this time?

'And I asked him to repeat it, told him to be a man and tell me what he said. He was just – he was like, scoffing, Abi. He was shaking his head like he was disgusted or something. And then Decky told us both to shut the fuck up, and I said he started it, and Jordy said…' Jack trails off, then takes a deep breath. 'Jordy said, *you started it when you raped that wee girl on Monday night, you fucking creep.*'

My heart stops. What is most sickening is I can imagine this from my second brother, can picture his face contorting as he says those words, can imagine the exact pitch of his voice as he hisses them. It's as if he's there in the room with us.

'He said that?' I say. 'He really said that? And then he… ?'

'I started it,' Jack says, looking uncomfortable. 'I punched him – not hard! Just in the chest. He's massive, he probably didn't even feel it but… It was like he was waiting for me to do it, Abi. Like he had this… This anger in him. I've not seen it before. Like he wanted me to do it so he could hit me back. If Decky hadn't been there to pull him off, if Dad hadn't come in to see what all the noise was…' Jack shivers. 'I wish you'd never left. It's been shit without you anyway, and now this.'

Guilt tries to creep up my spine, but I won't let it. The flat is mine, the space is mine. I've never had a place that's *mine* before. *You've also never had a person that's just yours before,* I think to myself nastily, imagining Max walking to his car in the dark, heading back to his wife.

'I don't want to be there,' Jack says. He holds his head a little higher. 'Not if that's what my own brother thinks of me.'

I nod. 'Yeah. Yeah, okay. You can stay here as long as you like, you know that.'

Jack looks gratefully at me, then down at my hand. I squeeze the condom wrapper more tightly in my fist, still unable to think of a good reason—

'So,' Jack says. He half-smiles and clears his throat. 'Mr Murray, then?'

I feel my cheeks redden. In any other situation I'd be flat out denying this, would be embarrassed beyond belief... But it's been a strange day.

'Yeah,' I say.

'How long... ?'

He isn't judging me, isn't horrified. Instead, he looks a little bit embarrassed and a little bit... impressed?

A thought hits me. 'Did you know?' I ask. 'Did you know it was him?'

My dad and brothers have known I've been seeing someone for the last seven or eight years. I obviously haven't been able to introduce them to Max as my boyfriend, because he is no such thing, and I never told any of them who my 'Secret Boyfriend' was. Not even Jack.

'Kinda figured,' Jack shrugs. 'A few years ago. Did it start when you were in school?'

'No!' I say quickly. 'No, no. I was nineteen before we actually...' I trail off, look away, shake my head. 'Anyway. A few years now. His – his marriage is really shit – they aren't—'

'You don't need to explain,' Jack says. 'Honestly. I know you. You're not a bad person.'

I used to think I wasn't.

'Thank you,' I say quietly. Some part of me registers that of course I have a person who is just mine. I've had him his whole life. I take a deep breath. 'Neither are you.'

*

Jack has been asleep on the sofa for only a few hours when the buzzer goes again.

I haven't been able to get back to sleep, have instead been scrolling absently on my phone for five hours, my legs outside the bedsheets, trying to get cool.

There is nothing official, nothing on the news about Katie's supposed attack. Instead, social media is peppered with a few whispers, but no names.

Girlies, be careful when out and about in Vetobridge this summer – have heard some nasty rumours about sexual assault in the area. When will this end? #MeToo

Stick together, be vigilant, be careful. #Educateyoursonstoprotect yourdaughters

This is fine. I expected this. These posts are nothing new, sadly. A woman was attacked in Oldry just last month, and the same people posted the same things. It isn't news, nobody is really looking into it. It's just women being attacked, that's all. No big deal.

Nobody has specifically said that it's Jack who is being accused. Not yet. Not until the newspapers get hold of something concrete, and if they haven't already…

When the buzzer goes, I'm there in a heartbeat, thinking it might be Jordan, come to finish what he started, making sure I'm standing between him and Jack when it happens.

'Yes?' I ask, as clipped as I can.

'Abigail Campbell?'

A woman's voice. A woman I don't recognise. Jack has raised his head from the sofa and looks blearily at me.

'Y-yeah?' I say.

'Can we come in? We're from the PPB. My name is Detective Constable Mathers and I have with me Detective Constable Pollock. We'd like to ask you a few questions.'

'What's the PPB?' I whisper to Jack, my heart pounding. 'Is this about you?'

'Public Protection Branch,' Jack says. He has stood up and is hurriedly fixing the sofa, as if trying to conceal all evidence that he has slept there. 'The... the Rape Crime Unit people. Mathers was in my interview yesterday. She was okay. She was nice. How do they know I'm here?'

I hesitate, my hand hovering over the button to let them in. Jack runs his hands through his blond curls, pulls at his crumpled T-shirt. They're going to think we don't bother with ironing in his family.

I finally push the button and hear the two officers coming up the stairs.

'I think they want to talk to me,' I whisper. I open the door and go to stand next to Jack. 'It was my name they said. It's fine, it'll just be background stuff. Don't look so—'

'Hello?' A pretty woman sticks her head through the door before she enters. Her colleague, a bigger, older man, follows her, unsmiling, but looking around the flat with great interest.

'Hi,' I say, more confidently than I feel. 'Come on in...' I look around, very aware of the lack of a table or suitable chairs.

'Oh, hello again, Mr Campbell.' Mathers throws Jack a wide smile and Jack mumbles an awkward hello and smiles back. 'Didn't know you'd be here so early.'

'Just... visiting,' Jack says.

Mathers frowns at him. 'What happened to your face?'

'Slipped,' Jack and I say in unison. It sounds suspicious, so I try to roll my eyes in a good-natured, sisterly way. Jack nods determinedly.

Mathers continues to frown. 'We were lookin' for a wee word with Abigail,' she says, '... privately.'

Jack continues to nod, then realises what she means. 'Oh. Oh, grand. I'll just – I'll nip to the shop, then. Think you're out of milk anyway.' He swallows and puts his hands in his pockets, goes to the door without bothering to lift his jacket, or his wallet. I hope he has his tenner.

We watch him go. We listen to his footsteps taking the stairs two at a time, and there is a collective intake of breath as the door downstairs slams behind him.

I look around again. 'Sit down, if you like,' I say, gesturing to the sofa. I am determined not to be overly friendly, not to be too kind. I don't want them to think I'm overcompensating. They have to know that I believe – that I know, for sure – my brother is innocent of the horrible things Katie Waltz has accused him of. Should I be more hostile? Is that how the sister of an innocent boy – man – would behave?

I don't think I have time to figure out the answer to that question. Too much psychology involved, too much thinking, and the two officers have already sat side by side on the sofa.

There's nowhere for me to sit. Unless I snuggle right up to Pollock, and he doesn't look like he'd enjoy that any more than I would.

I hope to God I haven't forgotten any other condom wrappers.

'You a gamer, Miss Campbell?'

I shake my head confusedly at the first of Constable Mathers's questions.

She is smiling, jerks her head into the corner of the room where Jack's Xbox sits, cables wound around each other neatly, controller perched on top. He left it with me last week when I moved in, saying he would never get any studying done while it was in his bedroom, and could I please confiscate it until such time when he allowed himself to play again. We'd laughed about it.

'Oh,' I say. 'Oh, yeah. A bit.' I have no idea why I haven't told the truth.

I go to the semi-circular window and rest myself on the sill, crossing my arms and trying to look concerned and welcoming at the same time. I'm glad there aren't any mirrors in here yet.

'Miss Campbell,' Mathers says, taking out a flip notebook. 'Just wanted to confirm a few things. Is that okay? It's just about the events of Monday night.'

I nod, my mouth dry, emphasising the concerned and welcoming face.

'Your brother Jack tells us you had a housewarming party – is that correct?'

Another nod.

She looks around the flat, smiling. 'Nice little place, this. Handy if you're a Vaper.'

I choke out a strained laugh that makes Pollock look at me with raised eyebrows.

'When did you move in?'

'Oh – just last week. Had the party on Monday night because I work in a bar. The Rooster, just up the road. You know it? Impossible to get weekends off and my friends don't mind having a drink on a school night.' I close my mouth deliberately, aware I'm waffling. Why do I feel so guilty? Why am I making myself so suspicious? The police do this to innocent people, I suppose. Max says walking through airport security is the most nerve-racking thing imaginable, says he always feels like he's accidentally forgotten about the machete in his laptop case or the bomb in his pocket. I've never been in an airport. Never actually left Ireland, come to think of it.

I blink at Mathers and she blinks back.

'So yeah. Had the party on Monday,' I conclude.

'And Jack arrived at this party at what time?'

I think hard. I was mingling, serving drinks, talking to people I hadn't seen in years, cursing myself for not taking Max up on his offer of providing collapsible seats from the school. Everyone had to stand, some sensible people darting for one of the two spaces on the sofa any time the sofa-sitters got up to get another drink or use the bathroom.

I remember Jack coming inside, looking around. I went to him immediately, because of course I did. Told him to get himself a drink, asked him about the exam. But I was in the middle of a slightly heated text argument with Max, who'd said he'd come down for a few hours but hadn't.

It was going to be a debut of sorts. The first time I'd introduced Max to any of my friends or family. Granted, he knew the majority of them, as he had taught them all at some point. His marriage was essentially over in all but law, so he'd said he'd come. Be with me, in front of people for the first time. And then he hadn't bothered. Had chickened out.

I pull my phone out from my pocket, hastily slide the Twitter app and its awful comments away, and open WhatsApp. A new message from Decky:

Did Jack stay at yours?

But I ignore it. I scroll through my conversation with Max.

'It was… it would have been about half-eleven when he got here,' I say finally. 'I remember him coming through the door as I was sending a particular text.'

'And how did he seem?'

'Jack?'

'Yes.'

'He seemed…' I shake my head slightly. 'Normal. Like himself. He'd just done his last exam, maths. He's really clever, you see. Like, super smart. Way smarter than the rest of us, and these exams are really important because we want him to go to MUSE in September. He's set for all A-stars.'

Mathers is nodding encouragingly, as if I'm in a job interview and giving perfect answers.

'Okay. That's great, thank you. He wasn't agitated, then? Nothing unusual?'

'No.'

'And what did you talk about?'

'We… We didn't talk much. I had maybe twenty people here. I just said hello and got him a drink and left him to it.'

'Was he drunk?'

'No,' I say quickly.

'Oh.' A line appears on Mathers's brow for the first time. She shuffles pages in her notebook, then looks up again. 'Are you sure? Jack says he was very drunk on Monday night. Before he got to yours. Says he has a lot of blank spots, can't remember some things.'

Pollock stares at me too, one eyebrow raised. He still hasn't said a word. I feel my pulse quicken.

'Well, I'm not sure,' I say hastily. 'Like I said, I barely got a chance to chat. He could have been drunk. Yeah. In fact, yeah he was.'

'You seemed quite sure a minute ago that he wasn't.'

'I know. But he was.'

I know my cheeks must be blazing, but if I think about that, I'll make them worse. I readjust my bum on the windowsill, trying to get comfortable, then take a glance down at the street below, just for an excuse to look away from them. I can make out Jack, standing outside the bakery, three doors down from the Vape shop, a plastic carrier bag in one hand. He is leaning against the window, looking across the road towards the promenade. I am about to look back at the officers when Jack's face changes. He straightens up and makes to leave, but then another figure joins him. A figure in a black jacket that is much too warm for the weather and a black baseball cap. He's been running to catch up with Jack, and Jack stops and looks at him.

Mathers is talking again. '... Left at? Miss Campbell?'

'Huh?' I ask, looking around as though caught doing something embarrassing.

'Can you remember what time Jack left at? Left your party?'

'It was...' I trail off, pretending to think hard, and look out of the window again.

The figure and Jack are speaking with their heads close together. The figure is gesturing, pointing a finger at Jack's chest, and Jack is nodding, trying to step away. The figure in black points up, directly at me, without looking up. I blink in surprise. Then he turns on his heel and strides across the road and back towards the beach. Jack slumps against the wall next to the bakery, looking after him.

Then he looks up towards the flat and we catch each other's eye.

Only for a second.

'It was...' I say again, turning to the officers. There is no point in lying, they probably already know this. 'About one. I think. Everyone kind of left then, including Jack.'

'And do you have any idea where he was planning on going?'

'I – I thought he'd go home—'

'Ah, but he didn't,' Mathers says, flicking through her notebook again. 'No, we have his phone pinging off a mast near Murphy's Arcade at… one-thirty. That's not near your brother's house in Pine Street, is it?'

It's not a real question. They know where Pine Street is, they know where Murphy's Arcade is.

'Why didn't he just go home? Why did he go to the beach, back through town?'

I swallow. 'I'm not sure.'

'That's the last time we have his phone,' Mathers says. 'It seems the battery died, not long after and, according to Jack, the handset itself is missing. He says he must have dropped it somewhere on the beach. Does that sound like him? Is he careless with his things?'

I feel a ripple of irritation. 'No. He's not careless at all. He's really careful. He has a job in the garage on the Oldry Road and he keeps a car, he studies, he's not like… He's not like…'

I'm not even sure what I'm trying to say. *He's not like the others, not like those little shit friends he's had since he was a child, Jack is different, why don't you—*

'Have you spoken to Jack's friends?' I ask, surprising myself.

Mathers exchanges a glance with Pollock. 'Which friends would these be?' She readies her pen.

'There's a bunch of them. All from school, though only one of them actually stayed on with Jack.' I remember the boy we saw in Tesco, and his name jingles something in my memory, so I can reel off, 'Ben, Fitzy and Fergie.'

'Ah.' Mathers doesn't write anything. 'Yes. We have.'

'What have they said? Did they say Jack was with them the whole night?'

Mathers nods thoughtfully. 'Yes. Yes they did. They were a bit worse for wear on Monday night as well, hard getting any definite times out of them, but they've confirmed Jack met them on the beach after one and they had a few drinks, smoked a few joints, messed about. They've confirmed Katie was with them, but that she left to go and meet a friend.'

I nod, trying for casual. The same story Jack told me, the same story Jack told the police.

Mathers continues, 'It seems the other three boys all walked home together, they stayed in the house owned by Jonathan Ferguson's parents. That's where our officers found them all yesterday afternoon when they went to speak with them... Mr Ferguson's father confirms he heard the three of them stumbling in around quarter to three.' She seems to consider something for a moment. 'It's a pity Jack didn't think to walk back with them, to stay at the Fergusons'. He'd have an alibi then.'

I am still nodding. Then I stop. 'Well, he doesn't need an alibi,' I say reasonably. 'Only guilty people need alibis. He left his mates and went home.' I take a deep breath. 'Look... I'm really sorry that Katie Waltz had a bad night on Monday. If something happened to her then... That's obviously awful. Obviously. But it didn't have anything to do with my brother. The poor girl is confused. They had spent time together earlier in the evening, at the party in Springhill Manor, on the beach... She's got mixed up.'

'Mm,' Mathers makes a thoughtful noise, her eyes on her notebook. 'But the thing is, Miss Campbell, Jack can't account for what he did after he supposedly left his mates on the beach. Pine Street is... what? A fifteen-minute walk from the beach, maximum? So, if Jack left at the same time as his friends – his friends who were home at quarter to three... why didn't he get in until after four in the morning?'

I am calm. I will not show her how my heart is thudding. I will not let her hear it.

'I thought he couldn't remember the timings,' I say.

'No, he can't. You're right. It was your brother – Jordan? – who told us that.'

I stare at her.

'He woke up to use the bathroom about four o'clock on Tuesday morning,' Mathers says. She's not reading from her notebook now. She doesn't have to. She knows this. 'They share a room, is that right? And Jack wasn't in his bed. He hadn't come home yet.'

Jordan had spoken to the police and he hadn't even told me. Dad hadn't told me. Nobody fucking told me. They want me to fix everything, but they won't do me that one fucking thing. The police must have spoken to them after Jack was arrested yesterday morning.

'So after Jack left here, around one o'clock in the morning,' Mathers continues, as though she hasn't just collapsed the remaining pillar of my world, 'you didn't see him again? Until he was arrested on Tuesday morning? Is that right?'

She's told me that about Jordan to test me, says a voice in the back of my head. What did she think I would say? Did she think I'd break down and tell her of Jack's guilt?

'Right,' I say. My throat is dry, and I am suddenly aware that I didn't offer them any tea or coffee. Would it have been helpful for Jack's case if I had? Start character building now? The last ten minutes have shifted my perspective, somewhat.

'Right,' Mathers echoes. She and Pollock nod at each other. 'We'll leave you to it then, love. Good luck with the new flat.'

It feels like a jibe. Like she's poking fun at the tiny flat, with nowhere to sit and no TV to use the Xbox, and… I look at it as they let themselves out and do a double take.

The shelf Max put up last night.

It isn't even fucking straight.

10

The Dreamer

When my brother Jack was eight, his interest in physics became almost unbearable for everyone except me. I loved having a brother who was so clever, who did his homework without my having to ask him, who stayed behind for Science Club, for Maths Club, and for Art. But physics was his real passion, the thing he talked about, thought about, and it did his brothers' heads in so they mostly ignored him, even Decky. Ciarán was living in a flat in Oldry and – by some miracle – had been single for almost two whole months, but we still only really saw him at weekends. Jordan was spending a lot of time in the gym and wasn't really going out: he was saving up to buy a car, as he was jealous that my careful saving had allowed me, his little sister, to buy one before him. Granted, it was an ancient Renault Clio that had already broken down twice in the first six months, but it was still more than he, or indeed any of my brothers, had ever had for themselves. Decky was flitting. That's what he called it. He'd stayed on for his A-Levels and had left the year before with his three C grades, and since then he'd had seven jobs. Seven. He was finding out what he wanted to do, but so far all he knew for sure was that he didn't want to be a kitchen porter, a care assistant, a receptionist, a dog walker, a machine operative in a warehouse, a ticket taker at the cinema or a professional online gambler. The last one was a desperate attempt for him to earn some money for Christmas, but he lost everything he had and made us all cards by hand that said 'Sorry this is so shit'.

None of this was of any importance to me. I walked about beaming, delighted that I'd done such a good job with Jack, who was literally perfect. I ignored invitations to parties because I didn't want to waste my precious weekends being away from Jack – we would go to the library together, get the bus to Belfast to go to the museum, go for nature walks where Jack could tell me about all the wildlife and shrubbery. I worked four evenings a week in The Rooster, fitted my A-Level studies in when Jack was in bed, and more or less forgot that I'd turned eighteen over Christmas and really should have been socialising with boys my own age.

Jack had decided the year before that he no longer wanted to be a pilot. His interest was still firmly up in the air, but had extended beyond airports and flight routes. Jack wanted to be an astrophysicist, and already knew the exact course he wanted to do at university, even though he wouldn't be going for another ten years. He'd already read every single one of the children's science books in the library – thrice – and was almost finished making his way through the relevant adult books. The librarian was kind and helpful when I asked if she could order a few more in, but their budget was already pretty stretched, so as soon as Jack had read through those, I didn't like to ask again.

I had an idea in the back of my mind.

Mr Murray, who had taught me from first to third year, was Head of Science and the school's only physics teacher. I hadn't taken any sciences myself, but I knew a few girls in my year who had scraped the grades for physics *just* so they could spend a few hours a week in his presence. Max Murray *was* admittedly gorgeous. I'd had a crush on him when I was younger, like ninety per cent of the girls, but I barely saw him around the school after my first few years, so I'd almost forgotten about him.

I thought I could organise a meeting with him, tell him about my younger brother's interest in his subject and ask if there were any books or websites I could point him towards. He'd be the expert.

It was March.

We'd just had a long weekend for St Patrick's day, but instead of feeling rested, I was utterly exhausted. I'd taken on extra shifts at The Rooster to help Norm with the celebrating crowds and I'd had about four hours of sleep across the weekend.

And so it was with a huge, ugly yawn that I knocked on the door of Mr Murray's classroom at breaktime. I wasn't sure he'd be in, maybe he went to the canteen at break, but I didn't want to start knocking when he was in the middle of teaching.

'Come on on on on in,' he called, in that specific way that slightly awkward Northern Irish people do.

'Hi,' I said, closing the door carefully behind me. 'Mr Murray. You probably don't remember me, I'm—'

'Abigail Campbell,' Mr Murray cut in. He was sitting at one of the high student desks, both his forearms resting on the well-worn wood. His sleeves were pushed up, and his shirt looked a little crumpled. If I didn't know better, I'd have said he was—

'Napping,' Mr Murray said, as though reading my mind. He grinned guiltily, then yawned as if to prove his point. 'I do it at break. And sometimes lunch. And if I have a free period. Don't mention to anyone, will you?'

I laughed, an awkward bark. Then I yawned, and Mr Murray laughed. 'Sounds like you want to join me!'

There was nothing in it. I know because I checked his face, feeling my cheeks flush.

'What can I do for you, Abigail?'

Mr Murray stood up and straightened his shirt, took his glasses off his nose and inspected them.

'It's a bit of a random one,' I said, feeling suddenly very conscious of the fact I hadn't washed my hair that day, of the fact I'd picked at a new spot before school that morning. Why couldn't I look effortlessly put together, chic and carefree and beguiling? Why did I always have to look so... harried?

'Great!' Mr Murray said.

'It's about my brother—'

'Ah, dear old Decky.'

'Not that one.'

'Jordan, a quiet boy if ever—'

'Not that one either.'

Mr Murray laughed and darted behind his own desk, looking a little more awake now. He indicated I should sit on a stool next to his computer chair, and I perched there, very aware of the length of my skirt and my years-old tights.

'How many brothers do you have?'

'Too many,' I said automatically. It was my answer when people asked me this. 'But this is actually about my littlest brother. His name is Jack. He's only eight so you'll not have met him yet, but I've told him all about you. Well, about the physics classes, I mean. Not specifically you. Though you do feature in my stories.'

You do feature in my stories, what the fuck does that mean.

'He loves physics, you see,' I carried on hurriedly. 'He's all into… like, space and shit. I mean, sorry, he's into space. Astrophysics. The universe. Black holes. Dwarf… holes? I'm not sure. But he's read everything I can find him in the library, and I was wondering if there's any websites I could sign him up to, any other resources you can recommend? I know he's only eight, but he's really advanced. He's cleverer than me, on some things…'

I trailed off. Partly because I was waffling, partly because I registered that it wouldn't be hard to be cleverer than me on some things. What did I know, really?

Mr Murray didn't seem to notice. He sat nodding enthusiastically, even after I'd finished speaking, as though he was delighted to have been asked.

'Love that,' he said. 'He sounds great. Little boys are always interested in space, but it sounds as if he's really taking this seriously. Has he read anything by Lance Mars?'

I nodded, remembering the dog-eared textbook Jack had followed me around the house with for a week.

'Ah, clever little man. Okay, what about *Parallel Worlds*? That's a personal favourite of mine.'

I hesitated. 'I – I'm not sure. I'll have to check his library card.'

Mr Murray leapt up from his chair so fast it sprang backwards and knocked off the whiteboard behind him. He dived over to the cabinet in the corner and opened a door, crouching to inspect the contents. I couldn't see what he was doing, but finally he emerged with a book held up high in the air.

'There we go. Try him on this one. If he likes the Lance Mars books, he'll love this. This edition has the most beautiful images as well.'

I scrabbled in the pocket of my blazer for a pen.

'Thank you,' I said breathlessly. 'I'll just write down the name—'

'Ah nonsense! Abigail, please, take it. If he's read it, you can bring it back to me, if not, he can keep it for as long as he needs. No, I insist. Honestly. Nothing makes me happier than a young mind thirsty for physics. God, was that the cringiest thing anyone has ever said?'

I giggled. Actually giggled. Like I was eight myself. But Mr Murray grinned, as though delighted to hear me laughing. He held my gaze for a moment, and then another.

The bell rang and we both turned to the clock above the whiteboard.

'Third period,' Mr Murray murmured, unnecessarily. 'Year 10. Forces.'

'Contact and non-contact,' I said, remembering. 'Gravity and... and tension.'

'Oh, yes,' he said. He met my eye again. 'Tension.'

Jack was delighted when I got home with his new *Parallel Worlds* book. He beamed and hugged me and sat cross-legged on the floor in front of Dad's armchair for the rest of the evening, reaching his arm up in the air to show Dad some of the more interesting pictures he found, speaking loudly over *Coronation Street* to share what he was learning.

Dad kept nodding off, and would sit up in alarm when Jack yelped his latest facts, mmhmming and ahhaing at all the right times, a pro at barely listening to his children.

I lay across the length of the sofa, enjoying having the others out of the house. Yes, Jack was excitable, but at least he didn't grunt responses or smell like an explosion at a Sure deodorant factory like his brothers. I had *The Canterbury Tales* on my lap, but I hadn't read a word. I was supposed to be revising for my repeat exams in May, but Chaucer read like another language and I despised him as a writer and as a person. Instead, my phone was glued to my hand, and I couldn't stop scrolling through Caroline Murray's Instagram page. Everyone knew Caroline Murray, Mr Murray's wife, and though I'd glanced at her page once in the past, I'd never paid much attention, had never needed to.

But I was thinking about the look Mr Murray had given me, the way he'd awkwardly coughed and bowed me out of his classroom shortly after. The way he too smelled like deodorant, but something... deeper, something muskier than I'd ever known before. The way his shirt sleeves had rolled up his surprisingly thick wrists.

There was nothing about him on Caroline's Instagram. It was mostly professional, pictures and videos of her showing off her tiny waist and toned arms in various yoga poses, none of which I stood a chance of copying even if I'd wanted to. She was younger than her husband, I thought. Maybe halfway between my age and his. Come to think of it, just how old was Mr Murray? Early... *mid*-thirties at a push?

Far too old for you, Abi Campbell I heard my mum's voice scolding, though she'd not lived long enough ever to impart any romantic advice to me.

'Abi? Aaaaaaabbbbiiiiii?'

I jumped and clutched the phone in my hand. 'What? What, Jack?'

'I saaaaaid.' Jack was rolling his eyes comically. 'The chances of life on another planet in another universe are quite high. Did you know that? Andromeda is not the only—'

'Ann who?' I asked, grinning. It was Jack's favourite joke, and he immediately rolled onto his side laughing.

'Yeah, yeah,' I said, over his giggles. 'Life on another planet. I'm sure that's true. If a life force from Barbaradromeda comes to try and take you away, you will send me a postcard, won't you?'

*

I dreamt that night that Caroline Murray was standing over me, but she didn't look like herself. Instead, her face was green and she had two antennae sticking up from her head. She was forcing me into ever-more-painful yoga poses and rolling her eyes when I couldn't do them.

'Hire beautee was hire deth, I dar wel sayn!' screamed the alien Caroline, and I woke up with my heart pounding. It took a moment for me to comprehend the ridiculousness of my dream, and I was almost about to give a tiny laugh of relief when my bedroom door flew open.

The door banged off the bottom of the bed and swung back on itself again, leaving just enough time for a blindingly fast creature to scurry from the doorway and jump into my bed with me.

'Abi,' Jack sobbed. 'I don't want them to take me, if they do exist, if they are real, if they're after us, I don't want to go with them, I want to know, I just wanted to know, and to learn, b-but I don't want to go with them, will I be able to tell them that? What if they don't – don't speak English?'

I stared at Jack, at his Arsenal pyjamas that were still far too big – a hand-me-down from Decky that he'd begged for – and his blond curly hair, mussed and a little flat from sleep. Then I realised what he was saying and physically groaned.

'Oh, darling,' I said quietly, and I put both arms around him. 'Did you have a bad dream? I'm sorry I said all of that earlier, about other galaxies or whatever, I was having a joke with you, you know that—'

'I know,' Jack insisted, a little too loudly so I shushed him. 'But it *could* happen, it could be real! I dreamt they looked just like us, and it was hard to tell them apart, and there was one who looked like you, and one who looked like Dad, and even *Ciarán* and I couldn't tell which one—'

'It was a dream,' I said firmly, though I hugged him tighter. 'It was *not* real.'

'But it *could* be!'

'Not if you tell yourself it wasn't. You have control over your own brain. If you tell yourself it didn't happen, it wasn't real, then it won't be. *You* decide. Okay?'

Jack considered this.

'Say it,' I whispered. 'It wasn't real. It didn't happen.'

'It… it wasn't real. It didn't happen.'

Jack blinked at me in the dark, and the streetlights outside my window reflected in his dark blue eyes. I wasn't much older than him when I lost my favourite person in the world, I thought. I won't let Jack experience that, ever. I wasn't sure what put it into my head, but it was suddenly there and I felt it was important to think about it.

'Is that how it works?' he asked at last.

'Yes,' I said. 'I'm very wise. That's how it works.'

He nodded and shuffled in under the covers next to me.

'It wasn't real. It didn't happen.'

'It didn't happen,' I said through a yawn. I thought of Caroline Murray, of her stupid alien head and her Chaucer quotation. 'I had a dream about Mr Murray's wife,' I told Jack.

'The nice man who gave you the book for me?'

'Yes, him. I dreamt she had an alien head.'

Jack giggled. 'That's silly. How do you know her?'

'I don't. I was looking at her online earlier.'

'Why?'

'Just to see her.'

'But, why?'

'Just because.'

'Well she doesn't have an alien head, I bet,' Jack said. He yawned too and he patted my hand under the cover. 'Just tell yourself it wasn't real.'

11

The Shielded

I decide to walk instead of drive. To approach quietly.
It only takes an hour.

I haven't told Jack what I'm up to; I've left him in the flat.

I think, technically, this is illegal.

But if the police are wasting their time talking to Judas Jordan and to me, then they aren't grilling Katie about what actually happened on Monday night.

I have to talk to Katie Waltz myself. Beg her to see sense.

The seagulls, so at odds with what is happening on the ground, laugh with each other somewhere unseen up above me.

I stand for longer than is necessary, checking the number of the house.

6A Sandy Mews.

The A of a house number always implied to me an afterthought, a tiny addition to a proper-sized house but… 6A Sandy Mews was anything but an afterthought. We could fit Dad's house – his whole row of terraces, actually – in the courtyard. They have a fucking courtyard. I've been here once before, but I am still not over this.

The gate is closed over but it isn't locked. I push it and it swings forward obligingly. My trainers crunch across the stones and I am struck with the memory that my own dad laid these stones. I can remember Norm telling me years ago – maybe as many as ten years ago – that his daughter was building a house on the outskirts of town. I had told him my dad was working on a landscaping job on the same road and we established it was the very same house. We joked about small town life.

Me and Norm joking, I can't even imagine it now. Laughing about how you couldn't sneeze in Vetobridge without your cousin's boyfriend's hairdresser saying bless you.

There is a doorbell next to the front door, but I knock on the wood instead. Rap three times, quickly, then step back and turn to face the courtyard, giving myself time.

There is a pink Mini Cooper parked on my left. I didn't even notice it at first. There is a tiny teddy bear hanging from the rear-view mirror. A rainbow flag draped over the passenger seat. R Plates. Katie's car.

It isn't Katie or her mum who answers, but I don't have time to be relieved. It's an older woman with grey hair in a bun and a roll of kitchen towels under her arm.

'Hello?' she says uncertainly, as though she is answering the phone.

'Hi,' I say. 'How are you? I was looking for Katie. Is she in?'

The woman glances behind her as though looking for Katie. 'I'm sorry.' She lowers her voice. 'She's... Katie's not very well at the moment. Have you tried phoning her? Texting, instead?'

I mirror her tone and nod seriously. 'Oh, I know how she is.' I haven't walked almost three miles to be turned away at the door. 'That's why I'm here. I was speaking to her yesterday and she said to call round. I'm a...' I hesitate. To say I am a friend is a lie. I'm not going to lie outright. Eventually I decide on, 'I went to Seaview High, too.'

It's not a grandmother, it can't be – Norm's wife died young, of a rare type of cancer I can't remember the name of, and I'm pretty sure Katie's never had a dad in the picture, so it can't be a paternal grandmother either. She must be a cleaner. A housekeeper, they'd probably call it. They literally employ someone to clean. They have an employee. The woman seems happier now I've uttered the magic words 'Seaview High', and she smiles for the first time and shuffles to the side to let me in.

'Oh. Okay. She's just up in her room. You go on ahead – what did you say your name was?'

'Abi,' I say automatically. Then I wince. Should have at least lied about that. Should at least have said Abigail – barely anyone in my life knows me as that, it's as good a disguise as any.

If the woman has heard of me, knows I'm a Campbell, she doesn't register. She just smiles vaguely and shuffles again, this time in the direction of what must be the kitchen.

While I've been to the house once before, I didn't go inside then, and the entrance hall – they have an entrance hall – isn't quite as grand or modern as I was expecting for a family who have a cleaner and live in a new build house with a sea view. The place is really cluttered. It's just full of *stuff*. Piles of books on the telephone table and a bright yellow Nintendo Switch teetering on the top, threatening to fall off. Glossy magazine covers with names like *ChitChat* and *Bliss*. I wonder if they are Katie's or her mum's. A glasses case, open and empty, a set of keys, a handbag.

The stairs, in contrast to the clutter, are shining. Wooden and clean. Not a smudge anywhere on them and no sand. There's been sand in Dad's hall and on the stairs in that wee house since I can remember. It doesn't matter how many times any of us hoovers, sand just doesn't leave in Vetobridge. It's a part of us.

But it is not a part of Katie Waltz.

The stairs twist and I follow them to the top. I find myself staring into a bedroom with pale green painted walls and a green and white checked duvet cover.

'Who was it at the door, Faith?' calls a voice from inside. 'Was it my wool delivery?'

I can't see Katie but her voice is just familiar enough. I have imagined it a lot over the last day or so, wondering how she could have said those things. My stomach churns at the thought of Jack's explanation of the police interview. More clutter covers Katie's bed – jumpers, sweatshirts, a pair of tights, all scattered haphazardly. All colourful, everything bright. I remember her unique sense of style, think Jack might have mentioned once, a long time ago, that she was bullied in primary school for a while because of it.

At the very end of the bed, a pile of neatly folded, clean laundry. Her mum – or the cleaner – leaves her clean laundry at the end of her bed. Just like I do with Jack. Just like I did, before I left.

What if I'd never left? Would this have been different? No housewarming party, a different chain of events…

I wait, paused at the top of the staircase, unable to move myself any further forward. The churn in my stomach turns rock hard and I feel angry all over again.

She's waiting for a delivery. In her massive bedroom, in her massive house with a sea view and a cleaner, she's waiting for a wool delivery. While Jack lies motionless on the sofa in my flat, unable to eat or drink, worry and fear etching lines onto his bruised and sore face far too early.

'Faith?' Katie calls again, uncertain.

I am aware of this being a pivotal moment in my life, which is something we are very rarely aware of as it is happening. I cross the landing and enter her bedroom, hoping I'm leaving sandy footprints on the cream carpet, hoping I'm ruining this one small thing, just in case this – whatever this is – doesn't work out the way I want it to.

There is another door visible at the far side of the room. It leads to an en-suite, and the pale face of Katie Waltz peers out of it.

She drops the face cloth she had been holding and it makes a splat on the tile below.

We look at one another for a moment, blinking.

'What are you doing here?' she whispers finally.

I haven't seen Katie Waltz in person for years. Not since that day she emerged from our living room, her face lined with tears, looked at me, and never came back.

She has lost her puppy fat. She's turned into a curvy, beautiful girl with the kind of boobs I'd kill for.

I feel sick as soon as I think this. Is that really my first thought, looking at her?

What is wrong with me? What is wrong with us all?

Then, a new thought. Why is my baby brother fraternising with this... this *woman*? It's jarring to me that she is such an adult, nearly a full year older than Jack, turning nineteen over this coming summer if I remember right. She's taller than I am by an inch or two. I had expected – had wanted, had needed – to have a quick talk with a child. I wanted to talk sense into a little girl who was telling fibs.

But Katie Waltz is no child.

Her hair, long and red, is clean, and she has a butterfly slide keeping her fringe back. She is wearing what looks like a handknitted crop top in a bright patchwork pattern, a pair of bright purple cotton tracksuit bottoms I recognise as designer. A pair that would cost me half a week's wages, and she's wearing them to lounge around the house waiting for a delivery.

'Abi?' she whispers. 'Why are you here? You shouldn't be here. You're not allowed to talk to me.' She folds her arms protectively around herself and I see her eyes dart to the door.

Somewhere downstairs, the hoover starts up.

Nobody will hear her if she calls out.

Why would she call out? I'm not going to attack her.

Am I?

'Why are you saying all of this about Jack?' I wanted to demand it. I wanted to be assertive for once in my life, to get my apology, have her confess it was all a mistake so I could go home and tell Jack I'd made it all better, I'd made it go away. But I'm whispering too. 'Katie, why are you saying all this? Why?'

Her eyes fill with tears, but they don't spill out. She just looks at me, her mouth slightly open, those tears surely burning her eyes. Her folded arms and her stupid-looking crop top. She takes after her mum in her unusual sense of style. They're the kind of people who have a lot of money – her mum does something in human rights law, defends people – that they use on buying fabric and expensive, erratic designer stuff. They both wear a lot of colour, and usually they'll pair garish tights with an otherwise pretty dress or pinafore. They both like chunky boots, but they swap out the laces for rainbow-coloured ones. Thick knitted cardigans, worn in the summer over skimpy dresses. I've always quite admired that they don't care about trends or what other people are doing. I like that they are unique, that they look thrown together in a happy, chirpy kind of way. It matches the Waltz personality.

Or, what I thought the Waltz personality was.

I first met Katie the day after she was born. Norm was proud as punch that his only daughter had given birth to a wee girl of her own. He brought her into the bar where I was sitting drinking a Coke and eating Bacon Fries with Dad. Mum was at home with the others. She mustn't even have been pregnant with Jack. There was a football match on, and Dad had a fiver on it and was watching the screen above the bar intently. I was sitting on the high bar stool next to him, swinging my legs and pretending I understood the game, cheering when he did and clinking my glass with him when one of the teams scored. Norm had to clear his throat before we turned to him.

He had the tiny bundle in his arms and was beaming at us.

'This here is our Milly's wee one. Six pound exactly. Born at three-forty in the morning there yesterday.'

I thought it was weird to give an exact weight for a baby. It's not like I went around introducing myself as Abi, born in December 1994, currently weighing six stone. I didn't like babies then, so I stayed quiet, smiling so Mr Waltz knew I was a nice girl.

Dad loved babies, so he held his hands out for her and said, 'What a wee dote, congratulations, Norm. I'm sure you're over the moon. What's she gonna be called?'

'Katherine,' Norm said. 'That's our Katherine. Ralph?' He directed this to the gormless teenager behind the bar. 'Give Pat and his wee woman another drink, on me.'

'Awk, Norm, you've no need.' But Dad didn't protest too much. We accepted our pint and Coke and I slid off my stool to peer more closely at the bundle in Dad's arms.

'She has your cheeks,' I gasped, and the adults laughed. I blushed. 'She does.'

'I know!' Norm was delighted. 'I know, she does. Not be long 'til yours start giving you grandkids, Paddy.'

'Be a while yet,' Dad said, pointing a finger at me mock-sternly.

I giggled, imagining myself with a baby. Completely unaware that I'd have one a year later.

The girl that stands before me now has kept her grandfather's high cheekbones, still has her mother's airy fairy hippie sense of charity shop style... but she has a fierceness all of her own. At least, a fierceness I've certainly never had reason to see on either Norm or Milly Waltz. I hope I never do.

I have nine years on her, but now the shock of my appearance in her bedroom has worn off... she's not one bit afraid of me.

'Abi.' She takes a deep breath. 'Everything I said to the police on Tuesday morning is true. I'm not allowed to discuss it with you because it might—'

'Why?' I demand. My own eyes have filled. Fuck. This isn't going how I wanted it to. 'Why would you say that? You and Jack... You're *friends*. He's your friend, he always has been. Whatever happened on Monday night... You can fix it. You can talk it out. Did you – did he—'

I look around wildly, as if her framed paintings might help me. My eyes stop on a particularly strange painting of a clock that looks like it's dripping down off the canvas. I stare at it, my mind blank, unable to think of how to word my next question. Aware that my presence in this girl's room might well make things worse for Jack instead of better. Why didn't I think of that before?

'The police said I'm not allowed to talk to any of you,' Katie says quietly. She lets her shoulders sag and goes to the bed where she sits down and pulls her feet up underneath her.

What does a rape victim look like?

I don't know anything more than what I've seen on TV.

Not like this, says a voice in my head. *They don't look like this.*

How do you know? How the fuck would you know, Abi Campbell?

'I'll be honest I...' She hesitates, shakes her head. 'I didn't want to get the police involved. It was my mum who... did it. She knew something was wrong, she got it out of me. It was her who…' she shrugs, 'got the ball rolling. I didn't want—'

'Didn't want what?' I ask, seeing the lifeline, clutching at it. My heart is beating so fast it's taking my other organs with it. My lungs are vibrating. 'You didn't want what? Didn't want Jack to get into trouble?'

She gives me a strange look then. As though she can't see me properly. As though she's looking through a frosted bathroom windowpane to try and see if anyone is inside.

'No,' she says. 'Not that. I'm not supposed to be talking to you…'

'What didn't you want?' I ask, hearing the desperation in my own voice. I imagine myself leaving this house, going straight to Oldry Police Station, asking for Mathers by name, telling her that Katie Waltz said to my face that she didn't want any of this – that they can drop the investigation, stop asking questions.

Katie looks down at the colourful crop top as if contemplating the pattern. She picks at a hole near the bottom that I think might be a deliberate part of the design. 'I didn't want the police,' she says finally. 'A distant cousin of mine went through something – something similar – a while ago and it was horrible. Awful. And in the end they didn't even bring it to court.'

It might not go to court it might not go to court it might not—

'But the things she went through. The things I've been through already. Repeating the story dozens and dozens of times. The tests they do. The… scrutiny. The people accusing you of *lying*.' She eyes me at this and against my will I feel my face flushing. 'It's fucking… It's awful. You've no idea. It's just the worst – it's the worst—' She chokes, stops herself before she can cry. 'It's the worst thing in the world,' she finishes. 'I've thought so many times… it would be better if it was all just, just over.'

My heart, still banging against my ribcage, starts to soar.

She won't go through with it she won't go through with it

'But he did do it.' She slides off her bed and goes to the door of her room. It's already open, but she holds onto it, pulling it wider. A clear indication that she wants me to leave. She blinks at me, her eyes sad and tired. 'My memory of that night is fucked but... I know it was him.'

My feet are rooted to the cream carpet. The carpet is too new, too high, for the door to move easily, and even though she's pulling at it, it sticks. They need those doors shaved. She must have had her room done up recently. Yes, I think. Maybe I can still smell the fresh green paint. And the high carpet. I'll look at the high carpet, at the glossy door. I'll just look at that while I ask my next question. It's easy to look at a door.

'If your memory is fucked,' I say slowly, 'how do you know it was Jack who – who hurt you?' In my head I hear *if indeed anyone did hurt you*, but I can't say that. I can't look a woman in the eyes and say that.

But when she doesn't respond I do look at her.

Katie's eyes are green. They're really nice eyes, but they're bloodshot and puffy, though she has done well in not crying during my visit. Her skin is pale and the bags under her eyes look like bruises. To match Jack's real ones, I think. But she is staring right back at me as she answers, 'Because I remember seeing his scar. I remember his hand. Clear as anything. I was at the rockpools... I was being attacked. And I could see Jack Campbell's scarred hand.'

I descend the stairs so quickly I almost slip down the last five, but I right myself, throw open the front door and slam it behind me.

I glance at the pink Mini, then put my head down and walk quickly away from the house, thinking the teddy bear on the rear-view mirror is dangling as though he has hanged himself from it.

When I step through the staff door of The Rooster later that afternoon, I'm hit by the smell of stale smoke and spilled beer, and even though it's been the scent of so much of the last fourteen years, it makes me feel suddenly sick.

I'm about to take over from Norm. What is he going to say? Does he even know yet? I know he sees his granddaughter a few times a week. They're close, really close the three of them. Does he know the details? Does he know I visited Katie just a few hours ago? My heart beats quickly when I think about her standing in her bedroom, picking at the hole in her top, looking at me as if disgusted.

I'm angry... but I'm disgusted with myself too.

I glance at the wall behind the ice machine. Norm has forgotten to turn the outside lights on. I reach for the litter picker that we keep for just this purpose, angle it upwards and jab at the switch, too high up on the wall for either of us to reach without help.

I step carefully around a little puddle in the centre of the storeroom and make my way through to the bar, tying my apron around my middle as I go.

What started as a backdoor boozer for Norman Waltz about forty years ago has gradually turned into a reasonably high-end bar and restaurant, with a stream of regulars and tourists, especially in the summer months like now. When I was twenty, Norm took over the lease of the hairdressers next door and we expanded – and it really, really worked. People love that there are no windows, that the interior has been designed like a speakeasy, and the tables are pushed close together, giving it a super intimate feel. Where we were busy enough during my younger years, we've become rushed off our feet as time goes on. As I become more confident, better, Norm becomes weaker and weaker, taking on fewer shifts as the years fly by.

In the bar, a head of glossy black hair leans over one of the beer taps, and beer spills onto the floor.

It's not Norm.

'Toby?' I ask, uncertainly.

The boy at the taps looks up and lets out a dramatic sigh that moves his whole body. 'Abi, thank fuck you're here. Here, will you do two Harps for table six? I keep fucking up the head.'

I grab the glass from him and pour the pint.

'Where's Norm?' I ask, going for casual.

'He's not in,' comes a voice from the other side of the bar. It's Sasha, the receptionist we hired when the phone lines were too busy for us to keep leaving the bar to answer. She and Toby run the food as well, and do the desserts and starters while Kev does the hot food. She smiles at me, her thick, fake-lensed glasses taking up the majority of her face. 'Some family emergency or something. He asked if you'd be able to cover him for the next few days, do a few double shifts?'

I put the pints on a tray and Toby takes them gratefully away.

'Aye,' I say. 'Okay. Do you know what happened?'

'No idea,' Sasha says. 'His daughter rang looking to speak to him. Sounded urgent.'

Norm doesn't have a mobile phone, so phoning The Rooster is how Milly Waltz always contacts her father.

'What time was that?' I ask, wiping my hands on my apron.

'Yesterday.' Sasha yawns. 'He left yesterday lunch time and hasn't been back, said not to bother you on your days off.'

So Norm hadn't known the details when he asked me to cover.

'Toby's had to do the bar, bless him, he nearly boked when I told him. His pints look like shite. So you're okay to cover for the next few days?'

I nod, and Sasha flounces off down the corridor towards the little desk that passes for reception.

I stand looking after her, feeling at once both immeasurably grateful that I don't have to face Norm just yet, and worried that the worst is yet to come.

The shift goes quickly, and Louie, 'the other wee bar man' as he's known by the regulars, shows up at seven o'clock to help me with the evening rush. Louie's incessant babble helps to pass the time, and I feel calmer than I have for the last two days. I'm in my zone, in the place I can be useful, where I'm good at my job and know what I'm doing. Where my regulars love me.

Everything will be fine. It's all about perspective.

By half-eight, the restaurant is cleared and there are only four or five regulars remaining in the bar. I tell Louie I'm going to leave early, that he can lock up and call me if there are any issues. I'll be pulling thirteen-hour shifts for the foreseeable, if Sasha's words are anything to go by.

Then I text Jack that I'm going to see Dad for a few hours. Decky got him a temporary replacement phone from the tech repair shop he works at in town. He dropped it round this afternoon, careful not to mention Jordan.

I stop at the off licence on my way to Dad's and pick up a box of Guinness for him. It feels like a peace offering, but I can't explain why.

'Only me,' I call, stepping through the front door.

I have a horrible feeling of déjà vu. How was it only yesterday morning that I came through this door, my arms full of coffees instead of Guinness?

'Hiya, love!' Dad calls from the living room. 'How are you?'

I go into him and smile. 'Got you these, Daddy, but I see you're way ahead of me.'

He grins and raises a can of Guinness in the air. 'You read my mind! This is my first one and I only realised I've none left. You're a wee life saver. Stick them in the fridge for me?'

I can hear music on in the boys' room upstairs, but I don't ask after either of them. If they want to talk to me, I'm sure they've heard me come in.

Jordan is moving out of their bedroom and into mine, now that it's free. Or, that was the plan. He might even have done it already. Judas Fucking Jordan.

I feel suddenly as though I've been moved out for months.

'About Jack and Jordan...' I say, coming back into the living room with a fresh can and a pint glass. I hate it when he drinks from the can.

Dad sighs and nods. 'I know. He was out of order. I've spoken to him.'

'... Right,' I say, unconvinced. Jordan is lucky I've calmed down in the last few hours. 'Well, obviously Jack can stay with me for the foreseeable' – an image of Jack and me wrapped in blankets, shivering with the cold in the unheated flat after Norm sacks me flashes into my mind – 'but I think Jordan really hurt him. Not physically. Well, physically, yes, he's much bigger and stronger than Jack, so that was out of order, but Jack's really... Well, he's upset about it all.'

Dad nods again, seriously. 'Yes, Jack's bound to be upset.'

I try not to let my nostrils flare. 'And Jordan told the police Jack wasn't in the house until after four on Monday night. Can you believe that? His own brother, trying to drop him in it.'

Dad blinks at me, pours his drink into the glass.

'I mean, why did he have to say anything? Why not just say fuck all?'

'The police wanted to talk to us all yesterday,' Dad says quietly. 'We had to. I think he... I think Jordy just didn't want to lie. But he was out of order, punching Jack,' he finishes quickly, seeing the look on my face. 'That's not right.'

'Right,' I say. 'So can you talk to Jordan, please? Get him to reach out and apologise. What he said was completely fucked. It's not right. This has been so stressful for Jack.'

'I'll talk to Jordan,' Dad echoes. 'Yes, love. I will. Not tonight, though, eh? Just you have a wee drink with your old man.'

I smile weakly. 'I'll have a cuppa tea, Daddy. Working doubles for the next wee while until...' I trail off, unwilling to talk about Norm in front of him, unwilling to say their names in this, our safe space.

Dad doesn't notice that I've cut myself off.

He's had four by the time I realise he's drunk. I don't think he was on his first when I arrived, never mind what he said. We've been sitting in the same position, taking it in turns to get him another can of Guinness but not moving an inch apart from that. It's re-runs of *One Foot in the Grave* back-to-back, and we've been *hmmph*ing little laughs obligingly for two hours. It feels nice to sit there. Just me and Dad, our eyes on the TV, not saying anything. Not having to say a word. The house is warm, as Jordan monitors the oil levels carefully, and it's nice that now everyone is an adult and can contribute, none of us ever has to be cold. I think about Norman Waltz, his family emergency. What is he doing now? How much has he been told?

When he finds out what Katie is accusing my brother of, will I lose my job?

How will I pay the mortgage on my new flat if I can't work any more? Decky would lend me the money, but Decky has no money to lend, and neither has Dad.

The theme tune plays at the end of another episode and I take a deep breath, readying myself to put my hands on my thighs and say, 'Right, I'm away,' but a glance at Dad stops me dead. He is crying, silently.

It is not a sad show. He's not crying at that.

'Dad,' I say quietly. A sentence and a question and an invitation all at once, he knows. I've seen him cry quite a lot – he's not too proud or too manly to let his children see him cry. The only difference is usually his tears are happy. He cried when I passed my driving test, cried when I got my GCSE results. He cried when Decky got his too, but only because he put so little effort in that everyone expected him to fail everything. He cried when the four of us – Jack was too little – clubbed together to get him Sky TV for Christmas one year, and he cries every year any time anyone on a talent show sings something poignant. But these are not happy tears. These are thick, fat tears, sliding down his lined face and dangling off his chin. He gives a sniff, the first sound he has made for an hour, and shakes his head.

'I thought I was doing a good job,' he says thickly.

I furrow my brow. 'A… a good job of what, Daddy?' I don't mean it to be offensive, but I'm pretty sure he hasn't actually worked for a month now. Maybe an old job was done wrong, and he's having to answer for it? Maybe somebody was unhappy with their garden?

'Of this.' He draws an invisible line between us on the sofa, moves his finger back and forth, shaking his head. 'Of being your dad. I thought I – I thought *we*, me and your mum—'

That really chokes him up. He closes his eyes and lets himself cry. He puts his glass on the floor and puts his face in his hands and sobs.

'We tried so hard to – we tried – raise you all to—'

I take a breath as if to speak but find I can't think of anything to say. Does he mean Jordan? His violence? Or does he mean…

I just watch him as he cries and chokes.

He pulls himself together and wipes his nose on his hand.

'We used to say yous got better. That we got better at it with each one of you. Ciarán—' He chokes out a laugh that comes with a new tear. 'Ciarán was a wee shit. He was such a wee shithead, Abi, he really was. And then Jordan – well, he was hard work too, but we had – we had some things down – down to a tee. And Decky was a good bit easier. Still h-had his meltdowns, but he was okay. Got better as he g-got older. And then you.' He looks at me and gives me a watery smile. Then he closes the gap between us and takes my hand. I squeeze him back. 'You were just… just *perfect*. Never a minute of bother, never a thing. Just my perfect wee girl. And now *this*.' The last word comes out as a whisper. He sniffs again. 'I've been thinking I was so blessed with you, you were – you are! – so good, and that's why all this has happened. I was spoilt with my lovely—'

'It's not Jack's fault she's saying this,' I say, surprised to hear my voice coming out as a whisper. Surprising myself with that a lot today. 'Jack's great too. It's not his fault she's made this up.'

He nods mechanically and pulls away from me to wipe his eyes. 'I know, love. I'm only sayin'.' He picks up his Guinness again. 'I'm being silly, ignore me. We used to tease Ciarán as well, that each one of our kids got smarter and better looking.' He grins and shakes his head. 'Just teasing but… They do.'

I try to smile back. 'It's not his fault,' I say again. 'It's not Jack's fault.'

'I know, love,' he says again. 'I know.' He takes a swig of his drink. 'It's not his fault.'

There are footsteps on the stairs and Dad wipes his eyes again and clears his throat.

I look at the door, stony-faced, knowing the exact tread of each of my brothers.

Jordan's face appears at the door. 'All right? Not working?'

'Clearly not,' I say.

He tuts and goes to leave.

'What the fuck is your problem?' I demand, standing. Dad reaches for my wrist, murmuring my name, but I pull myself away and follow

Jordan into the kitchen. 'Literally what the fuck is wrong with you? Our brother has been accused of something fucking horrible, and instead of standing by him and protecting him, you decide you'll throw your weight around and throw him under the bus? Is that what family means to you?'

Jordan pauses, the kettle in his hand, and turns around. Instead of fury or shame, he surprises me by looking calm, then twisting his face into an expression of mild concern.

'I'm sorry,' Jordan says. 'I'm confused. I thought I was speaking to my super feminist sister.'

'What?' I spit.

Jordan turns and fills the kettle, his back to me.

'What the fuck does that mean?' I demand. 'How does me being a feminist have anything to do with this?'

I push his shoulder blade and he turns to face me.

'All I did,' he says calmly, 'is tell the police the truth—'

'And punch your baby brother in the fucking—'

'He is NOT,' Jordan says, his eyes widening, raising his voice for the first time, 'A FUCKING. BABY, Abi. He's a grown man. A grown man who, on Monday night, wasn't at home when he should have been. And now a WOMAN, a girl Jack LIKES, is saying she was raped. It isn't very feminist of you to accuse her of lying, is it?'

'I'm – I'm not, I'm just—'

'None of us was there on Monday,' Jordan says. He pushes the button on the kettle and moves away from me again. 'None of us knows what happened. I just gave the police the facts. It's up to them to do their job.'

'He's your brother,' I say. 'You could show some support.'

Jordan folds his arms and rests his back against the counter. Still in his tracksuit, not a hair out of place, his smooth skin totally clear, with just a hint of stubble starting to grow. I want to punch him in the jaw, in the chest, I want to hurt him. Standing there, almost smug. Not caring about Jack. Not caring about anyone else but himself. As usual.

'None of us was there,' I echo, mimicking his voice in such a childlike way I can hardly believe I've done it. 'If that's your logic then surely you accept that it's innocent until proven guilty?'

'I believe the victim until it's proved otherwise.'

'THE VICTIM,' I scream, 'IS JACK!'

I notice that Dad doesn't bother coming in. If Decky is at home, he doesn't either. There is an awful lot of not bothering in this family.

Jordan looks as if he's trying to decide whether or not to say something. The smug look is gone, but I can't tell the look that's replaced it.

The kettle clicks, boiled.

'We'll see,' he says finally, moving away from me. 'But it's not like Jack doesn't have form.'

12

The Jealous

When my brother Jack was nine, I started having an affair with a married man. I was nineteen, very much single and absolutely not looking. But it is in these exact circumstances that things seemed to happen to the girls I read about in books, so I went with it, thinking it would last a few months and be something I could do – the one thing I could do – that was entirely for myself.

After that first day in Mr Murray's office, when I borrowed the book, we'd stopped in the corridors or in the foyer to chat for a minute or two, any time we'd seen each other. Nine times out of ten, it was he who made a beeline for me, his eyes widening and rushing to catch me up as though I was exactly the person he happened to be looking for. I heard some of the girls in my English class commenting on it and chose to ignore them. I liked the attention, I'll admit. Liked being noticed by someone so obviously attractive, someone so universally liked by staff and student body alike. Usually, he'd start by saying he'd thought of another book I could buy for Jack and we'd chat from there, but every now and then he'd catch me up just to walk next to me.

'Where are you headed?' he'd say in his soft voice, hands leaving the security of the pockets of his chinos to clean the lenses of his glasses.

'Health and Social Care,' I would say, raising my huge textbook each time as though proving I was telling the truth.

'Ah, I'm just nipping over to see Mrs Ferris, I'll walk with you.'

And we'd chat about TV shows, usually. We both loved the same ITV dramas, and we'd share our theories on the murderers. We talked about books a bit too. For a science teacher, he was extremely well read, and I found myself lying and saying I'd read some books that, actually, just sat on my tiny bookshelf at home gathering dust. I became an avid reader during that period of my life, trying desperately to remember the names and plotlines of the classics Mr Murray had said he particularly liked, in case he ever brought them up again.

I liked the way he laughed, the way I could watch his Adam's apple bobbing, the way his throat was covered in stubble even by lunch time. I wasn't sure what my type was – I had been fairly sure I didn't have one – but looking at Max Murray from under my fringe, walking slowly beside him to draw out our time together, I thought maybe he might be it.

'Well, this is me,' I'd say awkwardly when I got to my classroom. My fellow Health and Social Care girls would file into the room past me, some of them smiling or saying hello, most of them eyeing Mr Murray suspiciously before they went inside.

'This is you,' he'd say. 'Well, I'll see you tomorrow, Abigail.'

He'd use the palm of one hand to tap me on the shoulder of my blazer. I found myself both dreading and longing for that moment each time we walked together, desperate for that tiny, physical connection, but hating that it meant the end.

'It's Abi,' I finally plucked up the courage to call after him one day.

He turned to grin at me. 'Abi,' he said, nodding. 'Yes, it is.'

I noticed he never did go in the right direction to see Mrs Ferris.

Or anyone else.

At the end of my final year, on the day of my last exam, I went looking for him to say goodbye.

I felt stupid, ridiculous. A pathetic schoolgirl crush had taken over my life for months – any time I wasn't in work or with Jack, I was just thinking about Mr Murray. About his chinos, the stupid socks I could see poking out of the top of his stupid shoes – the fact that he seemed completely oblivious to the fact that in so many ways, he was a cliché. I liked that he didn't seem to think about what anyone else was thinking.

I'd imagined more than once us going for walks along the promenade, hand in hand, getting ice creams, maybe even going out for dinner. I'd never been on a date before. Maybe those were old fashioned ideas of what would happen on a date.

I found him in his classroom, tapping away on his computer.

He looked up when I knocked and grinned from ear to ear.

'Abi!' He sounded genuinely delighted to see me and came to the other side of his desk to lean against it. His hands stayed in the pockets of his chinos, now. He only cleaned his glasses when he was nervous. 'How did it go?'

'Fine,' I lied. I hadn't a clue what I was waffling on about in my English repeat. Something about *The Canterbury Tales*, the theme of money, something bollocks. 'Just wanted to say bye before...'

I trailed off and shrugged and smiled.

'Ah. Yes, of course.' Max bit his lip, nodding. 'Well, I have to say, I hope I get to teach this wee brother of yours. He'd be coming... when?'

'He's only nine,' I said, glad to be able, for the first time that day, to waffle about something I was an expert in. 'He'll be a few years yet. But I've told him all about you, about how great you are and how good a teacher. He can't wait for Big School. He wants to do a degree in physics. Imagine a nine-year-old wanting to do a physics degree!' Mr Murray had heard this all before, of course, but he smiled along. I had a peculiar feeling, as if the moment was charged with something I'd never experienced before. I didn't know what it was called. It was as if neither of us wanted to be the first to leave, to say goodbye, but we didn't have anything to say to one another that we could say in these circumstances. Me in my school uniform, technically still a pupil, him leaning against his desk, his navy shirt on today, the one with the darker pattern if you looked really close, him smelling of aftershave...

'Well,' he said, 'it's been lovely getting to know you, Abi. I... I really hope our paths cross again.'

I felt like a balloon deflating, and willed myself not to cry until I was safely in my car.

'You too,' I said, my voice strangely high. 'Thanks for… it all.'

'Ah!' Max held up a finger as though he'd only just remembered something. 'One more book I have for you. This time, actually for you!'

He went around to the other side of his desk and fiddled in one of his drawers. He took a minute or two, doing something I couldn't see behind the computer, and when he emerged, he passed me a battered-looking, huge-sized novel. I took it to read the cover.

Ulysses

My heart sank. It would take me forever to read this. Maybe I could just get the SparkNotes? Although, what would be the point? It wasn't like I'd ever see him again.

I thanked Mr Murray for the book and left his classroom with it, carrying it in both hands.

I sat behind the wheel of my car – the awful, battered Clio – and thought I was handling my first heartbreak pretty well. If you could call it that.

I opened the first page of *Ulysses* to see what I was up against, and felt my stomach jolt. Max had scribbled a message, in pencil, inside the cover.

A book for my friend, Abi,

With love from Max x

And underneath, he'd written his phone number.

The first time we met up, it was *almost* by accident. We'd started texting the same day he'd given me *Ulysses*, long into the night when my family and – presumably? – his wife were sleeping. My eyes stung with tiredness every morning when my alarm went off, but it was worth it to see Max's name on my screen, something innocuous he'd said the night before. I'd agreed to take a few day shifts off Norm, now that I was officially no longer a student, and I liked the longer days, liked being able to say, 'Sorry, working' when schoolfriends invited me to the beach or to a party. We texted all day… every day. All through the summer, and when the new school term started again, Max still found a way to send me a message at break, at lunch, between classes.

It made me smile, thinking of him pulling his phone out from his desk drawer, sending me funny quips, asking me what I was up to, putting a kiss at the end just often enough to have my heart racing every time I opened a new message. It wasn't sexual, not then. It was just a friendship that every now and then would creep into something like flirting and quickly back off again. I thought about asking him to meet up, but since he was the one who had given me his number, since he was the older one, the one with an actual career and a wife... I felt it wasn't really my place, and I waited and waited for him to ask me.

He never did, so I made it happen.

It was a Saturday afternoon in January. I was starting my shift at four o'clock and had safely deposited Jack at Ciarán and Gemma's (she the love of Ciarán's life, for then) for the afternoon, since Dad was off on a job somewhere and Jordan and Decky were nowhere to be found. A message from Max popped up as I was driving home from Ciarán's flat in Oldry. A photograph with a short text underneath.

Just starting this one, have you read it?

The photo was of a wooden table, a copy of a book called *We Need to Talk About Kevin* perched on top, the thumb of Max's left hand marking his page as he showed me the cover. I let my eyes flash between the road in front of me and the photograph on the screen of my phone.

I thought I recognised the background: it looked like Lesley's, a tiny little bookshop just outside Vetobridge town centre, with a room upstairs that had a self-serve coffee and tea kiosk and a few rickety tables. I could just about make out the window that looked out over the fields behind it.

I didn't think about it, not properly.

I just kept driving, never fully opening the message, until I was parked up in the tiny car park behind Lesley's. I checked my appearance in the rear-view mirror, glad I'd put some eyeliner and concealer on that morning, but gutted I hadn't packed a hairbrush in my bag. It was a dull, dark day – barely two o'clock, but looking like the evening.

Lesley's was busy enough, considering there was only room to walk around in a perfect square, given the huge table in the middle of the floor, stacked high with contemporary paperbacks. The shelves that lined all four walls were piled on one side with textbooks, biographies, encyclopaedias, and classics and fiction on the other. Two men were flicking through a huge historical tome, stopping to point at pictures, and a woman had crouched on the floor near the doorway to inspect a book about crocheting hats. I smiled at Lesley, behind the cramped counter, and she gave me a wave, pushing her leopard-print glasses up her nose. She was busy dealing with a woman and three toddlers, who were thrusting their colourful books at her and all trying to ask her questions at once, and I was glad she didn't have time to chat. She only knew me as Jack's sister, I thought, though she had asked my name once, a long time ago. Jack was the real reader, the one people wanted to talk to, the one people were impressed by. For a pre-teen, he had the confidence of a practised politician, and could hold his own with anyone, adult and child alike.

I glanced at my phone.

Max's message had come through fourteen minutes ago. Was it possible he was still here? I knew he didn't often drive – he was able to walk to work and into town, and from what I could gather his wife usually took the car away with her most days, so I couldn't check the car park. How long could you spend upstairs in a tiny bookshop? On a dull day like this... maybe all day?

I decided I'd let him find me, if he was still here, and if he wasn't then nothing was lost. I couldn't quite bring myself to walk up the winding wooden staircase in search of him. Much harder to pretend our meeting had been coincidental, if I did that, and I had deliberately not opened his message so I could keep the conceit alive.

Instead I pushed past the crochet-book lady and found a quiet corner in which I could browse the crime shelf.

I'd read a few classics by then: *Rebecca, Little Women, Dracula*, but I just... couldn't really bring myself to like them in the same way Max seemed to. I loved that he was a physics teacher who read. To me, that ticked every box. What else was there but maths and English? And he could do both, could talk about both. To say he made me feel inferior was an understatement, but he absolutely didn't do it on purpose. He always listened to – or read – what I had to say with great interest. Even if some of the ideas I had had came directly from the internet.

I liked crime novels, though. Those I didn't have to fake a love for, so I took advantage of not being overlooked and ran my finger over the spines.

'Abi?'

I physically jumped, snapping my head around at the sound of Max's voice.

He must have moved soundlessly down the stairs, and had one hand on the door of the shop, but he'd stopped and was beaming at me.

'Did you… get my message?' He glanced around, though he didn't look too worried.

I was an ex-student, I supposed, not a current one. And there was nothing wrong with saying hello to a teacher in a shop, surely.

So why was my heart beating, ready to burst out of my chest?

'No,' I heard myself saying. 'No, I didn't. What do you mean?'

He moved away from the door to let the mother and her children leave with their purchases, squeezing himself into the same corner as me so they could manoeuvre themselves out the door. I had almost forgotten the smell of his aftershave.

When the door closed after them, he pulled back, and I was disappointed.

'I texted you a picture of the book I just bought,' he explained. 'I thought maybe…' He looked embarrassed, suddenly, and shook his head. 'Never mind. What are you up to?'

'Oh, just… browsing.' I motioned towards the shelves. 'Jack's with my other brother today.'

I wasn't sure why I had to say that, as if I had to defend myself from an accusation that hadn't been made, but Max nodded enthusiastically.

'Great, so does that mean you're free? I've just had two coffees in a row but I'm sure I could face a tea.'

I blinked at him, unsure what he was getting at. It hadn't been a direct question.

In work, I liked being the person in charge of the questions. *Would you like a slice of lime, have you booked, would you mind terribly asking your son to stop pulling out the contents of that lady's handbag?* Was… was this an invitation to go on a date, of sorts? Or was it simply two friends who hadn't seen each other in a while, catching up?

I thought I'd made a horrible mistake. Had I bullied him into asking me to get a drink with him? Did he feel sorry for me? That was one thing I couldn't stand: pity. I hated it if the subject of Mum came up, if I had to endure the tilted heads and the slow nods. Hated it more if anyone seemed to think I'd had Jack thrust upon me, that I was his primary carer and had stepped into my father's shoes because I *had* to. Like he was a burden, not a brother.

But, no. Max wasn't like that. He didn't pity me, didn't treat me like a hard-done-by child… It was an invitation to have a coffee. Just two people, having coffee.

Until it was so much more than that.

It wasn't sexual at the start. We kissed in the car after our first bookshop 'date' of sorts. I offered to give him a lift home, and he accepted. It was raining by the time we left and he'd taken the bus. Made much more sense for me to drive him back. It was just… sensible. Easy. Though we kissed for such a long time that I ended up late for work, arrived in a blushing tizzy, the sides of my mouth sore from Mr Murray's – Max's – stubble, and smashed two glasses during the shift.

As soon as it became sexual, I was convinced everyone I saw could read it written all over my face… and in a way I was right. I wasn't deliberately being different. If anything I was trying hard to act normal, natural, not look at my phone too much during work so Norm and the others would have no reason to question me. But I gave myself away in the way that people who are falling in love slowly tend to do.

Surprisingly, it was Jack who mentioned it first.

The Blindspot

'You're different,' he announced one morning as he ate his toast and jam.

I didn't look up from my phone, where Max's good morning message had just arrived. 'Why do you say that?'

'You're being weird,' he said. 'You're not like Abi any more. Why are you obsessed with your phone?'

'I'm not,' I said, feeling guilty that he thought this, but not guilty enough to put my phone down.

'Decky and Jordan think you're in love.'

I looked up, then busied myself in buttering my own toast. 'Decky and Jordan are two Buttheads, as well you know.'

Jack giggled, but quickly became serious again. 'Who is he? Do I know him? Is he your Valentine?'

Jack had been talking about Valentine's Day for weeks. They had an anonymous box in their classroom into which the pupils could post their handmade cards. The teacher was going to hand them out the next day.

'Is he?' Jack insisted.

I hesitated. I hadn't ever lied to Jack's face, not about anything important. How do you explain to a nine-year-old that you do, sort of, have a boyfriend, but that it's a secret?

'Sort of,' I settled on. 'He is sort of my... Valentine. But it's not very serious yet.'

'Sounds pretty serious. Is he getting you a card?'

'I don't know.'

'Do you love him?'

Another pause. 'I don't know. Maybe.'

Jack's face fell unexpectedly. 'Oh. Will you move out and marry him?'

I laughed at the thought, then sighed. I picked up Jack's empty plate and my full one and moved them to the draining board. I looked out of the kitchen window, into the little garden with its overgrown, muddy grass and the broken fence. You wouldn't think our dad was a gardener. 'I don't think so,' I answered Jack finally. 'Probably not. We'll see. Get your school bag.'

*

Whatever Jack took from our brief conversation about Max, it wasn't correct.

I had the day off, but when I picked him up at the school gates a few hours later, he had his head down and his hands shoved in his pockets, and he didn't grin when he saw me like he normally did. He looked like Ciarán, I thought as he ambled along beside me, his shoulders shrugging any time I tried to ask about his day.

'Did… did somebody say something?' I asked hesitantly, unable to keep my eyes from flicking to Jack's hand, though as both were still deep in the pockets of his puffy jacket, I couldn't see the scars.

'About what?' he demanded, and I flinched. He was usually full of beans after school, keen to tell me stories about all the funny things that happened, to modestly inform me of his test results, his good spellings, his homework marks.

'You know,' I said. 'The boys in your class who aren't very nice. Did they say something, is that why you're in a bad mood?'

'I'm not in a bad mood,' he said. 'And they're my *friends*, Abi. I keep telling you over and over and over again. They like me.'

They don't, I thought, but I didn't say it. How anyone could dislike Jack I had no idea – I figured it was probably a jealousy thing. He was smart, the best in the class, and he was funny, and he was beautiful, and quite good at sports and really good at art, so I figured that was quite enough for a group of average boys to dislike Jack. Nonetheless, Jack hung around them day in, day out, seemed obsessed by anything they said or did or thought and had started in recent months to model himself after the ringleader, Ben. He had a habit of saying drily, 'Whatever, man', if I asked him to tidy his room or take the bin out, and it was doing my head in because I just knew without even asking that this was something he'd taken from Ben.

'Then why are you being so grumpy?' I persisted.

My phone bleeped in my pocket and I fumbled for it. Jack glanced over and tutted as loudly as he could before he strode away.

'Wait for me,' I called, hurrying to keep up with him. 'Jack, stop.'

The Blindspot

We were two minutes away from home, could probably see our little terrace if we squinted down the road, but I didn't like Jack to be too far from me.

'Why?' he called, looking over his shoulder without breaking stride. 'So you can ignore me and text your stupid secret boyfriend?'

I rolled my eyes—

Then my heart jumped into my throat.

Jack put one foot out onto the road, intending to cross, and there was a squeal of tyres as a lowered black Honda braked.

Jack stepped back quickly and his bulging backpack crashed into me, and we both stumbled and just about managed to keep our balance.

'WATCH IT, YOU DOPEY WEE PRICK!' The young driver had rolled down his window and stuck his head out, his baseball cap pulled low so we couldn't see his face.

I couldn't speak to defend Jack or apologise, and the car pulled away, the baseball-capped head shaking side to side.

'Fuck sake,' I heard myself panting. 'Be careful, Jack! You could have—'

I stopped when I saw his eyes were full of tears. He saw me looking and turned away, wiping his eyes with his palms.

There was something about men – boys – that made Jack different. I could tell him off for being cheeky and he'd apologise and we'd still be friends, but if Decky or Jordan or even Dad tried to say anything to him, he became defensive, argumentative, then cold and finally devastated. I couldn't put my finger on how or why, but it was as if he wanted his brothers and Dad to think he was someone other than who he was. As if he had a mask on around them, the mask of a perfect little boy, and nothing could get in the way of that.

I felt sure that if the driver of the car had been a woman, he might not have been so upset.

'Oh, Jack,' I said, my frustration rumbling away like the car's engine, into the distance.

'Don't even act like you care,' Jack snapped, though his nose was running, which took away from the severity somewhat.

He looked both ways, then crossed the road ahead of me and strode home in silence, me following behind and watching the back of his head, unsure what I'd done to make him so angry.

The next day was Valentine's Day and I was as surprised as anyone when I brought a small handful of post into the kitchen which included a red envelope with my name on it. Just my name, no address, which meant—

'That's been hand delivered,' Jordan said, looking over my shoulder.

'Fuck me, check out Poirot,' Decky said with his mouth full of cereal.

I snorted and Decky and I grinned at one another. Jordan glowered as he checked through the pile of letters.

'Anything for you?' Decky asked our elder brother.

Jordan blushed and shook his head. 'No, why would there be?'

Decky shrugged. 'Just our little sister who's popular today, then. Go on then, Abi, tell us who he is.'

I shook my head, clutching the letter more tightly than was necessary, sure one of them might pop up and grab it without warning.

Jordan rolled his eyes dramatically and busied himself looking at his phone.

'You gonna tell me?' Decky asked, looking amused and interested.

'I can't,' I said quietly. 'Not... not yet.'

Decky shrugged, smiling. 'Fair enough. Your business.'

Jack came into the kitchen just then, his hair still wet from the shower, dripping onto his white school shirt and making it see-through. Before I could tell him to go back and get his towel, he nodded at the envelope in my hand.

'What's that?' he asked.

His bad mood seemed to have dissolved, just about.

'A card to our sister from her secret, super serious, super mysterious boyfriend,' Jordan said before I could answer. Sarcasm was dripping from his tone. 'We're all just gagging to know who he is. Don't think I'll be able to concentrate in work all day today if I don't find out.'

'Careful a barbell doesn't fall and crush your neck, then,' Decky said mildly.

'Oh,' Jack said, and he turned away to make himself cereal.

I was working at four that evening, as we had bookings in the restaurant starting early.

'Couples'll be smoochin' across the table all night,' Norm had warned me, mock-sternly the week before. 'Bring a sick bag.'

I had time to pick up Jack from school before I went, so three o'clock found me standing at the school gates beside the parents and childminders. Most of them knew me, but a few of the newer faces were giving me strange looks, I could tell from the corner of my eye. I was used to the calculations, people thinking I looked far too young to be standing at the gates, then a sort of understanding as a nine-year-old came towards me, and not a nursery-schooler, the realisation and acceptance that I must be a young childminder or an older sister.

It was cold, raining, and I had my hood pulled up and my phone in my hand.

I'd thanked Max for his card and grinned from ear to ear when I thought about it, which was once every five minutes. He'd been up bright and early that day, he said, and thought it might cheer me up, considering I had to work that night. We'd been imagining all the things we could be doing that day, were it not for my shift in the bar, and our texts were making me grin all the more.

When I looked up again, Jack was almost at the gate – but he was hand in hand with a girl from his class.

My eyes widened and I smiled confusedly at him. I beamed at the girl, who looked down, shyly. I had seen her in the nativity play and on sports day, but I couldn't place her. Maybe Jenny? Or Emily or something. Or maybe she was one of the Lily-Roses. Or the Lily-Mays. She had adorable blonde plaits and high cheekbones, and I knew she'd be beautiful when she was a woman.

I pushed my phone in my pocket and took a step towards them, hoping Jack was about to introduce us.

Then they stopped and Jack turned and kissed the girl full on the mouth.

I blinked in shock.

Two of the mums standing closest to me looked at one another, and I found myself looking at them instead of at Jack. They looked amused. Then they looked back at the young pair, and concern took over their faces.

I looked back too. Jack's face was still pressed against the girl's, but his hand was behind her head, pulling her in—

No, not pulling her in.

Holding her there.

Against… against her will?

It was only a split second – a split second in which my trainers felt nailed to the tarmac and my mind raced in rings around itself—

And then they broke apart.

The girl pulled her hand away from Jack, turned on her heel and sprinted off in the opposite direction, blonde plaits swinging behind her. I hadn't had time to register her expression, or if I had I chose promptly to forget it.

Jack came towards me, his chest puffed out as if he'd just won a medal. His cheeks were flushed.

The mums beside me were still looking, their faces unsure. They kept glancing at each other, and I heard one of them murmuring to the other. I managed to make out a few words.

'Jack… I think.'

'… the sister, isn't it?'

I didn't say anything.

Not to them, and not to Jack.

'All right?' Jack said, his usual jolly tone back. 'Have a good day? What time are you working?'

We turned and started to walk automatically towards home.

Was Jack taller than he was yesterday? Had he always come right up to my shoulder?

'Yeah,' I heard myself saying. 'Fine, fine. Working at four.'

'Good.' We walked for a minute or two and then Jack added, 'That was my girlfriend.'

He beamed at me, and — *Why? Why? Why on earth?* — I felt myself smiling back.

I don't know what happened after that, between Jack and Lily-Rose. I don't even know if that was her name. But he never mentioned her again, and I never asked.

When I went to pick up Jack from school from then on, though, I found myself scanning the excitable heads in the playground for the girl with blonde plaits.

Anytime I caught sight of her, she was always determinedly looking in another direction, moving away from me and away from my brother, face set, and with a look in her eyes that made me think of someone much, much older, who understood more than they wanted to about the world and what it had to offer her.

13

The Liar

'How's Dad?' Jack asks as soon as I close the door of the flat behind me.

He stands from where he has been curled up on the sofa, stretching his long legs and his back like a cat in the sun. I feel myself calming at the sight of him. My blood, that had been boiling on my short journey home after my confrontation with Jordan, is cooling as I watch him.

'Dad's okay,' I say, hanging up my cardigan.

'Did you see Jordy?'

I hesitate. 'No, love. He must have been out. What did you get up to?'

Jack shrugs. 'Just Xbox. Feels so weird not having any exams to study for.' He gives me a tentative smile: he knows I like to hear about him studying. I smile back.

'Shall we watch something, or is it too late? I'm keeping this TV by the way.'

Jack brought the TV from his bedroom earlier today. Nipped into the house while everyone was out. Technically, Decky bought the TV, but everything Decky watches is on his own phone or laptop, so I can't see him protesting.

'Sure,' Jack says. 'You pick. I'm just gonna go and get a shower.'

'Did you eat?' I call, as his back retreats into the bathroom.

'Yep,' he calls back. 'Did you?'

'Yep,' I call back, before I realise it isn't true. I haven't had an appetite the last few days.

I sit on the sofa and it lets out a *poooof* of air. I sigh too, as if in response, and lift the remote for the TV. It's still on the Xbox channel: a purple-clad character has been paused on the screen. I'm about to change the source when a little box pops up. A message.

Hey

It's from someone with the username Fitzyboi04.

'Shall I log out of this?' I shout to Jack.

I can hear the shower water running already. Jack doesn't reply – he hasn't heard me.

Another message from the same person.

Did u get rid of the phone?

I blink at the screen.

There it is. Another of those moments in my life that have felt significant at the time. Moments that I've known, immediately, will change my life, will change the course of everything, forever.

The realisation of these words trickles. It's gradual. I stare and stare at the seven words on the screen and I let the meaning of them fill me up.

The sound of the shower stops and I'm not sure if it's been one minute or five.

The shower head still drips, even though it's turned off.

Did u

Drip

get rid

Drip drip

of the phone?

Drip

I tell myself all night that I'll ask Jack about the message in the morning.

We had such a normal, enjoyable evening, I couldn't bring myself to spoil it. I was able to press it out of my head, more or less, when Jack was right next to me. With his cricket-long legs pulled under him and his Sleepy from Snow White socks on display, how could I ask him what the message meant? When he giggled at something he knew was about to happen in a re-run of *Friends* (everything is re-runs with me, nothing is new, why is nothing new?), before it happened, how could I pause the TV to make him explain himself?

Now it is morning and my stomach is churning and everything hurts thinking about it.

I'll make it casual, I think, rolling over and squinting in the sunlight beaming through my window. I haven't got any blinds yet. That really should be at the top of the to-do list.

I'll just say, *Jack, I saw a bit of a weird—*

Before I can even form the thought in my mind, I feel bile rush up my throat. I throw the bedclothes off and sprint to the bathroom, make it just in time to vomit into the sink.

I stand shivering on the cold tiles, my arms and legs goosebumped despite the sunlight that floods into the bathroom too.

It's too bright.

Everything is too much.

One breath.

Two breaths.

I retch again into the sink, thinking far too late that I really should have done this into the toilet.

'Abi?' Jack knocks tentatively on the door. 'Are you being sick? Can I come in?'

'Yeah,' I manage between gasps for air. My whole body jerks forward with my next retch, and I feel Jack's hands pulling my hair away from my face.

He is so gentle, gripping my hair into an untidy ponytail with his fingers. I can see his concerned, tender face in the reflection in the mirror, and it's worse, somehow. My eyes, already watering from the vomiting, spill over, until I am crying miserable tears.

My lovely brother.

The message on the screen.

No. No. No. Please no.

'Was it something you ate?'

I spit into the sink, then nod. 'Must be,' I murmur.

'Oh, I'm sorry.' Jack uses his free hand to rub a circle on my back. 'Why don't you go back to bed and I'll get – oh, do you have a sick bowl in this house yet?'

Our reflections smile weakly at one another, both of us thinking of the huge glass bowl in Dad's house that has acted for all our lives like both a mixing bowl and a sick bowl. Disgusting, if you think about it.

'I'll be okay now,' I say, though my stomach is still churning. 'Thank you.'

I am lying in bed an hour later, watching my bedside clock move closer and closer to the opening hour of The Rooster, knowing I have to get up, shower, eat something and dress.

In the next forty minutes...

In the next twenty minutes...

I reach for my phone, see a text from Max.

When can I see you? How is all with J?

I quickly text back.

Working doubles for the foreseeable, will let you know. Yeah he's ok thank you. Love you x

I wait. Neither of us is a big texter any more, so usually it wouldn't bother me much if he didn't reply. But he does:

Love you too xxxx

I smile at the screen, grateful for this one small thing.

Max and Caroline have split up in all but logistics. When the summer holidays come next week and he has some time, he's going to move his stuff out of their shared Victorian semi – a house in which I've spent a lot of time during the last seven years, a house I've showered in, had breakfast in, had sex in, a lot – and rent somewhere a bit closer to the school. I'm not sure what it will mean for us.

Caroline is a yoga instructor on paper, but more of an influencer in reality. She travels a lot, to different parts of Europe, interviewing people on how they stay Zen, mental health, all of that stuff. Her Instagram – a page I'm ashamed to say I look at twice daily without following – is buzzing, and she has over 400,000 followers. She's not that famous in Northern Ireland, but is really big internationally, somehow. I once described her to a schoolfriend as 'pretty in a fresh-faced, childless way' when she came in to give a talk to us as sixth formers at Seaview High, but I sorely regret that, now that I'm sleeping with her husband and know from Max that she's a good person in her heart.

I type her into Instagram. *CarolineMurray_Healing*

I scroll through her posts, careful not to accidentally click like on any.

The latest she uploaded just an hour ago. A photo taken in their conservatory, the light coming through at a gorgeous angle, illuminating the expensive, immaculately clean tiles. Caroline is leaning on her hands, her neck craned far, far back, one of her feet reaching up to touch her head. The caption reads, Not feeling my best this morning, so a meditation session and some inner reflection before meeting with a dear friend for brunch to—

Fucking brunch.

Fucking meditation.

I don't even finish reading the caption, unfairly angry with this beautiful, lovely woman who has done nothing wrong, probably ever.

I click off her page and navigate to the news app.

I almost have to jump out of bed for a second time to throw up again. But I stop myself, my racing heart, my curiosity, my need to know, overpowering my sickness.

Woman, 18, raped in Vetobridge, Co Down after party

I click on the article with trembling fingers. It takes me to our local newspaper, the *Vetobridge Daily Review*, an entirely online affair that has more than once been known to post headlines with typos in them, earning itself the nickname of the *Vetobridge Howler*. I know two of the journalists who work there. One of them was in Ciarán's class in school, the other often arrives in The Rooster looking to get Norm's opinion as a 'local businessperson' on one story or another. This article is written by the latter, and my heart beats quickly, wondering if Norm has given an interview.

But, no. Jack is not named, nor is Katie. The article refers to a suspect and a victim, is vague enough that the entire story could have come from gossip. Very few facts, nothing new from the vague posts on socials.

I let out a slow sigh, relief flooding through me.

Until I get to the bottom of the article. To the comments.

Who was the guy???

Anyone know who this scumbag is?

Poor girl, sending thoughts and prayers to her at this time x

Can't be too careful, girls, always stay with your mates

Then a reply to that one, underneath,

--- Don't victim blame!!!!

My heart lurches as I continue to scroll.

Suspect went to primary school with me, always knew there was something!

Then, below that, five words of black on the white background:

Jack Campbell is a rapist

I drop my phone onto my bedcovers, cover my mouth with my hand as though to stop myself screaming.

My phone bleeps and I turn the screen over, expecting to see a death threat, a message from a journo, Norm's name, maybe?

It's a text from Decky.

Have you seen online?

I put my head in my hands, trying to steady my breathing.

Jack lost his phone – *the phone, the fucking phone, did u get rid of the phone* – and his laptop is still with the police, so if he stays in the flat today, he won't see any of this. He'll be fine.

I have to get ready for work.

I have to make what money I can before I get sacked.

It's a beautiful, sunny June day, and the drinkers and eaters in The Rooster haven't been glued to their phones reading the local gossip. Nobody bombards me with questions, nobody spits at me. The *Vetobridge Howler* is popular enough, gets quite a lot of traction, but I doubt anyone has notifications set up for it. Does anyone even read the comments? I doubt it.

It is a perfectly normal shift. I spend the majority of the afternoon making frozen strawberry daquiris for a hen party who have a party bus picking them up in a few hours to take them to Belfast.

During the lull between lunch and dinner, I lean my back against the counter, watching them absently.

The bride is adorned in a white mini dress, with a sash across her body that I can't read, but that says something like MRS WATTS TO BE. I try to imagine myself in something similar, a MRS MURRAY TO BE, and can't. Who would I have to invite to a hen party anyway? I never fell out with any of my schoolfriends, but I certainly fell out of contact with them. They'll call in, the odd Saturday afternoon, order a mini Prosecco and chat for half an hour, but they work during the week, during the day, and that's the only time I have off, so it was never meant to be, really.

Two of them came to my housewarming with their partners, but we barely got chatting. The majority of those there were Decky's friends, regulars from the bar, people our family just knew, in the way people in small towns all just know each other.

I'd have nobody to invite.

I don't think for a moment that Max splitting with his wife is a direct result of his affair with me – my ego isn't big enough to think that – but I know it's had a hand in giving him the courage to step away from his marriage. It's not toxic, not abusive, not awful by any means. It's just not really anything, hasn't been since the day we got together in Lesley's. They're friends who, twenty years ago, got married and moved in together. They're not in love, they don't hate each other. They're just nothing.

Are Max and I better than 'nothing'?

Yes, I decide. At least there's fun there. But really, I have nothing to compare it to, so what do I know?

When the party bus pulls up outside, I breathe a sigh of relief. The girls let the door swing closed behind them and I am left with a few stragglers, a family of four who are still eating their desserts, agonisingly slowly, and my own pale reflection in the mirror behind the gin glasses.

I start to clear up the hen party table. Straws shaped like penises, red confetti, plastic cards with dares on them. Then a cheap cardboard mask with a man's face printed onto it. Presumably the groom. Who could possibly enjoy this shit? Did Caroline Murray have a hen party like this? Did she print a picture of Max's face? Did he ever have a beard like this?

'Abigail?'

I turn, my hands full of glasses, to see Norman Waltz standing behind the bar. He must have come through the stockroom.

I nearly drop the glasses I'm holding, but I just about manage to cling on. We look at each other.

I swallow and come towards him, almost rubbing up against him as I make my way past, into the back to set the glasses in the dishwasher.

Calmly, slowly.

Like I've done a hundred times before.

But I've never thought about it this much, never noticed the smear of rust on the dishwasher handle.

He is the same Norm. There's none of that change that people talk about in the wake of a tragedy. He doesn't look older or paler or more haggard than he did last week. He's looked old and haggard my entire life.

He's not dressed for work, not in his usual black shirt and trousers, but in an old, cheap T-shirt and a pair of crumpled chinos. His white hair stands up and he hasn't shaved. I haven't seen him with this much stubble… not ever. That's the only physical change.

The way he's looking at me is different. That's what is so singularly shocking.

'Hi,' I say, not quite sure if I should start or let him.

'Hi,' he says quietly. He glances about the bar. It's still quiet. Nothing needs done. 'Just came in to do the safe.'

'It's all there for you,' I say, happy that this is one thing I can do right. 'Not too busy this week so far.'

He nods. 'You okay to cover a few doubles?'

'Yeah. Cleared it with Sasha.'

'Right.'

We look at one another until I can't meet his gaze any longer.

A part of my heart wants to say it out loud, wants to move this elephant into the centre of the room so we can look at it and point at it and comment on its ridiculousness. I want him to know that I believe my brother to be completely innocent of the crime of which he has been accused.

But then that fucking message resonates in my head.

Did u get rid of the phone?

'I'll be off for the foreseeable,' Norm says. He coughs and straightens up. 'If you could man the fort, I'd really appreciate it from a business perspective.'

'Yeah,' I say slowly. I've already said I will, haven't I?

'I'm going to spend some time with Katie and her mum.'

There it is.

I feel my cheeks burning and wish they wouldn't.

'It wasn't him,' I whisper, staring at a stain on the floor that we haven't been able to get rid of.

'What?' Norm says. He hasn't heard me.

'It wasn't him,' I say, not much louder. I try to look at him again. 'Norm, you know him, you know he—'

'My priority,' Norm says firmly, though his chin wobbles, 'is my granddaughter. I can't discuss the ins and outs of it. I don't – I don't blame *you* for what's happened. You're still – I mean… you'll always be like… Like another granddaughter…'

He doesn't pick up the thread of the sentence again. Instead, he looks at me, then shakes his head as though disappointed and walks away.

It's only as I'm mopping up later, almost ready to leave for the night, that I think about the fact that I've seen Norman Waltz almost every day for the last fourteen years and never, not once, has he said I'm like another granddaughter to him. He's told me how much he appreciates my work, and I feel sure he enjoys my friendship, but he's never said anything as deep or meaningful as *that* before.

It's unfair, I think, as I put my cardigan on over my uniform, ready to go home, that so many people don't tell anyone how they feel until it's far, far too late.

Jack and I aren't vocal. I don't remember the last time either of us said *I love you* – we don't have to. It's the most obvious thing in the world. It doesn't need to be said. We just both know it to be true.

It doesn't matter what the phone message from Fitzyboi04 meant, I reason, because I know in my heart that my brother did not hurt Katie Waltz, and that is the bottom line. That is the truth and that is the only thing that matters. I don't have to ask him to explain himself, to do so would be to question his innocence.

I think of Jack's slight flush at the sight of Max in my flat, the complete lack of judgement from him.

I won't ask about the message. Not outright.

He's still awake when I arrive home, curled up on the sofa where he now seems to live.

He smiles at me, grateful to see me, and my heart aches with how much I love him. How wonderful it is to be greeted by a smile, always.

'How was it?' he asks.

'Grand,' I say. 'Got some leftover beef stroganoff for you.'

'Brilliant, thank you.'

I set the not-quite-warm-enough dish on the counter and open the microwave, thinking carefully.

'Do you want this now?' I ask absently.

'Please.'

I put it in and hit the button, then turn around.

'Jack?'

'Mm?'

'What happened to your phone on Monday night?'

He looks over, his brow furrowed just slightly. 'I must have dropped it. I'm not sure.'

I shake my head. 'You're careful. Really careful with your things. You don't take things for granted; you know how much I paid for that phone. You would never have dropped it. And you weren't even that drunk.'

Jack looks at me. Just looks – he isn't panicking, isn't calculating how to get out of this, making up something to say. He just looks for a minute, and then says, 'I dropped it down a drain. On purpose.'

A beat. I don't let my pulse race. I concentrate on staying calm, concentrating.

'Why did you do that?'

'Lots of reasons. It made sense at the time.'

I wait, knowing he will come to me.

'I didn't want them to be able to contact me,' he says slowly. 'My – my friends.'

'Why?'

'I'm done with them, Abi. I never have to see them again, knew I didn't have to see them ever again after the other night. Didn't want to see pictures from the party, didn't want them texting me.'

'Okay. What were the other reasons?'

Jack takes a deep breath, then comes to lean against the counter next to me.

'I was at the rockpools on Monday night.' He is speaking quietly, like maybe the flat might be bugged. It might be, should I stop him talking? 'And – and my friends were being weird. Really weird. I thought they might... I dunno, vandalise something. Do something stupid. I didn't want to be associated with them. I just got rid of my phone.'

I stare at him. 'You thought your friends might commit a crime, so you got rid of your phone. Jack, that makes no sense?'

'I know. I was quite drunk.'

'You weren't.'

'I was. I just – I wanted a clean break, to be honest. Didn't want to know them any more.'

'Where did you put it?'

'Down a drain… Outside the Spar garage at the other side of town. Between the Spar and Wits End, you know that estate?'

'Jack,' I say slowly. 'Is there something on your phone you wanted to get rid of?'

'No,' he says immediately. He looks me in the eye, locks his pinkie finger around mine. 'I swear on your life. There is nothing on my phone I wanted to get rid of. I just did it because I thought I should. Because I wanted to. I know it doesn't make much sense.'

The microwave pings and breaks us apart.

14

The Frigid

When my brother Jack was twelve, and all his friends had been acting like teenagers for years, he invited Katie Waltz to our house to watch a film.

It was over the summer, a random Wednesday evening, and I happened to be off work. It meant I had to cancel Max – or rather, put him back a bit – as Wednesday evenings were one of our evenings. His wife, or *CarolineMurray_Healing* as I'd come to think of her, took back-to-back yoga classes at the community centre on a Wednesday, and we were guaranteed privacy in Max's house from four until nine.

I'd surprised myself by feeling not one ounce of guilt about what I'd been doing for the last two and a half years. If anyone had asked, I'd have said that yes, I was a good person, with morals and ethics and standards, and that I thought I was an excellent role model for Jack, but the evidence pointed in a strikingly different direction and maybe it was good that nobody ever asked questions like that.

I dropped Max a text around lunch time.

Can we take a raincheck for this evening? Jack is having a friend over and don't want to leave them alone xx

Max took an hour to reply, which wasn't unusual, but he was his usual amiable and flexible self.

Sure. Want to meet later on?

We agreed we'd see each other at ten, go for a quick drink at the golf club and… well, whatever happened, happened.

Jack came with me in the car to pick up Katie.

163

He was nervous, I thought, which gave me a secret little smile.

'What are yous going to watch?' I asked, trying for casual.

'Not sure,' Jack mumbled. 'I'll ask her what she wants to watch.'

'Good idea,' I said. 'Very thoughtful. Is it right up here?'

Jack leaned forward and squinted.

I tutted. 'Would you *please* wear your glasses! You're going to strain your eyes even worse, and what was the point in me paying for them if you don't wear them?'

'I do wear them,' Jack said quietly. 'It's a right turn here.'

Jack had walked Katie home from school a few times during their first year. I didn't like him arriving home later, but I did like the little flush he usually had, the spring in his step when he came through the door after his detour, so different to the morose and moody boy who came home on some other days, so I never said anything and quite looked forward to his walks with Katie.

I knew her to see. She'd gone to a different primary school, but she came into The Rooster the odd time with her mum to see Norm, and I always chatted to her and poured her a Coke or gave her a bag of crisps. She was shy, polite, a bit giggly when she was in the notion, and I liked her a lot.

I stopped the car at the pavement outside the gates of Katie's house. The door opened almost immediately, and the girl herself came skipping down the driveway, waving at Jack. She was dressed in multi-coloured stripy tights and a red pinafore that I thought, actually, looked quite calm and fashionable for the usually quirky girl.

'Should I let her in the front seat?' Jack hissed at me suddenly, his eyes wide.

'It's fine,' I said, laughing. 'Jack, relax. She'll be grand, we're not far away.' I hesitated, calculating the number of seconds I had before Katie opened the car door before I said, 'Is this a date?'

Jack's face flushed and he looked away without answering.

I took that as a yes.

Katie bounded in, her smile infectious, her teeth white behind her braces and her skin somehow tanned already, even though we hadn't had much sun that summer. Her face was round and her cheeks were a little chubby, but she seemed entirely unselfconscious. She had turned thirteen the week before, and Jack had been invited to her birthday party. It was there they had agreed that Katie would come to our house to watch a film and maybe have a go on Decky's laptop if Decky was feeling amenable.

I thought it must be a date and that Jack was handling the first date nerves a lot worse than confident Katie.

I liked that she still seemed young. So many of the other girls in Jack's class were overly keen to grow up, and looked and acted well above their not-quite-teen years. Katie was giggly, chatty, polite and she used my name, chatting more to me than to Jack as we made our way across town to Pine Street. I glanced at her as often as I safely could, and I liked that she wasn't wearing make-up yet.

I found a space right on the terrace for once, and couldn't help but compare the weed-ridden slabs of concrete outside our front door, passing for a garden, with the immaculate hedges and tended-to potted plants outside Katie's house. She didn't seem to notice, though, and that made me like her even more.

Jack and Katie settled themselves on the shabby sofa, a full seat cushion between them, while Jack fiddled about with the television remote. I filled one bowl with crisps and another one with the fizzy Haribos that Jack had told me were Katie's favourites, and brought them in.

'Do you want to watch it with us?' Jack asked me.

I raised my eyebrows, unsure if he was joking or not. He was still blushing fiercely, and I hadn't heard him say much to Katie – maybe he was so nervous he thought having his sister there would ease the tension. I glanced at Katie, who was smiling, non-plussed. Of course that wouldn't make it *less* awkward. Poor Jack.

'I'll not, mate,' I said finally. 'You two enjoy. I'm about somewhere if you need me.'

'Thanks again, Abi!' Katie said as I shut the door behind me.

*

For three hours, I moved quietly between my bedroom and the kitchen, not quite sure what to do with myself. Normally I felt there weren't enough hours in the day between work and looking after the house, but for once I was stumped and had nothing to do. I wanted to see Max, but I couldn't. I tried to read but my book was boring and I couldn't get into it. Ideally, I'd have done some chores, but I didn't want to put the hoover on in case it disturbed Jack's date.

Once, twice, I hesitated outside the living room door, considering knocking, checking if they needed anything, but between action-packed fight scenes (I thought it was some sort of superhero film Katie had picked), I heard the pair of them laughing and joking, and I didn't want to spoil it.

I put the immersion heater on for a bath and went to the kitchen to wait for the water to heat up.

I had a little secret smile on my face when Jordan came into the kitchen around eight o'clock, looking and smelling as though he'd just got ready for work, not like he'd just done a full shift.

'What's up with you?' he asked, sliding his gym bag onto the table.

'Jack's on a date,' I whispered, unable to control myself. I nodded to the living room. 'With Norm's granddaughter. You know, Katie? From his school?'

'Sure.' He was already opening and closing cupboard doors. 'Here, did you get any of them microwavable rice packets?'

I rolled my eyes at him. 'No, I haven't been to the shop.'

'Fuck sake,' Jordan murmured under his breath. He saw the look on my face and quickly countered with, 'Sorry, not you. Just fancied chicken and rice tonight, that's all.'

'You can be wild sometimes, Jordan, you know that?' I said sarcastically. He'd had that for dinner every night for about six months.

'I'll go!' He held both his hands up. 'I'll go, calm your tits. Do you want anything?'

'Hm?' I asked, not listening. My phone had just beeped – Max wondering if I could sneak away. 'No – sorry, no. I was actually going to nip out for a while myself; would you be able to look after Jack? Katie's mum is coming for her at nine.'

'Look after him? What looking after does he need, he's fourteen!'

'He's twelve, dickhead.'

'Same diff. We were all left on our own from much younger. He'll be grand here by himself.'

'I don't want to leave him when… You know. I don't want to leave the two of them.'

Jordan snorted. 'They won't be riding, Abi, they're babies.'

'He was fourteen a minute ago.'

'Fourteen is still a baby.'

'Never mind,' I mumbled, shaking my head. I typed out my reply to Max, my fingers punching the phone screen much harder than they needed to. Was it so much to ask for someone to take over every now and then? Did I have to do every single thing? Was I the only responsible person in the family?

I heard Jordan sigh but thought nothing of it. Next thing I knew, he had marched over to the living room door and flung it open.

I hissed as I bolted towards him, embarrassed.

'Brother dearest?' Jordan said, mock formally. 'We just wondered if you and your date would mind if we left you alone for twenty minutes? I'm nipping to Tesco and Abi is going to get her hole.'

'JORDAN!' I punched him on the arm as hard as I could, not caring that Katie would see and think me and my family lunatics. 'I'm not, shut up! Come on, leave them alone.'

Jordan was laughing, his awful, cackling laugh, pretending to push me backwards every time I reached for the door handle to close it.

Eventually I relented to the ridiculousness of it and started laughing too, too weak to put up any sort of a fight.

'Fuck off!' I cried, choking on my laugh. 'Jordan, stop it!'

He was jabbing me in the armpit intermittently, pretending to tickle me, as if we were children again, not twenty-one and twenty-five.

Katie was giggling too, and I noticed out of the corner of my eye that the pair of them had slid a little closer together – there was no room in between them now.

Jack, on the other hand, seemed confused and a little worried.

'Where are you going?' he asked me, unsure. 'What are you doing?'

'Getting her hole,' Jordan enunciated, as though giving an elocution lesson. 'It means she's meeting her secret lover and they're going to—'

'Jordan!' I said again, more seriously this time. I pulled on his forearm and he finally relented. 'I'm not going anywhere, Jack,' I added. 'I'll be here somewhere.'

'Don't let him cock block your poor boyfriend!' Jordan said. 'He'll understand someday how important all of this is. Someday. A long way off, not for years and years, isn't that right, Jacky?'

I tried to roll my eyes at Jack, to show how ridiculous his older brother was being, but I found myself laughing weakly again as I pulled the door closed and pushed Jordan back into the kitchen.

Jordan left for Tesco and I went upstairs for my bath.

I had just changed into jeans and a vest top when I heard a raised voice downstairs. I paused, my hairbrush half-way through my tangled fringe, straining my ears.

It sounded like Katie.

I heard the living room door open and I bolted to the top of the stairs, looking down.

'Katie?' I called. 'What's up, is everything okay?'

'Yeah!' Her voice was far too high. Far higher than it had been. 'I'm just going to wait on my mum outside! Everything is fine!'

I started down the stairs and she came into view.

First her thick-soled boots, then the stripy tights, then the pinafore, and finally her round, pretty face.

Only it was streaked with tears, now.

She made to open the front door, but it opened before she could. Jordan stood there with two plastic bags in his hands, a lot more than he'd gone out for.

'Got you both some ice cream,' Jordan said, sounding proud of himself. 'Didn't know what flavour you liked, so I just – oh. Oh?'

Jordan had copped Katie's red-rimmed eyes – not that she was hiding how upset she was very well. She was sniffing, loudly, wetly, her shoulders a little shaky.

Of course, Jordan looked at me for an explanation, and I shook my head, feeling droplets of water speckling my bare shoulders.

'Katie?' I asked uncertainly. 'What's wrong? What's happened? Your mum will be fifteen minutes yet, there's no point waiting in the dark.'

'I'll be fine,' she insisted. She sniffed again. 'Thank you so much, Abi. Thanks for the lift earlier. I'll see you later.'

Jordan moved out of her way and she sprung from the house without looking back.

He looked at me again. 'What's that all about?'

I didn't answer, but made my way down the last few steps and into the living room.

'Katie's upset?' I asked Jack. 'What happened? Did you fall out?'

Jack was staring at the TV.

It was *South Park*, a show I had urged my other brothers not to watch in front of Jack, and that I had half-forbidden him to watch – I found it gross. I tutted and reached across him to turn it off.

'Oi!' He snatched the remote back from me and turned the TV on again. It would have sounded harsher if his voice had broken, but it hadn't. He was just a little boy.

'Jack?' I asked, loudly. I could hear Jordan putting his shopping bags in the kitchen. 'Can you answer me, please? Why is Katie so upset? What did you fall out about?'

'It's none of your business,' Jack said coldly. He stared at the screen. The TV was old, so the show hadn't quite come back on yet. He was watching the loading screen as if he had to memorise it. His cheeks were flushed and, if I wasn't mistaken, he looked a little teary himself.

'Jack? It is my business – she's just sprinted from my house—'

'It's not your house, though, is it? It's Dad's house.'

'You know what I mean—'

'Don't be so cheeky.' Jordan was at my shoulder, his arms folded, looking like a bouncer beside me. 'Your sister is asking you a question, so answer.'

Jack snorted. 'What are you, my parents?'

'Why was that wee girl running out of here in a state?'

Jack shrugged.

The blinds of the living room were closed, but I saw headlights pulling up outside and prayed it was Katie's mum, there to pick her up. I also prayed she'd managed to control herself by the time she got into the car, but I wouldn't have admitted that.

'Did you try it on?' Jordan asked.

I looked around at him, my eyes wide. 'Jordan—'

'Did you, you wee prick?'

Jack was rubbing his scarred fingers with his healthy ones as if he was trying to create enough friction for a fire. He wouldn't look at either of us, and the tops of his ears were red.

'It was a date,' he said finally. He jumped up from the sofa and elbowed Jordan out of the way to go into the hall. 'I thought she liked me too. She didn't need to be so frigid about it.'

He stomped upstairs and I heard the door of the boys' bedroom close.

It wasn't a house you could really be dramatic in. Yes, he'd slammed the door shut. But if Jordan or Decky fancied going up to bed, they'd have to follow him in. Took away from the statement, somewhat.

Jordan shook his head at me and went into the kitchen. I could hear him shuffling about with his purchases.

'D'ya wanna cuppa tea?' he called.

'No,' I heard some version of Abi shout back. The version of Abi who was still in the house in Pine Street, who was still conscious and standing and having conversations. The other Abi, the real one, was wondering what exactly had happened in that living room just a few minutes before. How two kids could get along brilliantly all evening and then... Was it something to do with Jordan teasing me? Did Jack think it was *he* who was the butt of the joke? As if Jordan was calling *him*... frigid? Was that the word?

The Blindspot

I looked at the hairbrush in my hand, then went to the mirror above the boarded-up fireplace and continued to brush my hair.

I pulled into the car park of Green Swings and spotted Max's car almost immediately. I slid into the space next to him and raised one hand in greeting. He grinned, turned off his engine and switched into my passenger seat.

'Hi,' he said. He kissed me once, chastely, on the mouth. 'You took your time.'

'I know,' I said. I hesitated, unsure whether I should tell him what happened with Jack – he knew Jack, after all, had him for science classes three times a week. It was the most bizarre phenomenon of our relationship, and there were a few. 'Sorry.'

'Never worry. Do you want to go in for a drink?'

Green Swings Golf and Country Club was one of our frequented hangouts. Max was a member, and he played golf there every Sunday, but there was a certain... anonymity, he assured me. Yes, he knew everyone to see, and they him, but nobody knew his personal circumstances and he didn't think that would change any time soon. We often had a few drinks in the Club House, a rickety little bar on the third storey of the tiny building, and there were changing rooms and comfortable sitting rooms for the members to use... however they liked, apparently. I liked that it was twenty minutes from Vetobridge, that every member and drinker was at least fifteen years older than I. That there was no chance of seeing a schoolfriend or, worse, one of my brothers, there.

'Yes, actually,' I said, unbuckling my seatbelt. 'Will you drive me home later? I could use a drink.'

We chatted amiably enough for an hour, enjoying each other's company, enjoying how quiet Green Swings was at this time on a Wednesday night. Nobody was looking at us, nobody cared that Max's arm had slid around my shoulder, that he was stroking the top of my arm. Nobody noticed that he wore a platinum wedding band while his younger companion did not.

'How was Jack's date!' Max's eyes were bright as he remembered.

I happened to be on my third glass of wine, so naturally it all came tumbling out.

'I thought it was going well,' I said. 'She seems lovely – she is lovely. But then… I'm not sure. Something happened between them, I think.'

'Oh?' Max looks surprised and I shake my head.

'Not like that. I think – I think maybe Jack tried to kiss her and she freaked out or something.'

'Didn't she know it was a date?'

'Well. I'm not sure if it strictly was a date. I know Jack definitely likes her.'

'She likes Jack too,' Max said, taking a sip of his sparkling water. I shuddered to think what my brothers would say about such an old person drink. 'They don't stop talking the entire time they're in my class. And the way she laughs at his jokes – my God, no twelve-year-old boy is that funny, I can assure you. She really likes him.'

'Well then…' I watched absently as a group of three men came through the swing doors, golf bags balanced on their backs. 'I'm not sure what happened. She left in a bit of a state, crying.'

'It'll blow over,' Max said wisely. 'She'll just have panicked. Guarantee they'll be right as rain by the time they're back in my class in September.'

I watched as the men took off their caps and ordered drinks from the barman, trying to think of how to word my concern. The way Jack had spoken to Jordan, the way he'd so flippantly spoken about Katie the second she left the room. I hadn't ever thought about the fact that Jack didn't have any healthy relationship models in his life: Dad, widowed and grieving even twelve years on, likely to burst into tears at a particular song, a particular advert; Ciarán who moved from woman to woman, falling head over heels in love with one before promptly dropping her for the next one; Jordan, who wasn't yet comfortable enough to admit to any of us that he liked men; Decky, who didn't seem aware of anything beyond the basics of human survival, never mind women; and me. Me with my secret boyfriend. What kind of twenty-one-year-old had a secret boyfriend? Lies and secrets and love all pushed into one, what kind of example was that to set?

I didn't have a chance to put any of this into words, for just then, Max grabbed my arm and pulled me close to him.

'Shall we nip into the meeting room downstairs for ten minutes?'

'I... I might just finish this,' I said lamely, picking up my wine. I was far from in the mood.

'Take it with you,' Max said, standing and straightening his trousers. 'Those three have only ordered soft drinks, they might leave the bar soon.'

I glanced over at the men, wondering why that was relevant, and felt myself standing, against my instincts.

I didn't have the energy to explain how I was feeling, didn't want to face the half-joking pout Max might pull if I said I couldn't be bothered having sex with him. Or, worse, the unsubtle irritation and hints that he might as well have stayed at home.

We took our drinks downstairs and found the meeting room unlocked and empty as usual. I wasn't sure what kind of meetings the golf club members had, but there didn't seem to be too many of them, and while there were several chairs scattered around, there stood a huge pool table in the middle of the room, which didn't scream formal meeting to me.

'Shall we have a game?' I asked, hopefully, balancing my wine glass on the edge of the table and reaching for a cue.

'If you like,' Max said. 'I'm not bothered.'

I pressed the button on the side of the table and welcomed the loud rush as the red and yellow balls jostled their way into the tray. I wondered what Jordan was doing, what Jack was doing. Was he still stuck in his room? Should I have stayed to see if he was okay? Should I have pressed him further?

Max wasn't very good at pool, but he was one of those people who pretended he was good at everything and was just having an off day.

Should I have insisted Jack talk to me, refused to leave until I got the truth? Called Katie's mum and asked if we could all sit down and have a chat?

Is that what Mum would have done, if she were alive?

Max was on red. He potted one, then sent the white ball straight in after it. He tutted.

I potted a yellow. Then another.

'Did you ever read *The Count of Monte Cristo?*' he asked as I sharpened my cue.

I shook my head. 'No, who wrote it?'

Max put a hand to his mouth as if stifling a laugh, but I still saw it. 'Dumas.'

'Never heard of him.'

'No, I don't suppose you have.' He took a sip of his drink, smiling.

I potted another yellow and stepped back from the table to grin at Max.

'Doing okay tonight,' he said, nodding. 'You'll be a right wee pool player in no time. You can practice when you're in work.'

'Norm doesn't have a table,' I reminded him.

'Really? I would have thought with his clientele it would have been ideal.'

I wasn't sure why this remark would sting me – it didn't feel like an insult, but I furrowed my brow anyway, and missed my next shot.

'I think I need to talk to Jack about tonight,' I said, as Max positioned himself with one leg on the side of the table, like a dog having a pee. He was preparing for a complicated shot. 'I suppose I've never really talked to him about... Sex and all that.'

Max thrust the cue and potted his last red ball – but the white flew straight in after it. He cursed. 'It's not your job, is it?'

'What?'

'Jack. Shouldn't your dad be... or one of your brothers? Why is it always you?'

I considered this. It was a fair enough question.

'I'm afraid they'd say the wrong thing,' I answered finally. 'I'd rather do it myself, make sure he has all the facts, properly.'

'He's twelve, he'll know all the facts. What makes you think you'd know any more?'

I hated it when Max was like this. He sometimes went from sophisticated, intelligent conversation, to quite snippy and spiteful, if things weren't going perfectly his way, like the pool. As if he wanted to niggle at me, as if he got a perverse pleasure from it.

'Still,' I said. 'I'll have to talk to him.'

Max lifted the white ball and positioned it on the table, then went to try and hit the black ball.

'My go,' I reminded him. 'You just fouled.'

'Oh, yeah.'

'Getting a bit forgetful in our old age, are we?' I teased.

Usually we laughed about this. Max would roll his eyes and nod and agree, saying yes, thirty-seven was very, very old, and he would be senile soon.

He didn't smile or nod tonight.

I took my shot and potted my last yellow, then potted the black and took a joking bow.

Max clapped slowly, then downed his drink.

'Maybe we can talk about something else?' he said. 'Bit of a downer, talking about your kid brother.'

'Sorry,' I said automatically. 'I know.'

I'd said it to friends, said it to Max before, said it to my own dad before. *Sorry for talking about Jack. Oh! Sorry for waffling on about my family.* It was never 'my family' I was waffling about, of course.

It just came out.

'I'm not being horrible,' Max assured me. 'Just... don't want us to waste even a second. Our time together is so precious.'

It was. We saw each other twice a week – Wednesdays and Sundays, usually, but the odd time we could rendezvous at the last minute, just as plans could change at the last minute and we wouldn't be able to meet at all. It was he who decided where and when, out of necessity.

I had nobody to answer to. I told myself I was delighted by this, that I was, in a technical way, free and single and able to choose what to do and when. I didn't have to run anything past anyone, didn't need to figure out anyone else's plans, or not a partner's, at least. I think he liked that too, that I was ready and waiting more or less anytime he dropped a text to my phone.

So it was precious, this time. Max had to be home in an hour or so, so if we were going to have sex – and we were, of course we were – it had to be now.

Only...

Only what?

Well, I wasn't even remotely in the mood. Hadn't one iota of inclination to do anything sexy, not tonight. Not after the strange evening I'd had, not with everything swimming around in my brain, me trying to make sense of a crying girl.

I'd turned Max down twice in the two years we'd been together. The first time was fine, an understanding nod, but the second time he went from intelligent, well-read teacher to sulky teenage boy. And the sulk turned into a full-on foul mood, an irritating tut escaping his lips every time he denied his change of mood.

I couldn't be bothered with that tonight, I didn't have the brain space to deal with another pissed off person, couldn't face placating anyone else or having anyone else annoyed with me when I hadn't done a single thing wrong. Why did everyone take their bad moods out on me? It was something about my personality, I thought, as Max leaned in for a kiss. I seem like an easy person to be annoyed with for no reason. What's Abi going to do, really?

I kissed him back for a minute, let him put one arm around my waist.

It would be just perfect, perfect timing if we could hear footsteps outside the door of the meeting room right about now, I thought. The club was echoey and we'd hear them coming a mile off. Maybe the group of men would finish their drinks earlier than we thought and head down? Usually I was praying that nobody disturbed us, but tonight. Just tonight...

Max used one arm to lift me so I was sitting on the pool table, feeling the hard wood underneath me.

'I don't really want to—' He cut me off with a kiss.

There's bound to be something I can say, I thought. It's Max, I can talk to him. Why is this so difficult? Why can't I think of anything to say?

'Can we just—'

And then, a few minutes later, I thought, Why am I letting this happen?

Why are my eyes filling up? Wise up, Abi. Wise up.

And then, a few minutes after that, I thought, I'm enjoying this, it's fine.

Everything is fine.

[15.07.2016]
Jack Campbell 2157: *Hey, you get home ok?*
Jack Campbell 2230: *Hey, you there?*
Jack Campbell 2351: *KT?*

15

The Honest

June bursts into the flame of July and it's a hot one.

Jack's name has been put under a few of the news stories, but nothing official is reported.

That doesn't matter, though. Not in a small town.

He stops going to work, calls his boss to explain, and she is all too happy to accept his unofficial temporary resignation. He can't work behind the counter in the garage if every other person coming in thinks he's a rapist. Not good for business.

Then he stops going out entirely, ordering groceries on my laptop and having them delivered.

He goes to the twenty-four-hour gym in the middle of the night, sleeps in my bed all day while I'm at work, and gets out of it only when he hears my key in the lock. Then, for two or three hours, we are normal. Ourselves, eating takeaway or drinking tea, talking about the customers in the bar, not a care in the world. A completely normal family, in the dark.

He uses my car as he doesn't want to return to Pine Street to fetch his own.

He hasn't spoken to Dad or our brothers since this whole thing began.

So a completely normal family of two, in the dark.

We have both pledged to stay off social media, calling it a cesspit, the root of all evil, and we're right. No good can come from scrolling on it, Jack says, and so I de-activate my own accounts in solidarity and we don't miss any of the sites one bit.

Once, twice, three times, I think I hear Louie and Sasha in work whispering Jack's name, and I question them about it. They both stand straight each time, shaking their heads and making their excuses.

Norm comes in to empty the safe once a week, apparently. He chooses times he knows I won't be there, and he doesn't cover any shifts himself. Instead, a new girl appears one day, shiny-haired and white-teethed, with a tightly-fitting button-up black shirt that makes her the new favourite of the punters even before she knows how to work the till.

I lose interest in my job, then. I fall out of love with it the way you fall up the stairs: suddenly, and after quickly righting yourself, with little heartache or thought.

Towards the end of the month, a twenty-four-year-old man is arrested for the rape of a woman in Oldry back in May, and I feel our hearts lift. Maybe it is this man, this anonymous stranger, who hurt Katie. Maybe Jack's name will be cleared. It is a news story one day, and never mentioned again.

July rains into August, which is a muggy and wet one.

Although we aren't sure it has anything to do with the other arrest, the police call to advise Jack that though they don't need to speak to him again anytime soon, he is to continue to follow the terms and conditions set out during his initial interview. That is, he is not to contact or go anywhere near Katie Waltz. It occurs to me that the police must not be aware of my visit to her residence back in June. So she didn't mention it to anyone. Is that significant?

It feels like life is slowly, slowly, getting back to normal.

It is a strange summer, but it is not an unpleasant one.

Life, A-Levels, affairs, have got in the way of Jack's and my relationship for a few years now, so in an unusual way it is nice to spend uninterrupted time with him again.

He has lost weight, but he is sleeping a lot, and privately I'm delighted that he hasn't gone out with his friends since the night it all happened.

Those boys were a horrible influence, and I never liked them. I'm glad to have him to myself, glad he seems to have removed himself from them completely, just as he wanted.

I start to think – and I know Jack does too – that the whole thing has blown over. The police haven't contacted Jack for weeks, and surely, if the investigation was ongoing, someone would have spoken to him by now? Maybe Katie has remembered what really happened that night, and has named the actual culprit. I've read that that can happen, that trauma can stop you remembering the details. The brain protecting itself, cushioning the truth.

I book off the Wednesday and Thursday at the end of the month, as Jack's A-Level results will be out on the Thursday morning and we'll be going to the school together to collect them.

I can tell Jack is nervous about seeing his classmates again.

The rest of them have likely been out partying all summer, enjoying their last flings together before they go their separate ways.

Does his lack of socialising these last two months indicate a feeling of guilt? I hope that isn't how they see it. I am grateful that Katie went to college after her GCSEs and won't be there to pick up any results on Thursday. Jack probably wouldn't be allowed to collect his own if she was going. Ridiculous.

To relax him ahead of the big day, we decide to go to Portdawdle, a gorgeous wee beach town in the far north.

We get stuck in a queue of traffic that snakes on for miles, and the heat of the day makes us miserable for about an hour, but then the sea is there, bright and shimmering in front of us, so different, somehow to the one that caresses the stony beach in Vetobridge. So much bigger, full of possibility, blue water where the Vetobridge sea is always grey.

We are extraordinarily lucky and come upon a Fiat Punto reversing out of a parking space that overlooks the busy beach. I indicate and swoop in as soon as they've gone, and once the engine is off, we seem to breathe again, even though the car is stuffy.

We're lucky too, in that this is the driest, brightest day we've had all month.

'How are you feeling about tomorrow?' I ask. It's not the first time I've asked it, but it is the first time today.

'Okay,' Jack says, nodding. 'Physics and chemistry I think, yeah. Fine. Biology is a cert... I can barely remember the maths. Honestly.'

My heart clenches just a little. The day Jack did his last maths exam was the day he went to the party in Springhill Manor, the day I had my housewarming – was that really only two months ago? – the day something happened to Katie Waltz up at the rockpools. Something so terrible she hasn't been seen or heard from since.

Nothing further has been posted on social media. Katie's accounts have been silent too, I made Decky check for me since I have nothing myself any more. The police haven't asked any more questions. It really is as if it never happened. Like it was a tidal wave of emotion, stress, worry, pain, that broke and then immediately ebbed away from the shores of our lives, leaving only foamy white memory in its wake.

We get an ice cream each from a little van parked on the sand. A Flake for me, hundreds and thousands for Jack. The same order we've had our entire lives. We sit cross-legged, side-by-side, watching families building sandcastles, mums shouting to older kids not to go too far. A couple dressed in swimwear are splashing one another, ankle-deep in sea water and laughing loudly. A sleepy-looking dad pushes a newborn back and forth in a collapsible buggy, smiling at his children, looking like he wishes he was the one being rocked to sleep instead. I try and catch a glimpse of the baby when the pram moves close enough, and my heart clenches again.

'If it goes well tomorrow,' Jack says, his mouth full of sprinkles. 'I'll accept the residential scholarship, I think.'

I had been expecting this.

If Jack gets the four A-star grades that he has been predicted, MUSE has offered him the full four-year study scholarship, the research grant, and a residential scholarship. Jack spent all of last summer coming up with his idea for that telescope feature that he thinks is likely to transform the world of science, if it works. The university agrees with him, and they could not have been any more delighted to offer him

– a state schoolboy with no money – the chance to do his degree and work alongside their scientists to develop it.

He'd said he wasn't sure about the residential scholarship. Mingle University of Science and Engineering is down south, but you could make the trip from Vetobridge in eighty minutes if you went at the right time. Jack wasn't sure he was quite ready not to live in Pine Street any more, but that was then and this is… well, very different. He hasn't lived in Pine Street for nearly two months, and I don't think he misses it.

And it's not practical for him to sleep on my sofa throughout his degree.

'Yeah, I thought you might,' I say, trying to keep my voice light. I keep my eyes on the baby, thinking, thinking.

'I'll miss you like crazy.'

I blink and nod, though I'm not sure if Jack is looking at me. He knows I feel the same, I don't have to say it.

'But I don't think Vetobridge will ever be the same for me.'

There it is. Katie Waltz squeezing herself in between us, practically flicking the ice cream out of my hand.

'I was thinking…' Jack continues. 'You could come to Mingle.'

'Of course I will.'

'No, I mean you could come there to live.'

I snap my neck around to Jack so fast I hurt it. 'What?'

'Not with me, necessarily,' Jack adds hastily. 'Just… not far.'

I stare at him, unsure if I've heard him properly or if my brain is playing tricks.

Me, move out of Vetobridge, out of the *country*, half-way across the island of Ireland to the tiny city of Mingle. No beach, no Decky…

No Katie Waltz, adds a voice in my head. *No Norm, no police…*

Mingle was quite cute, I supposed. I'd been there on a visit with Jack to check it out the year before. It was up-and-coming, helped along by the relatively new university campus that pulled the best science students from across the UK and beyond. There were new houses, new restaurants, popping up every day, Jack told me.

'It's a stupid idea,' Jack says, misreading my serious look. 'Forget it.'

'No,' I say hastily, using my free hand to reach for his arm. 'No, it's not. Are you serious? You'd want me there, cramping your style?'

Jack lets air out through his nose, some semblance of a snort of laughter, then turns back to his ice cream.

'Hardly have much style, have I, Abs? No matter how much I like to think I have. No matter how much I pretend.'

'I'd love to,' I say. 'I think... Yeah, I think I should.'

'What? Seriously?' Jack is grinning. 'You'd move? What about The Rooster?'

'What about it? It's hardly my dream job and it's... well, it's been different recently. A bit awful.'

Jack looks down, but he's still nodding.

'I'll hand in my notice tomorrow.'

'Wait until I get my grades!' Jack warns.

'You'll get them,' I say, and I realise I've never been so sure of anything.

The drive home is an easy one, and we share a bright pink candyfloss stick as I drive. It feels like something has lifted from between us, and as we chase the sunset south back towards Vetobridge, I find I'm grinning to myself.

My little brother is about to get the best grades anyone from Seaview High has ever got. He's getting a scholarship to a prestigious new science school, where he'll put together his inventions and learn with some of the best minds in the country. And I get to go too.

The only thing is Max.

As the town centre comes into view, the cobbled street making a racket under my tyres, I let myself imagine Max coming with me, the two of us setting up together, miles away from here. Would he be prepared to leave Seaview High? The good thing about teaching was that you could do it wherever you went, surely?

Maybe, just maybe...

The Blindspot

We pull onto Old Droless road and I have to swing to a stop. The outside of the Vape Shop is surrounded by people, I can't get any further.

Jack leans forward, searching the crowds.

'What's going on?' he murmurs. He's squinting, as usual.

My throat catches as faces turn towards us, and then—

'There's a police car,' I say, my voice hollow. 'Maybe... maybe there's been an accident?'

I can't get any further, so I turn off the car and get out.

The tallest member of the crowd has seen me, and is coming near.

I recognise him as one of the police officers who was in my flat, and he has recognised me.

Pollock and Mathers have parted from the crowd and are coming towards us.

Heads turn, gradually, then all at once, to face us.

'Rapist!'

The word is spat from a window, and I jerk my head up, trying to figure out where it came from.

My breath is coming in short shallow gasps.

'There he is, get him!' shouts someone in the crowd.

For one horrifying second, the crowd surges toward us, but Pollock has them backing off with a single shout.

Mathers has reached the passenger side of the car, where Jack too has poked his head out and is looking, terrified, from her to the swarm of people blocking our way.

'Jack,' I hear her say to him, kindly, motherly, as always. 'We need you to come to the station. Now. Come and get in the car.'

'Why?' I ask. I am perched awkwardly, one foot in the footwell of the car, the other on the kerb, both hands resting on the door as though to shield myself behind it.

Mathers glances at me. 'Some new evidence has come to light. We need Jack to answer some more questions about the accusation Katie Waltz made on the twenty-first of June this year.'

Jack is shaking his head. 'No,' he says. 'No, you said it was over. Please, please—'

'Mr Campbell,' Mathers says, her tone low, her eyes full of something. Pity, maybe? Or just exhaustion? 'I can arrest you, but in front of all these people, I'd rather not. Come and get into the car with me and I'll explain. That's it, good boy.'

Good boy, I think, as Jack follows Mathers, bewildered.

You don't say good boy to a rapist.

She knows he's innocent. She knows as well as I do.

Good boy.

I'll cling to that. I'll cling to that.

She pushes his head down as he gets into the back of the police car. They do that on TV, I didn't realise it was a real thing.

Pollock is in front of me and he's said something. I tear my eyes away from the police car and focus on his face, having to look up. He must be over six foot three, I think. And he's so broad, so immense. I could hide three of me behind him. Did he look this big in my flat? How did he fit in the door?

'Sorry?' I say weakly. 'What did you say?'

'I said do you want me to get your car into the car park for you? They'll move for me.'

I look miserably at the crowd behind him. People have videoed this, I can see iPhones pointing at the police car, moving to Pollock's back. Maybe they're livestreaming it, providing audio commentary, my brother having his head pushed into the back of a police car.

It's over now. That's it. Whatever semblance of a life we created after Jack's first arrest has vanished, whatever tiny anonymity he was granted is gone.

'Yes, please,' I whisper, and I hand Pollock the keys. He's nice, really. He was only ever doing his job.

I walk away from my car, back towards the main road, and I lean against a wall for support. A wall. My support is a wall.

Pollock carefully manoeuvres my car into the car park behind the Vape Shop, hands me back my keys, and then he gets into the police car and reverses it expertly down the street until he can turn it around. He's right, the crowd moves for him. People are looking at me, staring at me. People have taken pictures and videos. My face will be everywhere, all over the social media that I don't have.

Rapist's sister.

Accused rapist's sister. Does the word make any difference on Twitter? I don't think so. I really don't think so.

Then the police car is gone and I haven't even been able to see Jack, make eye contact with him, give him anything of reassurance.

The world has flipped around, and it took a few minutes.

I walk away from Old Droless Road, not hurrying, not really thinking. I don't want to go through the crowd, don't care about going into my flat. They'd all know I was in there, how could I relax?

I feel strangely calm, and pull out my phone and call Dad. I ask him to text Francie's number to me. Why don't I have Francie's number, I wonder? Because I thought I'd never need it again. Because I put all of my hopes, put all of my life, on not needing that bloody number ever again.

Dad says the police were at the house looking for Jack, did they find him? Is it all sorted now? I don't say anything, don't confirm or deny either way.

I call Francie and he knows who I am immediately, recognises my voice before I even say my name.

'Is it Jack again?' he asks. He sounds like he's eating his dinner, even though it's so late. I don't think I'll ever eat again. I think of the candyfloss in the car and it starts to creep back up my throat. I swallow hard.

'Yeah,' I say. 'It's Jack.'

Francie promises to head to Oldry Police Station immediately, and says he'll keep us informed.

The next call I make is to Max.

I've only been able to see him once or twice a week recently, in the stolen hours after work, usually in the car. Caroline's been working from home a lot lately, so we can't go to Max's house, and I'm obviously not going to bring him over when Jack's living on my sofa, even though I don't think Jack would mind.

'Can we meet?' I ask, still my voice is so calm. 'At yours, or— or somewhere?'

'Abi?' He sounds like he's moving from one room to another, closing a door behind him. 'What's up? What's wrong?'

'I can't go home,' I say, and it sounds as pathetic and useless as I feel. 'Can I come over?'

'Uh. Yes. You can, yes. Can you give it half an hour?'

Of course I can give it half an hour, I'm walking.

I walk up the mini main street, into Vetobridge town centre, feeling every cobblestone under my trainers and focusing on that. Past Tesco, up the big hill. I walk past The Rooster, briefly wondering how The New Girl is getting on without me, and I find I don't care one bit. The place could burn to the ground for all it matters.

It's really dark now, after nine, and cold. I realise I left my hoodie in the car, and by the time I turn into Max's estate, my arms and legs are goosebumped and sore.

The lights are on in his living room, and there's no car in the drive.

It's a big house. Caroline's influencer wage must be impressive, because I know Max's isn't. He could never afford a place like this. There are four bedrooms, two of them with en-suites, and for absolutely no reason that I've ever been able to establish, they have two massive living rooms. One of them is a 'good room' that they never use, only if they have people over at Christmas, and more than once I've wanted to shake him and say, why the bloody hell are you saving a room for best? Why wouldn't you use it? And what's the point?

I knock in a code we've established, and he comes to the door.

He furrows his brow. 'Where's your car?'

'At my flat.'

'Okay.' He stands back to let me in, looking me up and down as though my appearance might give him some clue as to what's going on.

I wonder how I must look to him. Now and in The Before, when I was just a normal person whose brother was just a boy. And back when I was in a tatty school uniform. I experience an unusual, unpleasant jolt to the solar plexus when I think about that. It's not cute, it's not romantic, is it? That a teacher would fancy a pupil, even if she was eighteen. It's fucking weird. I think of Francie and his hairpiece, I think of Dad and his greasy beard and the complete lack of parenting on his part for the majority of my life. Maybe it's just men who are fucking weird in general. Maybe I've just had an epiphany.

'Sorry,' I say to Max, automatically making for the kitchen. 'I had nowhere else to go.'

'So I'm a last chance saloon?' He's joking, but I don't smile.

I sit at the marble island and look at his fruit bowl.

It's completely full with perfectly ripe bananas, apples, easy peelers. It looks like an Instagram picture. In fact, I bet if I pulled my phone out and looked at Caroline's page, she'd have taken a photo of this exact bowl only this morning. I fucking hate it. How hard is it to have cereal for breakfast, Caroline?

'Jack's been arrested. Again.'

'Oh.'

'New evidence. They have new evidence, they said. They... they have something on him.'

From behind me I hear Max sigh heavily, and he comes to rest his elbows on the counter beside me.

'I'm sorry,' he says. 'That's... that's so shit.'

'It's going to go to court,' I whisper. 'Isn't it? He's gonna be charged with this. There'll be a trial. He's gonna have to – he's gonna—' I choke, but I don't let my tears fall. Instead I shake my head, so violently my vision vibrates. 'He'll go to prison.'

Max puts one hand between my shoulder blades. Kind of a hug, but not really.

Kind of a relationship, but not really.

Kind of a good man, but not really.

'Just... just see what they have first. See what really happened. You – you never know. Maybe...' But he trails off, unable to think of anything that will maybe happen that doesn't involve Jack being in a cell. My Jack.

My brother, Jack.

I look down at Max's slippers – they're expensive moccasins that Caroline got him for Christmas, that make him look like an old man. He's wearing jeans and slippers to sit in the house. Why have I never thought about how weird that is before? Who wears jeans in the house?

I imagine him next to me in court, in his suit—

'You could be a character witness!' I say suddenly, looking up at him for the first time.

His brow furrows more still. 'What do you mean? When?'

'For Jack!' I feel my pulse quicken.

Max rubs his stubble in a gesture I know so well. 'I'm not sure...'

'It's perfect!' I say. I bounce off the stool and take one of his hands, looking at him seriously. 'You're an academic. A teacher. You've written papers, you've done research. And you've known Jack for years – he's your best pupil ever, you've told me so yourself! If you're up there, sticking up for his good character—'

'I'm a secondary school teacher, Abi,' he says. 'I'm not an academic.'

'You know what I mean,' I say using my hand to bat away his ridiculousness. 'You're respected. People would believe you if you stood up and said the accusations are impossible. Jordan was researching trials like this, and a lot of people have got off from—'

'Do you hear yourself?'

I stop with my mouth open, hanging on my words.

I stare at him. Properly look.

Max turned forty-three in May, to my twenty-seven. It had never really felt like much, not when I felt so much older than my years. It is only now, staring at him in his moccasin slippers in his designer kitchen with its designer Instagrammable fruit bowl that I really see it. He is... older. He is a bit old. Not in age by any means, but... in his eyes. In his mind and his opinions. He's not quite old enough to be my parent, but not far from it. He is a middle-aged man.

Why have I never noticed that before either?

'What do you mean?' I say.

'Do you actually hear what you've just suggested? I go up in court and say Jack's great and he, what, *gets off*? Gets away with forcing himself on Katie? Is that what you want? You think that would be a good thing?'

I can feel my pulse in my ears.

'But he didn't do it,' I say, quietly, weakly. With far, far less conviction than I have been thinking it for the last two months. 'He's innocent.'

'Oh, Jesus, Abi.' Max puts his head in his hands, lets his fingers push through his hair, which needs a cut before he goes back to school next week. He takes his glasses off and cleans them on his T-shirt without opening his eyes. 'Jesus Christ, Abi. You don't honestly believe that, do you?'

'What do you mean?' I repeat. I don't have any words to offer but those. Questions I can do, answers… not so much. Those will require a part of my brain that's currently out of focus and dizzy. I'm too fuzzy to think.

Max sighs again. It's rare people sigh in real life, but he's a sigher. He's dramatic. 'I know he's your little brother, and I know you love him… but if they've just found new evidence and come to arrest him *again* then I'm afraid… It's not looking good for Jack.'

'But if you gave evidence of—'

'I'm not going to be his character witness!' Max says, his eyes wide, shaking his head. 'Why do you keep saying that? I'm obviously not going to do that. Why would I? Why should I? I'm not getting involved. He's a student. A good one, granted, but that's all I know. And…'

'And what?' My cheeks feel hot, as if I'm sitting beside a fire. I kind of am.

He looks uncomfortable. Pulls away from me slightly, thinking. Then he grabs one of the easy peel oranges and starts to dig his thumbnail into it.

'And I heard something about a bet,' he says lamely, his eyes on the orange. 'I didn't want to tell you before because I was hoping maybe it didn't mean anything but… Some of the sixth form boys… Jack's mates, you know. That guy Ben and some of the other hangers-on who stayed for A-Levels. Before the summer break, they were talking about a bet. They didn't know I was right behind them in the queue for the canteen.'

I watch him, my mind blank, completely clueless as to what he is saying. I let myself fall back onto my seat, my brief thrust of optimism completely gone.

'Something about…' he uses the orange to gesture with his hands, 'the number of girls they could shag before the end of the term. They were all counting. Taking it seriously. And something about getting evidence of each.'

Evidence of each. Evidence of each. Like on a phone?

'That's just a stupid thing little boys say to each other to make them look like the alpha male,' I say quietly. 'It's just words, Max.'

'I have a feeling Katie Waltz wouldn't think it was just words. I heard Jack discussing numbers. He was in on this dopey bet. Abi… I think you have to accept that there's a chance every word Katie has said is true. I'm absolutely not getting involved in this. For a start, it could affect my career, my relationships with my students and the other staff.' He was on a roll now, orange forgotten in his palm. 'For another, next term Caroline's launching her new charity. A free, anonymous counselling service online for women and girls who have experienced sexual violence in any form.'

He sounds like he's reading off an advertising flyer. I wonder if he helped her come up with it.

'Since when?'

'Since… I dunno. A few months.'

'Oh. Well, I'd hate to get in the way of Caroline's new business venture. I don't know how I could sleep at night if I thought my brother's freedom had disturbed that.'

'Abi, *don't.*' He's literally just used his teacher voice on me.

'No, Max. *You* don't. Don't act like your wife is so fucking important to you all of a sudden, don't act like you give half a shit about her career – a career you once likened to that of a seventeen-year-old girl. And do you know what's funny?' I gesture around me, at the huge American fridge-freezer, at the patio doors that lead out to their immaculate garden, at the gigantic Aga and the sink. 'She's paid for all of this. It's all *hers*. You have nothing, and you're never done slagging her off. What makes you so much better? You teach twelve-year-olds the fucking periodic table—'

'A minute ago I was an academic. Stop acting like a child, Abi.'

'Oh my God.' I put my palms up to squeeze my temples. 'You're the child. You're the child, Max, and you can't even see it.'

'You can't see what's been right in front of you for months – your brother *raped* somebody, Abi. He *raped* someone. He's a *rapist*.' Max really is on a roll, his voice loud for maybe the first time ever. 'And you look pathetic, you look heartless, and horrible, and sick, and wrong for supporting him, letting him live on your sofa! He's a criminal. He deserves jail time for what he's done – and if this new evidence is up to scratch, he'll get it. No more technicalities, Abi, no more *oh maybe they had sex and she regretted it* – no. No more. He forced himself on someone who *did not want to have sex with him*. That's rape. He's guilty.'

I look up at Max, slowly. His old-man slippers. His jeans. A brown belt. A stripy polo shirt. Then his glasses, and the hairline that's receded significantly since we first got together.

'Is it?' I say, my voice hollow. 'Is that what rape is, to you?'

Max tuts and fires the orange down onto the counter. 'What? Yes, obviously.'

'You sure?'

He stares at me, uncomprehending.

Because he really, genuinely, truly, doesn't remember.

Or maybe – and is this worse? – he never realised in the first place.

Max and I don't say much more. There's nothing much more to say. We've barely seen each other for eight weeks, we aren't married, we have nothing shared that needs to be sorted before we go our separate ways. We're just done, at an end, like everything else that ever exists.

I walk home in the cold, in the dark, my heart aching, my blood boiling with anger, trying not to imagine what's happening to Jack. I can't go down that line of thinking or I might collapse at the side of the road and never get up again.

I find I walk to Pine Street instead of my own flat.

Home, because that is where my family will be.

I'm not sure I want company, but I definitely don't want to be alone, and unfortunately there's nothing that's in the middle.

The next few hours are an out of body experience. I am aware that things, important things, are happening to the Campbell family, but their impact does not register. The things do not happen to me. I see myself from above, sitting at the tiny table in Pine Street at midnight. Then at two. Then at four o'clock in the morning. Then five.

When the police have been questioning Jack for seven hours, they take a break to let him sleep. This we know because Francie leaves the station and joins us in Pine Street, taking up the rest of the space at the tiny table, and he talks us through it. Or rather, he talks the Campbells through it, and I'm there, on the ceiling, watching. His words have very little meaning. He's describing the plot of a TV show he's been watching. He's not talking about my brother. That would be ridiculous.

'A pair of tights were found, washed up near the Bloomin' Bridge,' Francie informs the Campbell family. 'About half a mile away from the rockpools where Miss Waltz claims... You know.'

Miss Waltz. He's graduated from *the wee girl*.

The Abi on the ceiling wants to roll her eyes but she's not capable at the moment.

'As the investigation wasn't exactly still active, they might have gone unnoticed, only a dog took an interest in them and alerted her owner, and her owner thought just to be on the safe side, he'd call it in. Katie Waltz confirmed they were hers. She gets clothes from a Swedish website, apparently they're very distinctive. Police got the DNA results back earlier this evening... Jack's DNA is all over them.'

Like the moment in the hall when Jack was first arrested, several times I nearly laugh aloud, but I sit silent. I don't speak even when people ask me questions.

Everyone is asking me fucking questions.

Why is it always up to me?

The tights are ripped and they have some blood on them, Francie tells us. Katie Waltz's blood. And Jack's DNA. A perfect match with the sample they took back in June when he was arrested.

'So, Jack's now changed his story,' Francie says finally.

I feel, rather than see, all heads snap up.

Decky is next to me, in checked pyjama bottoms and a grey sweatshirt, his leg shaking against mine. Jordan sits opposite me, his mouth clamped as tightly shut as mine, pale but still practically perfect, his dark fringe expertly gelled to one side. Dad is next to him, looking old and confused. He's had quite a few pints of Guinness, though, so his cheeks are red, and with his greying white beard and hair he looks a bit like a sad gnome. Pathetic.

Ciarán hasn't bothered to come over, but texted me four times.

He finally worked out I wasn't going to reply and is messaging Jordan back and forth instead.

'What's the new story?' Decky asks.

'He maintains it wasn't him who... attacked Miss Waltz. He's very clear on that. He says his friend did it.'

'His friend?' Jordan bleats. 'Who? Which friend?'

They all look at me, as if I'll reveal the truth I've been holding on to all along.

I ignore them all, staring at Francie, willing him to continue.

'Ben Ringwall. Jack says Ben did it, but that Jack was there.'

'Then surely they'll arrest Ben instead?' Decky says.

'They'll have to talk to him for sure. They'll probably go and lift him first thing in the morning.'

'And his other mates? They should talk to them.'

'Of course they will. But...' Francie trails off.

He's loosened his tie again, but tonight his hairpiece is staying motionless, as though it realises how serious this is, compared to the minor misunderstanding back in June.

'But what?' Decky asks.

'They don't like that Jack's changed his story. It looks... bad. A bit too... convenient, to mention it all now. Why didn't he just tell them all this when they first asked about it? And save himself a lot of trouble? Why would he keep this secret for the last two months?'

'Because he was threatened.' My voice is slightly hoarse, and I have to clear my throat and repeat myself, to make sure they've heard me. 'Because Ben Ringwall threatened Jack. Made him keep his mouth shut.'

'You knew?' Jordan demands. 'Why didn't you say?'

'I didn't know,' I snap back. 'I'm guessing. Obviously. But it makes sense, now. I saw Ben outside my flat one day, talking to Jack. Like the day after his arrest.'

I remember the figure in black, jabbing a finger at Jack's face while I was interviewed by the police in my flat, only now realising that he was the exact height and build of Ben, the boy we'd seen in Tesco the day before.

'He was threatening Jack,' I murmur. 'He must have been.'

Francie is nodding thoughtfully. 'Okay. Well, that's good. We can go with that. Jack says he was scared of Ben. Apparently, his brother is some,' Francie uses his index finger to twirl a circle around his ear. 'I dunno. Mad aul bastard. But at the same time, without proof...'

'If it's the truth, there will be proof,' I say. 'There will be. You'll just have to find it.'

When Francie has told us everything he knows, Dad pours him a beer and the two of them sit side by side, drinking away. As if this is a middle-of-the-night catch up between friends.

'How long can they hold him for?' Dad asks. The only real question he's asked this whole day, this whole experience.

It's I who should be holding Jack.

Is he in a prison cell, crying himself to sleep?

Would he be in a holding cell with someone else? With criminals, with bad men who do bad things?

'Another day,' Francie says.

I don't realise I'm crying until Decky puts the old throw from the sofa over my shoulders. He puts his arm around me too, and we sit like that for a while.

Jordan is checking social media, and he watches the footage of Jack's arrest from four different angles. I listen, but I don't look at the screen. I don't want to see myself or Jack, don't want to see my street, or Mathers putting her hand on Jack's head. Once was enough.

Jordan constantly updates newsfeeds and every now and then he'll interrupt Francie and Dad to read out statistics from other rape cases. Some of them are reassuring until I think about what they actually mean.

Sometimes he gets up and makes tea that nobody drinks.

It is the longest night of my life.

Francie leaves at half-seven, says he's going back to the station.

I want to ask him if he's planning on sleeping, on showering, if he's eaten anything. He won't be on form to help Jack if he's half-pissed and sleep deprived.

Is this the best we have?

The door closes behind the two of them and Jordan sighs.

'I'm going to bed,' he announces. 'Wake me up with any developments.'

'Why do you care?' I ask. My voice is croaky again. I haven't spoken for ages.

Jordan narrows his eyes at me, goes to say something, then just tuts and leaves the room.

'I – I think I will too,' Dad says nervously. He downs the last of his beer and stands up, a little unsteady on his feet. 'Been a long night. Let me know if there's an update? I told Francie it'll be better if he keeps you informed instead of me.'

'Of course you did,' I say. 'Why would you ever be the first point of contact for your own son?'

Dad is surprised and hurt by my comment, I can tell, but he mumbles something, pats me on the shoulder and a moment later we hear him padding up the stairs to bed.

Decky and I are alone.

'What time are the results out?' Decky asks.

I physically jump back.

Jack's A-Level results.

They're out today, and he's in a cell in Oldry. It's the most fucking ridiculous thing I've ever heard of.

On some base level, I'm surprised and touched that Decky has remembered this.

'We can lift them at eleven,' I say, checking the time on my phone. 'I – I'm not sure he'll be out in time to get them.'

And it's these words of mine, not the re-arrest, not the bloodied tights, not the fight with Max or the image of Jack in a holding cell, that make me lose it.

Any control I've ever had evaporates.

I can't see with the tears, and suddenly I'm aware that my throat hurts and it's because I'm sobbing wretchedly, painfully, from somewhere deep inside me that I didn't realise existed.

From behind a door that's just been unlocked and won't ever be closed again.

16

The Hurt, Again

For his sixteenth birthday, I threw my brother Jack a party in the bar of The Rooster and invited his entire year group. I let Dad and the boys take credit for it, but Jack squeezed my hand when he was thanking us, and we both knew what it meant.

Norm and I spent the entire day decorating the pub, prepping the food, cleaning the toilets, knowing that in a few hours a group of teenagers would probably trash the place, but we had to try. Norm had agreed to my suggestion to hold the party there on two conditions: one, that the sixteen-year-olds all had permission from their parents to be there; and two, that they stuck to beer and alcopops.

'No hard stuff,' Norm warned, waggling a finger at me. 'No dark spirits before you're forty, that's what my old man used to say.'

'Did he live a long life?' I asked, wondering why he hadn't mentioned his dad before.

'Nah, he was gone before I could walk. Was the drink that killed him, but my ma claims that was his life motto.'

I grinned at him and we went back to hanging Jack's banner.

By the time the birthday boy arrived, there were already fifty people gathered in the tiny space. The bars had been allowed to re-open the month before, after lockdown, but that night Norm had agreed to close to the public so we could have the main bar and restaurant area all to ourselves. I thought that was probably so he could take the social distancing rule with a pinch of salt, behind closed doors, but I said nothing and was grateful. I thought the number of people who had showed up proved how sick everyone was of staying inside. They were raring to go, arriving in small groups from half-six.

The usual tables had been pushed back against the walls to create a sort of dance floor, and we'd found loads of high tables in the store and placed them around in a circle so people could stand there.

Dad and Ciarán had been among the first to arrive, and were watching the horse-racing on the big screen behind the bar even though it was muted.

'Awk, go on Abi,' Ciarán moaned. 'Stick the volume on, sure barely anyone is here yet.'

'No,' I snapped. 'He'll be here any minute, and his friends are enjoying the music.'

'You don't need volume to enjoy the racing when you have your eyes,' Dad said, and he made it sound like a wise piece of life advice.

Jack walked in with Decky and Jordan on either side and immediately the crowd turned and shouted *HAPPY BIRTHDAY, JACK!* A few people even had party poppers.

Ciarán and Dad went to greet him first, darting forward, both of them holding pint glasses, to bash him on the shoulder.

'Happy birthday, wee bro,' said Ciarán. He chucked Jack under the chin, even though he was only an inch shorter. 'Practically a man!'

'He is a man,' Dad said, as though offended. 'Happy birthday, son.'

I was glad Jack didn't have the heart to point out that he and I had had breakfast with Dad that morning, and Dad hadn't remembered to say it then.

'Thanks,' Jack said, beaming. His face was flushed already, curls a little frizzy from the heat of the June evening. 'This place scrubs up rightly, doesn't it?'

'That's Abi,' Ciarán said, rolling his eyes as if it was a bad thing to put in the effort. I tutted at him and grinned at Jack, who grinned back.

The speakers were playing *Blinding Lights*, and a group of girls were doing the dance while someone else was filming and laughing.

The Blindspot

Everywhere I looked, people were laughing. Granted, it was a much younger crowd than we normally had, but the bar felt full of... well, happiness. It felt like the place to be.

I offered Jack a tumbler of champagne. 'Norm won't let us use the flutes,' I explained as he took it. 'Says they'd get broken.'

'He's probably right. Thank you so much, Abi. This looks amazing.'

'Glad you like it.' I lowered my voice and leant close to him. 'Those lovely boys that did the Junior Maths Challenge are over in the corner. They all showed up an hour ago and brought presents, I put them on that table over there. You might want to go and say hello, they're a bit awkward.'

Jack laughed and, as always, did as I asked.

The teenagers were much more mature than I thought – or maybe I had just been sheltered from the realities of being sixteen. I had been working almost full time, after all.

I did have to clean up one little puddle of sick, but the girl in question had made it right into the bathrooms, and had almost got it into the toilet, but not quite. I consoled one other girl whom I found crying in the storeroom about a boy, and I broke up an almost-fight between two skinny boys with a single shout. Apart from that, Jack's friends seemed to want only to laugh and gossip and whisper. They seemed... nice.

'Is Katie coming?' I asked Norm when we both found ourselves behind the bar around ten o'clock. Norm was sweating, and downing a pint of water, his shirtsleeves rolled up. The beer and alcopops rule was being adhered to, but he was rushed off his feet serving the teenagers while I did everything else. 'I was just about to serve the food, but I can wait on her?'

'Mm?' Norm swallowed the last of his water and shook his head. 'No, love. She's not coming.'

'Oh, that's a shame,' I said, thinking of Katie crying in the hallway in Pine Street. I felt my pulse quicken. 'Did she say why?'

Norm shrugged and lifted a bottle of WKD out of the fridge for a girl who looked like she still might need a booster seat for the car. We both made a cringe face at each other as she swished away. I hoped she had permission to be here.

'She didn't,' Norm said. 'Just didn't feel up to it, I think.'

'Right.' I thought it best not to ask any more questions. Katie obviously hadn't told her grandad about whatever had happened between her and Jack that night all those years ago, so it was best not to push the subject.

I left to lift more glasses, reaching behind Jack to get some. He seemed to be involved in some sort of photoshoot, and girls were taking it in turns to sit on his lap in front of the Happy Birthday banner to have their photos taken.

'Mrs Campbell, do you want to get a photo?'

I glanced up, unsure, to see a pretty, dark-haired girl shaking her phone at me and smiling.

'Mrs Campbell?' Jack barked a laugh. 'Melissa, that's my sister.'

'I know,' the girl said, confused. 'Does she not want a photo?'

I laughed, but I felt my heart sink. I was only twenty-five, was that really miles away from her age? Another glance around me at the tiny waists, high heels and perfectly contoured makeup made me think… yes, it probably was.

'Get a photo with me?' Jack asked, laughter in his eyes.

'Sure,' I said, wondering if it was a pity photo.

I set down the empty glasses and sat next to Jack on one of the comfy stools. He put his arm around my shoulders and leant his head towards me. He smelled of his David Beckham aftershave and the Malibu he'd been claiming to his friends all night was vodka (the beer rule didn't apply to Jack as I knew he hated the taste).

'Gorgeous!' Melissa said breathlessly, and I couldn't help but notice her teeth were shiny white and perfect. I wondered if Jack liked her.

'Thanks again for the party,' he said before I could stand.

'You're very welcome,' I said. 'You deserve it.'

I looked at him then. He was relaxed, happy. A little bit drunk, maybe, but not too bad. He was handsome, and tanned and perfect. She'd be lucky to have him, I thought.

The next time I saw Jack, there was a young man hanging off him and he didn't look any of those things.

I was clearing the empty plates, trying to avoid touching the smears of curry with my freshly painted nails, when Jack's three 'best friends' arrived and jumped on him.

'The bumps!' one of them was shouting. 'Give him the bumps, gwan!'

'Oh, he's a big man now, our Soupy!'

'Oi, you, get him a shot!'

'Get him a slippery nipple!'

'Get him a blowjob, that's what he needs!'

Chortles and laugher, louder than the music, it seemed.

I made eye contact with the girl from earlier – Melissa? – and she shook her head and rolled her eyes.

Jack pulled away from his friends and reached for his glass on the bar, I thought to stop them doing it again.

'Happy birthday, you big tube.'

'Cheers,' Jack mumbled, sipping his drink.

'Three beers!' one of the boys, the shortest one, demanded of Norm, holding up three fingers.

'Please, Norm,' I added in a loud voice as I moved towards them.

I wondered if Norm was glad that Katie had chosen not to do sixth form at Seaview High. She was going on to do art at college, and with these reprobates as her classmates, I was sure Norm would be delighted she'd be getting away from them.

'Do you want to take a wee break, love?' Norm asked me when I came behind the bar with him. 'Go and have a drink with your daddy?'

I heard one of the newcomers snorting and another one mocking Norm's voice, even as he handed them three bottles of beer.

'Sweet,' the tall, dark-haired one said, without thanking him. He took a swig and the others followed suit.

'I'm fine,' I said to Norm, keeping my eyes on the newcomers surrounding Jack. 'I'll stay with you.'

The tall boy caught my eye and spoke loudly as Norm sidled out of the bar. 'Jack, Jack, Jack. Aren't you going to introduce me to your big sister? We've been best friends since primary school and we've never been properly introduced.'

And that must be Ben, I thought, trying not to let my distaste show. Any time there was anything dodgy at Seaview High, you could bet Ben was behind it. I'd never met him, as he didn't spend any time at our house, but I hated the way Jack seemed different around him, the way he still picked up stupid phrases that I knew had come from him.

And the relaxed, happy boy from earlier seemed to have gone with his arrival. Instead, my tense and strained-looking brother was sipping determinedly at his drink as if he couldn't bear to let it out of his hand.

'This is Ben,' Jack said, smiling weakly and jerking his head at him. 'Ben, Abi.'

I looked him up and down and didn't smile back.

Norm and I went into the kitchen to fetch Jack's cake from the fridge.

'Is he having a lovely birthday?' Norm asked, lifting a handful of paper plates.

'I think so!' I nodded happily at him. 'Thanks again, Norm. You're a life saver.'

'It's my pleasure, love. I have to say, they're better behaved than I thought. Except those boys in the shiny jackets.'

I snorted with laughter. He was right: whether they'd intended it or not, Ben and his two cronies – one was Fitzy and one was Jonny Ferguson, I didn't know which was which – were wearing almost identical black sports jackets.

'They're like the – what do you call them?'

'The T Birds!' I laughed, properly.

'That's them!' Norm laughed too. 'Wee dickheads.'

'I know.'

'Hope your brother isn't getting too friendly with them.'

'I'm not sure,' I said. 'I don't like them either, but if I tell him not to be friends with them he might…'

'Might what?'

'Be annoyed with me,' I finished lamely.

I couldn't really put it into words. On one hand, yes, I wanted to mother Jack in all the ways our own mother should have been able to. On the other, I couldn't do that, because he could turn around and tell me to fuck off and he'd be completely entitled to. It was a thin line to walk and I was afraid of stumbling over it.

'Nah,' Norm said. He lifted the cake knife and balanced it on top of his plates. 'You should say something to him. He's your boy.'

We stood just outside the bar, lighting the sixteen candles, hardly breathing in case we put them out. Then Norm turned out the lights and we went slowly inside, my hand cupped around the candles.

A few people screamed, jokingly, and there was a lot of laughter and whooping.

Jack's classmates caught on quickly, and they started singing in perfect unison, some of them turning their phones to film it, some craning their necks to see where Jack was.

Happy biiiirthdayyyy toooo youuuuu

I glanced up too, unable to find his curls among the crowd. Then he came shyly to the middle of the dancefloor, where people clapped him on the back and squealed delightedly.

Happy biiiiirthdayyyy toooo youuuuu

I reached him and we grinned at each other.

Happy biiiiirthdayyyy, dear Jaaa-aaack

'Thank you,' I heard Jack whisper, even though everyone was singing loudly and cheering.

Happy biiiirrrthhhdayyyy tooooo youuuuu

'Make a wish,' I whispered back.

Cameras flashed as he leaned in, his lips pouting.

In the split second before he blew out the candles, I saw his face change. A slight wrinkle of his perfectly smooth forehead.

It was only afterwards, as I cut slices of cake and kept the smile pasted on my face, nodding at the kids who thanked me and rolling my eyes at those who didn't, that I realised I had absolutely no idea what he might have wished for.

17

The Over-Achiever

At ten, I phone Seaview High and explain, without giving details, that Jack can't come to lift his results, and I ask if I can lift them for him. I'm passed from the receptionist to the head teacher, Mr Goodall, who greets me like an old friend.

'Oh, Abi, it's so good to hear from you. Yes, of course you can. You're sure Jack can't make it? It seems an awful shame, we'd have loved to have seen him again before he jets off to uni…'

Decky comes with me to get my car as he has Thursdays off in lieu of working Saturdays.

We walk past the coffee shop, past the stationer's, towards my flat, two sleep-deprived little zombies, not speaking. When we turn into my street, Decky stops and swears.

I look around, panicked, until I see it.

The semi-circular window of my flat, the one that looks across to the Mournes, is shattered.

No curtain or blind billowing in the breeze, I still haven't got around to either of those yet, but the window has been broken in the bottom right-hand corner, sharp shards pointing towards the star of missing glass as if guiding us to it.

'Shit,' I murmur, and we break into a run simultaneously. Towards the danger, towards the hurt, always towards it.

The door is uncompromised, locked just as it should be.

When we reach the window, we both peer down into the street.

'It was broken from the outside,' Decky murmurs. 'What do you reckon? One of the onlookers from last night's public arrest?'

'Probably,' I say.

It says a lot about the events of the last fifteen hours that I am completely numb to this latest turn.

'Oh, shit. It was a brick.' Decky crouches to pick it up from beside the sofa, then looks up. 'Maybe I shouldn't touch it? Evidence on it?'

'I don't think I'll be calling the police, Deck.'

'Right.'

He lifts the brick and weighs it in his hand. 'Yep. That'd do it. Here, do you want to read this or shall I?'

He pulls an elastic band from around the red brick. There is a single white sheet attached to it.

'Nah, gwan, gimme it.' I take it from him.

It's handwritten, sealed in a clear plastic Poly-Pocket.

He says nothing or nxt time it will b ur skull

I am just about to read the note to Decky when there's a tentative knock at the door downstairs, and someone calls, 'Hello?'

Decky bounces up from the floor and goes to see who it is. I hear him speaking to someone quizzically, then footsteps.

Still, I feel nothing.

Decky re-emerges, then a beautiful face appears at the door, following him.

'This bloke says he works downstairs?' says Decky.

Indeed he does. I've seen this man, Vik, and his brother through the glass of the Vape Shop many times, and they always grin widely and nod when they see me. I've spoken to Vik, this elder one, twice, and he's always been kind and sweet and funny.

'Hello, Abi.' He looks nervous today, though pleased he's remembered my name. 'I have finally met one of your famous brothers!'

'Yes,' I agree weakly, trying to match his smile. What the bloody hell is this lovely man doing in my flat?

He seems to hear the unspoken question because he quickly becomes serious.

210

'I have come to tell you of something that happened early this morning. My brother and I came in early to clean as we have been busy lately – we arrived just after five. There was a man at your door. A very angry man. He was knocking very, very hard. We stayed and watched, to make sure he wouldn't hurt you if you answered. He was shouting many things. Then he left and we thought that was the end to things.'

Vik glances at the broken window and rubs his clean chin.

'I am very sorry to say we were wrong. He came back not one hour later and he threw that from the street. My brother, he wanted to call the police, but I said we should wait to ask you, in case this man is simply...' He gestures for the right words. 'A very annoyed boyfriend. We wrote down a description just in case. It is not the same glasses man who visits you sometimes.'

I glance at Decky, who is pretending he didn't hear the last part.

I had no idea Vik and his brother even thought of me, but by the sounds of things they... look out for me? Someone looks out for me, without needing to? I'm touched and surprised.

'What's the description?' Decky asks, looking from me to Vik and back.

'Big. Not very old, maybe early twenties. A big black coat. He had a bright green baseball cap with a white logo on it.'

'You could pick him outta a lineup?'

'I'm sorry?'

'Would you know him if you saw him again?' Decky rephrases.

'I believe so. Me and my brother. Between us, yes.'

'Thank you,' I say. 'I'm not sure we'll be pursuing it but... Thank you very much.'

'You have to pursue it,' Decky says. 'They've wrecked your window. They've threatened you. It's obviously...' He glances at Vik, who is standing with his hands behind his back, nodding seriously as though he completely gets the ins and outs of the conversation. 'Y'know. Ben's ones. His brother or their cronies.'

'I can't think about it at the minute,' I say. 'I can't make a decision,

I'll just… I'll deal with it later. Okay? Not now. Thank you, Vik. I really appreciate you looking out for me.'

'Yes, of course. Let me know if you want to talk some more. Okay? I will leave you now, have a great day.'

I bet it's what they say to customers leaving the Vape Shop.

I'd love to have a great day.

I'd settle for average, mediocre.

I'd settle for dull.

I pull up in the already crowded car park of Seaview High, aware suddenly that this is the last time I'll ever be here. I remember sitting here with *Ulysses* on my lap, feeling deflated until I saw Max had put his phone number in the cover. I think of a few months after that, when I picked up my own brown envelope that told me while I'd scraped English, I hadn't got my other two results. It was no surprise; I was too busy working to complete the coursework properly. What a stupid decision, I think, as we slam the car doors shut behind us. Why did I choose to spend my time behind a bar instead of revising or doing my school work? Why did I think that would ever be a good idea? Imagine if Jack had told me he wanted to pick up extra shifts in the garage instead of his chemistry homework.

But you don't care about you like you care about Jack, says a voice in my head. *Because Jack has been given every opportunity and every support needed to succeed, and you weren't.*

I can feel my heartbeat in my ears as Decky opens the door to reception for me.

It's been a night and a morning of revelations. Is this what it feels like to grow up?

There are groups of teenagers everywhere. Some with envelopes in their hands, hugging, some chatting seriously to teachers, nodding and listening. Quite a few people on the phone, either grinning and laughing or mumbling into the mouthpiece.

I have a feeling that, were this not such an important occasion for every student here, all eyes might well be on me. Surely everyone has seen the video from last night by now? That must be why Mr Goodall didn't question me too much. He didn't want to know the details.

We move into the assembly hall.

Snaking rows of brown envelopes sit across two tables, a new teacher whom I don't recognise perched behind them, her eyes narrowed slightly at us.

'Can I help you?'

'Yeah,' I say. 'I'm here to lift results for my brother. Jack Campbell. He can't make it.'

'It's been okayed with Mr Goodall,' Decky adds, and these are the magic words.

'Yes, of course! Jack Campbell, of course.'

The teacher, who might well be younger than me – how terrifying – starts to fuss through envelopes.

'Campbell... Campbell. Here it is.'

She thrusts an envelope at me, all smiles. 'I think I heard someone saying he's done well.'

'Really?' I ask, hating the pathetic hope in my voice.

Maybe he has done well, lady, but actually he spent the night in a police station, accused of rape

Decky and I have almost made it back out the front doors when I hear someone calling my name from behind me.

My first instinct is to keep walking – it'll be a classmate of Jack's, wanting to ask about him.

But Decky grabs my wrist and I turn around.

Mr Goodall is striding towards us, his arms outstretched dramatically. Aside from being the head teacher, he also used to teach drama, and still takes over if ever there's sickness. He's constantly in over-the-top dramatic mode. It used to do my head in.

'Abi Campbell, thought that was you! How have you been! Haven't seen you for ages. What are you doing with yourself now!' His questions don't sound like questions, more like learnt-by-heart soliloquies, and he is smiling like he has too many teeth to fit in his mouth. He comes to a halt in front of us, barely glancing at Decky.

'Have you had a look?' he motions to the envelope.

'Not yet,' I say, not bothering to add the lie that I'm waiting for Jack to have the first peek. How can I wait for that? He might never get the chance.

'Well, you might want to have a look now.'

'Why?'

'Just… just trust me.' Mr Goodall and his teeth make a point of raising eyebrows significantly. 'There's a photographer from the *Daily Review* hanging around interviewing happy students who've done well and I've told him Jack's story is sure to make the front page no problem. It's fine that he's not here, I thought you could talk to him instead. A bit of background about Jack. I've actually gone to the liberty of writing a little article myself.' He sniffs importantly and straightens himself. He already towers over us, now he's basically touching the roof. 'So, go on then, open them and we can get a photo of you. *Proud Sister Opens Clever Brother's Results.*'

'The *Vetobridge Howler*,' I murmur, my eyes scanning the clusters of people behind Mr Goodall.

I was wrong – some people are looking at me. They're noticing me and quickly looking away to whisper in the ears of their friends. Not just the students, their parents too.

'The *Howler*,' I repeat. I think of the article back in June, the half-informed, half-rumoured article… with Jack's name in the comments.

'Yes,' Mr Goodall says, impatiently like I'm stupid. 'They'll want to get a few words from you. I know what a support you've been to Jack. He's a wonderful reflection on you.'

'No,' I say. 'I'm sorry. I have to go.'

I'm back in the car a full minute before Decky, having practically run through the car park. Decky doesn't run. He doesn't hurry, ever. Likes to dawdle.

He also doesn't question why I've insisted on coming back to the car instead of opening Jack's results. I wonder if he knows, instinctively, in that way only a sibling can, exactly how I'm feeling and what's going

214

through my head or – as is more likely – if he just isn't asking because he is Decky, and he lets people get on with things as long as they let him do the same.

He settles himself in his seat and looks at me.

I look at him.

His skin is greyer than usual, his eyes hanging as though he's had a night on the drink instead of a night on the tea, in the kitchen. His T-shirt has a small stain on the collar. My brother Decky.

We don't speak. Instead, I tear at the envelope with shaking fingers, half afraid I'm going to tear the results page, half not caring one way or another.

I have to know.

This will change everything. If I can show this to the police…

The page is not the one I was expecting. In fact, it's a three-page letter, stapled together, with Jack's name, his address in Pine Street typed on the top. The exam board logo.

Oh fuck.

He's fucking cheated.

'What is this?' I say dumbly, staring at the words without reading them.

Decky eases the letter out of my hand and starts to read.

It is only then I realise there is another page inside the envelope. I pull it out – the results page I was expecting.

I stare at this page too, without reading it.

I don't have to read it. I can see the letter grades down the right-hand side. All four of them, exactly the way I've imagined in my dreams for the last two years.

Exactly.

Exactly.

Perfect, like Jack.

A* A* A* A*

'He's done it,' I sob, thrusting the page at Decky. 'He did it.'

And I bury my face in my arms and bawl all over again.

*

The letter that was inside the envelope is from the exam board, congratulating Mr Jack Campbell of 11 Pine Street, Vetobridge, County Down, Northern Ireland, for achieving the highest grades across the United Kingdom. Mr Jack Campbell, who never knew his mum, who refuses to wear his glasses because of what his classmates might say, who still eats Coco Pops for breakfast, and who spent last night in a police cell, achieved the best exam results in the country. A state schoolboy who never had a tutor, who studied a fair amount, but not constantly.

My brother Jack.

I read the letter for a third time, for a fourth time, and by the fifth time I can recite it from memory.

They want him to feature on their website, give an interview, and they've given him a prize. He is to contact them for more information.

Decky and I are seated opposite one another in the Clandy, Decky's favourite pub. It's attached to a hotel, but the bar is reasonable enough, and it shows the horse-racing and the football, and anything else you might like to watch. Decky says it's his favourite because he never sees anyone he knows in there, and he doesn't mind paying a bit extra for his pint if it means he's just Decky, and not *Decky Campbell, brother of x, son of y.*

I can relate.

'Now, who's having the pancakes?' the smiley waitress asks.

'Thanks, Ashley,' Decky says, leaning back so she can set the huge plate of pancakes and bacon in front of him.

'And the scrambled eggs and toast for yourself, then.' She sets mine down and bounces off back to the kitchen.

'Ashley,' I repeat, smiling as I take my knife and fork from its napkinned sheath.

'Yep. That's Ashley,' Decky says, grinning wryly. 'Ashley's a very nice, very competent waitress and barperson. I'm sure you can appreciate.'

'Oh, for sure.'

We tuck into our food, and Decky was right – I was hungry. It did help.

When I am half-way through my brunch I take the letter out and read it again.

'You'll wear away the words,' Decky says with a mouthful of maple syrup. He smiles at me – our mum used to say that – and I smile back.

'He's incredible,' I murmur, tucking the pages back into the envelope. 'I just can't believe it.'

'Yes, you can.'

'Yes,' I say. 'I can.'

'It'll sort itself out, you know.' Decky uses his thumbnail to dig something out of his back tooth. 'I promise you that. It will sort itself. Jack says he's innocent and… he must be. Granted, he's handled this whole thing terribly, but the right person will pay for what's happened. I know it.'

It's probably the longest speech I've ever heard Decky make, and it's touching.

Ashley has just cleared away our plates when my phone rings.

I swallow a mouthful of lukewarm coffee before I blurt, 'It's Francie!'

Decky's eyes widen as I answer the call.

'Abi? It's me. Listen – I just overheard something I wasn't supposed to and it's good news.'

Good news I mouth to Decky, who nods encouragingly. My heart is racing.

I have good news too, I want to scream. *Tell Jack, tell Jack—*

But I want to see his face when he reads the letter, want to be there to hug him as soon as he knows.

And I will.

I'll make sure of that.

'We took a wee break there,' Francie continues. 'And I went outside for a smoke, and who do I spot rushing into the station but Katie Waltz herself.'

'*What?*'

'I know. I followed her in, taking care not to be too obvious, hiding myself behind pillars and the like—' Francie actually chuckles, and I imagine banging his head off a pillar. 'She was demanding to speak to one of the officers on her case. Says her liaison has told her Jack's been charged, and she needs to talk to someone pronto. Guess what she's just *happened* to remember this morning?'

'What?' I repeat, more urgently this time.

'Well, she identified the tights a few days ago, right? No doubt they're hers. And the DNA came back yesterday confirming Jack's was all over it. Her liaison told her Jack had been charged with her rape, and she went to bed all happy as Larry.'

Hardly happy as Larry, I think, gritting my teeth. *The girl's been fucking raped.*

'But she wakes up this morning and sees the footage that's been plastered all over socials of Jack's arrest. You seen it?'

'No.'

'You don't look too bad, actually. You're only in it for a bit at the end. Anyway, she saw this, saw Jack being pushed into the police car and apparently something came back to her.'

Francie pauses for effect and I want to scream down the phone for him to hurry up.

'She remembers she cut her leg when she was walking that night. She was shouting this all over the reception because they couldn't get hold of her officers quick enough. Was like she had to get it out, bless her. She remembers she had to take her tights off to get at the cut, used her tights to kind of mop it up, stop it bleeding. And she remembers giving them to Jack.'

'She gave the tights to Jack? Why? Why would she do that?'

'Who knows. The wee girl was drunk, remember? She'd had a loadda drugs. She says she gave Jack the tights to... get rid of, or whatever, and that that could be why his DNA is on them.'

'Right...' My mind is racing. I'd hardly say that's good news, though it's not bad and I suppose I should be thankful things haven't got any worse. 'When you said good news, I thought maybe—'

'I'm not finished!' Francie interrupts. 'The receptionist saw me at that point and he knew I was involved as Jack's solicitor, so he told me to leave. Didn't want me muddying things by listening in. But then Katie says, *what? You're Jack's solicitor?* And I says, *Yes, that's me.* All the while I'm backing away, going back to the interview room, aware that I'm not allowed to fraternise with the victim.' *Supposed victim, Francie,* I think, *supposed victim.* 'But then she says, *I just want this all to stop. I want to drop the charges against Jack, I don't want this any more, it's too hard. Please can you tell them I don't want this any more?*'

I am staring at Decky's mug of tea.

Decky shakes his hand in front of me so I look at him, and he mouths *What?*

I shake my head, unsure what Francie is saying. In my mind's eye, I see Katie Waltz in her knitted crop top, in the police station on a bright and sunny Thursday morning in August, begging these men who think of her as a wee girl, to stop the chain of events that has evidently ruined her life as much as it has ruined mine and Jack's.

More, I think.

Of course, more.

This is nothing, nothing, nothing, compared to what Katie has gone through.

'So, what?' I ask Francie again. I'm so sick of hearing myself say that.

'Well, it's good news,' Francie says. He takes a deep breath and I think maybe he's sucking on a second cigarette. 'Obviously, it's not really up to her. Now that there's evidence, the case will still be investigated—'

'How?' I demand. 'How can it still be investigated if she's asked to drop the charges? She doesn't want this any more! It's her case, how can they still—'

'When there's evidence of a crime,' Francie says simply. 'They'll investigate it. But I wouldn't worry – without her evidence, with her explicitly stating she isn't interested in pursuing the charge, it's unlikely the CPS will deem it in the public's interest to go after Jack or even this Ben chap. They've got him in, by the way. They lifted him half an hour ago.'

Twelve hours ago, these words would have made my heart soar.

Now they only increase the sick feeling in my stomach.

I'm more confused than ever, feel less sure of the future than I did five minutes ago.

'Right,' Francie says. He takes another drag. 'I'll go and tell Jack the good news, see what I can wrangle with these officers. They're putty in my hands, Abi, I tell you.'

I hang up without listening to the rest of what he has to say.

'What?' Decky says. 'Is it over? Have they got Ben?'

'They have Ben,' I say. 'They're questioning him. But it's – it's not that. It's better, I think. I'm not sure.'

Decky listens intently as I explain what Francie overheard, his eyes brightening.

'So… It's over. She wants to drop the charges.'

'Francie says it won't be as straightforward as all that… But it's something, right? It's a step in the right direction.'

'If this Ben bloke did rape her,' Decky says, lowering his voice sensibly on the verb. He leans in closer to me. 'Why does she want to drop the charges? She knows she was raped, even if her memory is a bit iffy… Why does she just want it to end? Or why isn't she naming Ben?'

'Maybe she can't,' I say. 'Maybe she's coming to realise it wasn't Jack but she isn't sure…'

'But she knows she was raped,' Decky repeats. He leans back in his chair, looking defeated and confused. 'I don't get it. It's a crime. The worst crime, the worst one there is. Why doesn't she want justice for it?'

I think of Katie in her knitted crop top, in her en-suite, her wool deliveries and her laundry scattered around her. Of her reluctance to want police involvement in the first place. Of the cousin she mentioned. Of the look in her eyes that told me something awful, something horrible had happened to her. And of something else…

Acceptance, I thought. Acceptance that she couldn't change what happened. That she wanted to put it in a drawer in her mind and never let it out and pretend it didn't exist and that way, only that way, would it stop having power over her.

Put it in a drawer.

It's easier to pretend it didn't happen.

And I get it. I really get it.

'Even if she goes ahead with it...' I say quietly. 'You heard those stats Jordy was reading out last night. Even if she puts herself through a court case, scrutiny, accused of being a liar... That doesn't mean for a moment she'll actually get justice at the end of it. The truth isn't enough.'

We both let that sink in.

Decky's shoulders sink visibly and he lets out a long breath, his eyes wandering over towards the bar, where Ashley is cleaning some beer pumps.

'Is it too early for a drink?'

I shake my head. 'Might join you, actually.'

We sit for an hour, Decky drinking pints of Bud Light and me drinking pints of cider. Neither of us says very much, but we enjoy each other's company, enjoy watching the bar fill up with lunch time diners.

Then another hour. My blood is fizzing and my vision shakes a little when I get up to go to the toilet. I am relaxing, I realise, swaying slightly as I dry my hands. This is what it's like to relax. We toast Jack's grades without saying anything else about him.

We sit for a third hour. My tongue and my brain feel loose and too big for my head, and once, twice, I even giggle.

Ashley brings us two bowls of chips without us asking, grinning.

'I'm his sister, by the way,' I hear myself saying as she turns to leave. 'Not his girlfriend.'

I don't want her to think she's out of luck with Decky. I like the idea that one of us might actually have a healthy, functioning relationship. That one of us can be happy with no strings attached. If it can only happen for one of us, I hope it's Deck.

He blushes and shakes his head into his pint, refusing to meet Ashley's eye.

'I can tell,' she says. 'But it's good to know.'

And she sashays away without a glance. I'm in awe of someone so… normal? Confident. She likes that he's single, so she's more decent than me, who doesn't seem to care about these things.

'I split up with Max,' I hear myself admitting, swirling some warm cider around in my glass.

Decky lowers his glass and looks at me. He's better at handling his drink, and doesn't seem remotely pissed. 'Oh, right. I'm sorry.'

I nod and down the last of my drink before signalling to Ashley for another one.

'Are you… okay about it? Was it your decision?'

'Mutual, really.'

'I think it's probably a good thing.'

'Yeah?'

'Well. Yeah.'

'Have you all known for ages?'

'Yeah. He waited in his car at the end of the street a couple of times. Not exactly invisible. We figured.'

'Do you think I'm horrible?'

Decky tilts his head as though actually considering the question. None of the unconditional love from Decky. Maybe that's a good thing. Maybe I should be more like that.

Ashley sets down our two pints and goes back to the bar.

'I think you did a horrible thing,' Decky says finally. 'I don't think that makes you a horrible person.'

'I think I deserve this mild heartache,' I say. 'It feels like…' I pause, trying to get the right words, 'karmic retribution.'

Decky snorts. 'Fucking karmic retribution. What are you, some hippie yoga teacher?' I think of Caroline's Instagram page and my stomach squeezes uncomfortably. 'Look, whatever it's called,' Decky continues. 'There's just what you do and how you react to the things that other people do to you. I'm sorry you're sad about it… But maybe now you can meet someone—'

'Who isn't already married to someone else?'

222

'Ideally.'

'Where shall I look?'

'I don't think we're supposed to look. Do you fancy a game of pool?'

'No,' I say immediately, feeling my stomach churn again and forcing the image of a pool table out of my head. It isn't difficult, it happens easily because it's the only thing I can do.

I go to the toilet again, thinking about what Decky said, and find myself checking my phone against my better judgement. Nothing from Max – not checking in with me, checking in about Jack or his results.

Maybe he never cared in the first place.

Maybe he never, ever cared.

When I come back, I see Ashley lingering by our table, leaning down to speak to Decky as he types into his phone.

I walk slowly back towards them, not wanting to interrupt, feeling myself smile.

Max doesn't matter, because Max isn't my family.

Decky and Ashley sense me behind them and both turn around.

'Sorry,' I say. 'Do you want me to…?'

'No,' Ashley says. 'I was just giving Declan my number, he says he doesn't have Facebook any more.' She rolls her eyes at me as if to say, how ridiculous is he?

'Deleted it a few weeks ago,' Decky explains to my curious look. 'Couldn't be arsed with… with all the shite on there. Too much awful stuff, too many trolls.'

'Ha! You're telling me. There's an entire album of *awful* photos going around today as well. This girl, super drunk and messy. People are writing horrible stuff about her too, about how she faked an accusation against one of her friends and all this.'

A beat.

Decky and I look at one another.

'Can I see?' I ask. 'Sorry. I know that's a weird thing to say but – can I see them?'

Ashley frowns but shrugs, digging into her apron. She unlocks her phone, scrolls for a moment, and holds it out.

'It looks like some sort of slander campaign,' she murmurs. 'People accusing her of all sorts… people actually adding other photos of her to the comments. Do you – do you know her or something?'

I look, flicking through photographs that make my heart sink deeper and deeper into my chest.

The photos are not the worst part.

I am instantly sober.

I hand the phone to Decky and he looks, his expression darkening as he scrolls the comments.

'Who is it?' Ashley asks nervously. 'Is she a friend of yours?'

It's the thirteen-year-old Katie I think of, running through the courtyard of her house to get into my car. The giggling, excitable girl. Not the woman.

'She used to be,' I murmur. 'Yeah. She used to be.'

OLDRY POLICE STATION ELECTRONIC AUDIO TRANSCRIPTION FILE

Please insert case number here

For PART 1 of this interview, click here
18 August 2022 – 17.00 – Interview with Jack Campbell – Verbatim

JC – Jack Campbell

FF – Francis Finn, legal representative

PM – DC Paula Mathers, PPB

ZA – DS Zachary Andrews

[ZA]: Mr Campbell, I'm sure I don't have to emphasise how serious this is. You've kept important information from us that could – that would – have led to an arrest two months ago. You've put this woman through unspeakable torture, keeping your mouth shut. I understand you were under pressure from your schoolfriend but I really must reiterate: we are not finished with you indefinitely. You're free to go, now, and we thank you for your help today. Once our tech team has managed to have a look at the evidence on the mobile phone, we'll know a little more what's happening... but for now.

[FF]: For now, he's free to go. Thank you.

[JC]: I'm really sorry.

[FF]: Come on, Jack, we can go. The charge has been dropped.

[JC]: Can you tell Katie, when you see her, that I'm really, really sorry. I wish I – I wish I'd done something. I wish I hadn't just... just stood there and—

[FF]: Jack. Come. Now.

[JC]: I am really sorry.

[ZA]: I think it's a bit late to say sorry, Mr Campbell. Don't you?

18

The Free

I get into bed at seven o'clock, unable to get warm.

It might be something to do with the shattered window that I haven't bothered to even try and cover, but it doesn't feel like an external thing.

I left Decky and my car at The Clandy. The former will probably be there all night.

I re-activate my Facebook account just so I can see it.

I hate it, I don't want to see it, it's the last thing I should do.

But I can't stop myself. I need to see it again.

It doesn't take too long to find it: at least ten of my friends have reacted to the post in some way, so it's the first thing that pops up when I open my newsfeed.

Why has this not been taken down yet?

An account known only by the name DR Justice has posted five photographs. Katie Waltz is the main feature of all five, though there are other girls with her in some of them. The first shows her in a mini skirt and crop top, leaning over a toilet bowl in what looks to be a nightclub. Her legs are curled under her on the sticky floor, and her hair is covering some of her face. She has one hand up to the photographer, but she's laughing. The next shows her in the same outfit, undoubtedly taken later the same night, but this time she is lying on the floor in someone's living room, a small circle of vomit up by her head, touching her hair. Her crop top has ridden up. The others follow a similar theme, all seemingly taken on the same night, all showing a progressively drunker girl in various positions. From the look of her I'd say they were taken in the last year or so, she looks seventeen or eighteen.

DR Justice has written nothing in the caption. They – he, undoubtedly – didn't have to.

Social media has done its thing. The pictures have been reacted to over three thousand times, and there are hundreds of comments.

Bit by bit, the general public of Vetobridge and County Down beyond has pieced together what the pictures supposedly say.

I scroll through once again, feeling sick to my stomach.

This is the wee girl claiming she was 'raped' over the summer – from the state of her I think we can all safely assume this is yet another case of girl-regrets-being-drunk. CRINGE

What a mess, surprised she even remembers it

Is this the night it was meant to have happened? How the fuck would she be able to name anyone?

There are messages of support, of course.

This is atrocious, who made this account?

Why would you post these and what do they have to do with a rape accusation? How are the two related? Is it because of what she's wearing?

An absolute coward has posted this #victimshaming

I went to school with this girl and she is honestly the nicest, quietest girl you'll ever meet. These photos were all taken on ONE night as you can clearly see – so she had one messy night out one time, who here hasn't? Absolutely disgusting that these would be posted as if to prove she's lying

And then a comment that hurts me and lifts me all at once in equal measure.

Jack Campbell is innocent, I think we can now all finally agree on that one

A girl has posted it – a girl I have never heard of, and don't recognise even when I click on her profile. But her comment has seven hundred likes, and has jumped all the way to the top of the chain, so it's right under the photos. His name in a thread about a rape… but seven hundred people jumping behind his innocence.

The Blindspot

I've looked at it all day, watching the number grow steadily, and I still have no idea how I feel about it.

I exit the app and text Francie for the third time.

Hi, any news? Can he come home yet?

Before I can send it, I hear a car outside. I can hear everything, now, with the window broken, and I know it's stopped right outside the Vape Shop.

I get out of bed and go into the living room and peer down.

It could be the brick thrower, back for more.

I don't care.

It's Francie's gold Toyota.

My heart beats and my legs shake and I back away from the window, not wanting to watch in case it's bad luck. Not wanting to know just in case Francie is alone and has come with bad news. Wanting a few more moments of peace, to hope. To breathe, to be alive, to hope, to hope, to hope.

The downstairs door is unlocked.

Jack has a key. I had one cut for him last month.

But he could have given it to Francie?

But he wouldn't but he wouldn't but he wouldn't

There are footsteps.

I know the exact tread of every one of my brothers.

But there is no tread I know better than that.

I stare at the door, willing, wishing, hearing the blood pounding in my head, feeling sure I will pass out. I will faint.

The door to the flat is unlocked, then pushed open, and then my brother Jack stands there in the doorway, and he looks right at me, immediately, like he knew I would be standing exactly here, in this exact spot, waiting for him.

Like he knew the world would come together, eventually, and it would be me standing at the edge of it, right behind him – right beside him.

Where I've always been.

*

229

He is ravenous.

I put bacon in the oven, but he can't wait for it, so he puts bread in the toaster and has two slices. And then another two, hardly waiting to butter them.

'They fed me well,' he admits, when we're sitting cross-legged, facing one another on the sofa, finally, bacon sandwiches apiece. 'I wasn't hungry at the time, obviously, but they offered stuff constantly.'

I watch him reach to the floor for the ketchup bottle, and he squirts more ketchup onto the side of his plate. The ketchup inside is never enough for him, he likes to dip the crusts in some extra.

'And they let me have a shower and everything. It honestly wasn't too bad today.'

Today, I think. That must mean it was awful last night.

I take a bite of my bacon sandwich and almost gag at the taste. I spit it out subtly, not wanting to put Jack off his. I hate bacon recently. I didn't think to make myself anything different.

I put my plate on the floor and sit back up, watching him.

'Mathers was nice. I think... I think she liked me. Pollock was really sound too, once – you know.'

I know.

Jack has been cleared for the charge of rape.

Ben Ringwall's fate is less certain, but with Jack's word against him and with Fitzy and Fergie finally admitting the truth, there might be a chance of a conviction.

'Katie won't even have to go to court,' Jack says, not for the first time. 'She can do it on a video link streaming thing. She won't have to see him.'

Jack seems to think it is over, that Ben will admit it all eventually, and that that will be the end.

I haven't made up my mind yet.

This afternoon, around about the time Decky and I were sinking pints in The Clandy, Jack and a few police officers drove to the Spar garage on the edge of town, and Jack pointed out to them exactly where he dropped his phone down a drain.

And another phone that would provide the crucial evidence for the police.

I don't have all the ins and outs of it yet, and I'm not quite sure what the phone is supposed to prove. Perhaps that the group were at the rockpools at the time of the attack? I haven't asked for specifics because I'm afraid to know.

Because of Jack's willingness to help and his – eventual – honesty, it seems the police won't be too hard on him for keeping his mouth shut about the truth of that night.

'I couldn't say anything,' Jack says. Again, this is not the first time he has said this, but it feels as though something has come loose in Jack, that the words he has so desperately wanted to say for the last two months are tumbling out and he can't stop them, doesn't want to. 'Ben said he and his brother would... would kill you, if I said a word.'

I think of Ben dressed in black, pointing at my flat.

'Damo is honestly a completely psycho, Abs. He would have done it. He really would have. I couldn't say anything – they knew where you lived.'

We both look at the shattered window as if for confirmation. So it was Damo who sent me the brick.

'So I just... didn't say anything. And then when nothing happened, I figured Katie must have... I dunno. Given up with it. I still can't *believe* she named me.' He sounds outraged at this, not wholly fairly. 'That she thought I would do that.'

'She knew you were there,' I hear myself saying. 'She remembered seeing your scarred hand.' I realise Jack still doesn't know about my trip to see Katie, doesn't know that she said that to me, so I hurry on, 'It's no wonder she thought it was you.'

'I would never do that, though.' Jack chews thoughtfully. 'Though... I suppose I didn't think Ben was capable of it either.'

I wonder what's going on behind his eyes. If he's reliving it. How does it make him feel?

Now that the initial elation of his arrival has worn off, I'm starting to feel sick and wary again. He watched someone get raped... Just watched it. Yes, he was scared but… Surely there was something, *anything* he could have done? My clever, resourceful—

'Oh!' I leap up off the sofa, nip into my bedroom and come out with the brown envelope in my hands.

Jack's eyes widen and he puts his plate on the floor. He knows exactly what this is.

He reaches for it, runs his finger along the torn edge.

'Is – is it?' He looks at me, the silent question in his eyes.

'Open it,' I say.

He does. He looks at the results page first – I can tell which page is which from the way they are folded and the way my hands have shaped them already. He is nodding constantly, blinking and nodding, blinking and nodding. He lets out a long, wavering sigh that he has been holding in for probably two months. Maybe longer.

He looks up to grin at me, lets a single tear fall and gives a shaky laugh. Then he starts to read the letter.

It takes him a few minutes to read the full three pages.

I stand in the living room, feeling the breeze on my bare arms from the broken window, and I watch him reading.

I don't have a handle on my brother. I can guess how he is feeling but I can't be absolutely sure.

I thought I knew Max.

I thought I knew everything.

I thought I was doing a good job, I thought I was doing the right thing…

Katie Waltz was raped and my brother watched it.

My brother, the boy I held from the day he was born. The boy I taught to speak, to say please and thank you, to hold doors open for people, to make eye contact, to smile. Where did it all go so wrong?

How can one boy – one man – be so many things at once?

'Amazing,' Jack says finally, and he beams at me. 'I can't believe it's actually happened. Did you read this, about the award and the interview?'

'Yeah,' I say quietly.

He sets the pages down on the sofa, stands and comes towards me.

'Thank you,' he says. The smile is gone, instead he looks serious, his face set. 'Thank you so, so much, Abi.'

'What? What for?'

His eyes look around the tiny room, then he gestures to the ceiling, all around him. 'For everything. For being… just, everything.'

I find my smile just in time and give it to him.

Easier not to fuss, there will be time for fuss.

He looks behind me, then gives a small laugh. 'Abi? Are you ever going to fix that shelf? I can do it for you, if you like.'

I look around, see the skewed shelf, still empty, and give a nod.

'Yeah. Yeah, please do.'

I don't show Jack the photographs on Facebook. He'll see them eventually. Something that viral can't stay secret, not from someone who is actually mentioned by name.

But there will be time for that, too. Plenty of it.

After he straightened the shelf, he went to sleep on the sofa. He was out like a light, and I can hear him snoring, loudly.

I have another look before I go to sleep, just to see if there's any more likes for Jack's innocence. Instead, an article from the *Vetobridge Howler* has been linked under the photographs, and it is this article that has become the top comment. Two thousand likes.

County Down Boy Receives Best Marks in UK Plus Cash Prize

My heart is in my mouth as I click on the article.

They've done well, considering they didn't get a photograph of Jack or any comment. I don't even notice any typos; maybe this is Mr Goodall's own article.

A young man from County Down has been awarded a prize from ALEUK for achieving four A* grades in his A-Level exams this summer. Jack Campbell, 18, from Vetobridge, attended Seaview High for the duration of his school career, and will receive his prize and certificates in a ceremony in September.

'He was always a model student,' says Seaview High Headmaster Mr Brooks Goodall, 60. 'Since he arrived in first year he showed an aptitude for all things science, reading at a much higher level than an eleven-year-old should. He continued to excel during his seven years here, and we're very proud of what this young man has achieved.'

In fact, Mr Campbell achieved full marks in his A-Level maths exam papers, full marks for his chemistry exam and coursework, and was one mark short of full marks in his physics paper. The young academic's fourth A* grade was in biology.

'Jack was offered a scholarship for MUSE,' Goodall continues. 'He has a grant to carry out research alongside his degree in Practical Physics, and will work with Dr Miles O'Hagan to develop an eyepiece for a telescope. He really is such a bright boy.'

Jack will take up his place at MUSE next month.

He and his family were too busy celebrating to comment.

The article is accompanied by Jack's school photograph from last year. He didn't want one, said practically nobody else in sixth form was getting one, but I insisted, and I'm glad. He looks great – his blond curls framing the face that could *almost* belong to a man, in the right light, but the cheekbones and the cheeky smile of a boy grin out at me. I have it framed and hung up in Pine Street, I must bring it with me for my flat.

Maybe I was too hard on the *Vetobridge Howler*. They only have what other people tell them, really. It would have been worse if they hadn't reported the attack on Katie, as if that wasn't important enough to mention.

The comments in support of Jack are flooding in below the article, under the photographs. Dozens… hundreds, maybe. The article has another hundred likes since I first started reading.

I'll frame the article too, I think, as I lock my phone and turn over to sleep.

I'll put it next to Jack's photo, maybe on the shelf in the living room.

I'm chasing Caroline Murray down a long hallway.

It looks like Seaview High, but there's a long bar at the end that's shrouded in darkness. Her hair is flowing out behind her like she's underwater, and I can hear her laughing at me. She's not angry, she doesn't seem hurt. She's just laughing. Because I'm a joke.

I'm trying to catch her because I want to explain myself, but I'm not sure how I'm going to word it.

Your husband isn't the man you think he is. I know I'm awful, but surely he's worse?

She stops just before she reaches the bar and turns to face me. She's wearing a stripy, knitted crop top.

'Did you make that yourself?' I ask, my mouth too big.

'Yeah,' Caroline says sadly. 'No point though.'

I wake because my phone is vibrating somewhere in the bed.

I use one hand to fish around, thinking – assuming – that surely, it must be Max. Calling to apologise.

I find my phone and drag myself from the depths of sleep to press the accept call button.

'Abi?'

It's Decky's voice. I'm surprised and don't say anything, trying to work out why on earth my brother would be phoning me in the middle of the night.

'Abi, are you there?'

'Yeah,' I mumble finally. I'm still in the hallway with Caroline. 'Are you okay?'

'Abi, Katie Waltz is dead.'

19

The Girl

I lie on my back, my eyes open, tracing the crack in the ceiling that I've never noticed before. Should I have had this place surveyed before I bought it? How much would that be?

I am waiting for Jack to wake up. It's nine o'clock in the morning and he's still snoring. Maybe he'll sleep forever and I'll never have to tell him.

Blinds and curtains.

Paint.

A coffee table and a new sofa.

In that order?

No, a sofa seems like something I should do now, first.

Paint last.

Katie Waltz will never make these decisions about her own house.

At half-past nine, the snoring stops.

I hear an exaggerated yawn. A happy yawn. The yawn of someone who is planning to go back to bed, maybe. Who is sleepily looking around and smiling.

I hear him padding to the bathroom, hear the extractor fan come on, the door close.

I hear him peeing.

The flush.

The tap.

Take your time, I think. Enjoy this, please take your time. Look out at the sun, feel it on your face, think about your grades.

The door opens and I get up, slowly, one hand on my stomach.

I go barefoot into the hall, and Jack turns at the sound of me.

'Morning,' he says. 'Shall I make pancakes or do you want to go out?'

I shake my head.

'No to pancakes, or no to going out?' he says, with a grin. He must read something in my face because his own clears. 'What's wrong?'

'Sit down,' I say. I'm not sure where this has come from, but it's what people say. In case their legs give out underneath them, probably. Yeah, I can understand that. My own feel weak, and I feel faint, though I've felt faint for a while now. For weeks.

'What?' Jack says. 'Tell me.'

Not here in the hallway, I think. Don't make me say it here in the hallway where I have to walk every day.

He isn't budging.

He's in just his boxers, his chest slightly glistening with sweat.

No hairs, not a man, really.

Just a boy.

A boy whose heart I have to break.

'It's Katie,' I say, my voice stronger than I thought it would be. I have to be strong, have to be strong for Jack, for everyone. Always. 'Jack, I'm so sorry. Katie killed herself last night.'

He snorts. His first response to what he assumes is a sick joke.

He sees I'm not smiling and twists his lip up.

He doesn't say anything for a very, very long time.

'No,' he says finally. 'No. It's over, now. Why – why would she do that? She didn't.'

His lip stays up, a horrible, obscene half-smile, showing half of his perfect teeth. He's looking at me as if I'm insane, as if I'm a liar.

'I'm sorry,' I say again. 'Decky found out last night from a girl who works in The Clandy. She's called Ashley.' I have no idea why I'm telling him this. Because it's easy, maybe. 'There was something on Facebook, some girl posted an RIP thing… then a few more people. Decky went to The Rooster to see and, yeah, it's true. Last night. Her mum found her about seven o'clock.'

Jack is moving his head back, shaking it, looking obscure and obscene and horrified and horrific. Everything, all at once.

'No,' he says again. 'She wouldn't do that.'

I want to say, I know she wouldn't. But I never knew Katie Waltz. I just picked her up from her house one time, brought her to watch a film, let her leave, crying, didn't insist on knowing why. I just accused her of lying about a rape, just pressured her into retracting what she'd said. I didn't know her.

'Abi, no.' This last comes out as a moan. Animal, not human.

And then a six-foot, half-naked man-child is sliding down the wall in my hallway. Not a rapist, not a murderer… and yet responsible for a rape and a death.

'No,' he says again. He is choking, staring at me.

He knows I wouldn't lie, not to him. He knows that if I am telling him this, there is no doubt.

'Dead?' he chokes.

'Yes,' I say.

It takes an hour of sobbing for Jack to calm down enough for me to speak to him. He sits on the sofa and hiccups, his eyes still wet but more in control.

I have never seen him like this. Never.

I take a mug of tea to him and look around, hating that there's nowhere to put it. I'll start today with my list, I have to start today.

'You know that girl Sasha I work with at The Rooster?'

Jack nods and takes the tea from me.

'She says Katie took an overdose. Her mum's pills. She didn't know the name.'

'Fuck,' Jack whispers. He's summed the whole thing up with one word.

'Her mum rushed her to hospital but there wasn't… It was too late.'

We sit and think about that for a second.

'I think… I think I might know why,' I say.

Jack looks blankly at me.

'I might know why *now*,' I clarify. 'What happened to her was awful. Awful, awful. But it got worse yesterday.'

'Worse?' Jack is paying attention now, his eyes flashing between mine, trying to understand me.

'She wanted to drop the charges against you—'

'I know.'

'But she didn't – or couldn't – name anyone else. She just wanted it to go away—'

'It might have!'

'Jack, listen. Yesterday afternoon some… dopey, anonymous account on Facebook posted some photos of her. Sloppy, messy, drunk ones. The comments underneath…'

'Let me see,' Jack says, looking wildly around for my phone.

I hesitate, then take it from my pocket and give it to him.

He navigates around for a moment or two, then thrusts it back to me.

'Where is it? I can't see it.'

I have a go at trying to find the pictures, the post. Anything.

It's all gone.

When I type in the username, DR Justice, Facebook informs me that this user no longer exists.

The post has been removed.

Fifteen hours too late. Why is everyone always too late?

What the bloody hell was supposed to be on that phone Jack pushed down the grate?

I sink back into the sofa, my phone in my hand, thinking.

When I look up again, Jack's eyes are huge and wet, and he's crying once more.

'I really loved her, you know. I was really in love with her.'

I consider this for a long time. I consider it as I pour us bowls of cereal that neither of us touches, as I boil the kettle again. I consider it as I mute my phone to the constant rings and texts and messages from co-workers, friends and my family.

Dad has phoned six times, sent texts asking about Jack.

But he hasn't bothered walking the ten minutes to my flat, so I'm not in a rush to get back to him.

I consider it as the morning becomes the afternoon, as the afternoon stretches into a bright evening with a low sun. A breeze whistles in from the broken window, and we listen to it. It gets stronger, then even stronger, so I busy myself looking in cupboards, trying to remember if I have any newspaper lying about, knowing I definitely don't have any Sellotape and I'll have to nip out for that.

There is a crash and I jump, banging the top of my head off the cupboard.

I whirl around.

It's only the shelf. It's fallen down in the breeze.

Jack's jumped too, and is standing, a hand clutched to his chest.

We look at each other and he gives a single-syllable, shaky laugh.

He was really in love with her.

Really? Was he?

Was I in love with Max? A man who, more than once, forced me to have sex I didn't want. A man who didn't realise he was patronising me, who didn't hear himself when he put me down. Who laughed at my jokes, told me I was beautiful, beamed when he saw me... and went home to his wife at the end of every day and pretended I didn't exist.

No, I realise with a tiny jolt. Maybe once I thought I was, but that can't be it. That can't be all there is, that can't be the feeling they write songs about.

'I can't believe what I did to her,' Jack says a little later. He looks wretched, like he's aged over the course of the day into the man everyone was accusing him of being. 'Why didn't I say anything? We could have hidden you away somewhere. I could have told someone the truth. I didn't have to lie.'

I think of something I said to Jack once. When he had a nightmare as a child, or when he was upset about something that had happened in school, I can't really remember. Something deep and meaningful about lies, something that I taught him. Another one of the things I taught him that turned out to be wrong, wrong, wrong.

I can't quite grasp it, so I don't say anything.

I'm done with advice, with trying to teach anyone anything.

He takes a deep breath, and lets it out in a shuddering, body-racking sigh, as though the weight of the world is resting on his chest.

Then he scrunches himself up smaller so he can lie across the sofa and put his head on my lap.

I put one hand on his hair automatically, knowing the shape of his skull before I stroke it, knowing every contour of his ear.

He did his best, did what he thought was the right thing...

And so did I.

He falls asleep in the living room and I leave him there.

I sit on my bed feeling more than exhausted, much too tired to sleep. I catch sight of my reflection in the tiny mirror I did manage to put up on the wall, and I look like a different person. I look at this girl and I don't know who she is either.

Though DR Justice's collection of photographs have been taken down, the *Howler*'s article about Jack has gained more and more traction over the last few hours. I navigate to the original post on their Facebook account, note the four thousand likes with a kind of numb shock, and scroll slowly through the comments. Why did this make my heart soar yesterday? His grades, yes. They're fantastic. Unheard of. He is a genius, and now everyone knows it.

Massive congratulations Jack C! I remember you in my P6 class and I just knew you'd do great things. Mrs K

This is amazing, putting our wee town on the map! And our wee country. Amazing.

What an impressive young man, well done to him and best of the luck for the future

But every now and then, in the comments, there comes a reference to the accusation. A reference, only half disguised, to Katie's rape. To the rape of the girl that Jack thinks he was in love with.

And most of them, more than half, are not scathing. They aren't affronted, offended by the article proclaiming Jack's brilliance. They're righteous, as if this article is his defence.

Fantastic achievement. Hope this young man can put those awful unfounded accusations behind him and move on with his amazing academic life

The truth comes out in the end, well done Jack! X

You weren't there, u don't know the truth ??

Neither were you x

LOL I got 3 Bs and I was delighted – well done mate!! Never believed what they were saying for a minute

I wonder how big the jump is, then, to

Your Honour, my client could not possibly have committed this crime. I'd like to enter into evidence this, Exhibit 9, an article from the Vetobridge Howler...

Outpourings of grief are added to Katie's Facebook page every few minutes. Mostly girls, mostly just love heart emojis or RIPs, but every now and then a slightly longer comment, or a memory.

You drew my dog for me in second year and it's hanging up in my bedroom – I won't ever take it down. Rest in peace KT

We will never forget you Katie. Another angel in heaven

There are no references to the photographs, but if I'm not mistaken some of the same names that came up in the hateful comments under those are the same ones appearing on this page now, leaving condolences. People move and change like the tide, I think.

My eyes swim and my head grows sore trying to read all of the memories, but I make myself go through them all, scrolling back and back and back. For Katie.

Now that Jack knows, now that I've shared the burden with him, I feel heavier instead of lighter. As if I had no permission to grieve until he knew, until he could mourn her first. As if it was his right.

I think of her laughing in the living room in Pine Street, thanking me for the lift, smiling with her braces on show, completely unselfconsciously. The difference between thirteen and eighteen is so much more than five years.

I think of her at the rockpools, dizzy and confused and scared.

Of the weeks that followed where the sun shone into her huge and beautiful bedroom and she stayed there and waited for deliveries, wanting to go back in time and change everything.

Then I think of her putting pill after pill into her mouth and swallowing. Sure of herself, of her decision. Going on until there were no more left.

And then I think of Jack, and how he could have spoken up and put a stop to her suffering.

Weeks ago.

I reach the end of the memorial posts on Katie's page and find myself clicking on the last picture she ever uploaded to Facebook, six months ago now. Just a selfie, just of her, in the en-suite I saw when I lied my way into her house. Just her face and her smile, a little bit of makeup and no filter. Twelve likes.

I lock my phone and sit up.

I watch as the girl in the mirror clenches her fists and lets hot tears spill down her cheeks. She's shaking, completely silent.

Shaking with rage.

The police find one phone down the drain. Just one – not two. Jack told them he dropped both his own phone (which he maintains he wanted to get rid of so Ben and the others couldn't contact him again) and Fergie's phone down the drain that night. It is Fergie's phone the police are really looking for. Jack has told them what is on it, and they're keen to see.

The police call at the flat again that evening, Pollock and another woman I don't recognise, to ask Jack if he's sure about the location of the drain. Is he sure he didn't put one phone down that drain and the other down another? Jack is sure.

'It changes things a little,' Pollock says. 'I suppose there is a chance someone could have found the phone, and there is a chance it's been swept away further than we thought. We'll keep looking. It would have wrapped things up nicely, it's a pity.'

'What about Jonathan Ferguson?' I demand. 'What's he said? And the other one – the Fitz boy?'

Pollock nods, sucking his teeth. 'We've spoken to Mr Ferguson and Mr Fitzhugh. They've confirmed Jack's version of events. Of course, in light of recent developments...' Pollock glances over to the windowsill, where Jack is leaning, his head lowered, his arms folded, still shaking. He hasn't stopped shaking all day. Pollock doesn't have to ask if we've heard about Katie's death. 'We're not sure where we stand. The phone would have been nice but... Look, don't worry. Just wanted to update you, Mr Campbell. We'll be in touch.'

I join Jack at the windowsill after they've gone and I watch as Pollock drives expertly away. Just another day on the job, nothing special. He'll go home to his wife or girlfriend tonight, not think about Jack again.

'What was on the phone?' I ask quietly.

Jack doesn't answer. He stares at the ground.

'Jack. The police found *your* phone down that drain. What was on the other one, Fergie's phone? Why did you have it and why did you get rid? What evidence was on it?'

Jack chews his lip. 'Why can't they find it? It should have been there.'

I don't answer. I refuse to lie to him.

He's not a child any more.

'Jack Campbell.' He looks at me, finally, his eyes bright red. 'Tell me right now what was on that phone.'

I think for a moment he isn't going to tell me.

But then he does.

Of course he does.

20

The Woman

The cafes and shops are covered in twinkling colourful lights, so the whole of Vetobridge is like one enormous Santa's Grotto even though it's only the first day of December. It's pretty, really pretty, and for the first time I am glad that the locals put in so much effort this time of year, when businesses struggle and tourists are nowhere to be seen and we're left staring at one another. The energy they've dedicated, the fake snow they've sprayed on the windows... it's for them, or for us. Nobody else. There's something beautiful about that.

I stand with my back to the sea, watching people hurrying to the car park on the edge of town, their day of work over, keen to get home. It's freezing, and almost pitch black already, even though it's just gone five.

I've never been so grateful for my huge, padded jacket, for more than one reason.

I lift my phone from my pocket to check the time and am about to roll my eyes when Decky calls my name.

I turn to grin at him.

Just finished work, he is shuffling towards me, hands deep in the pockets of his black hoodie which is nowhere near warm enough for the evening. Now I do roll my eyes. You'd think at twenty-nine, he wouldn't need his sister to remind him any more, but since I moved out, I genuinely don't think I've seen him with a coat on once.

'Sorry,' Decky says as he reaches me. 'Some woman wanted to trade a Switch Lite for the regular Switch and didn't understand why I had to charge her more. Stood and argued with me for twenty minutes about it. Is it a bit cold for our walk?'

'Not for me,' I say. 'For you?'

'Nah, I'll warm up in a few minutes. You know me, I'm like a furnace.'

He holds his arm out and I push my own through it, and we walk along the stony beach, listening to the soft crash of the waves.

We've taken to doing this the last few months. It's good for both of us to get out of the house. Decky says that without Jack, without me, Pine Street feels more cramped, smaller somehow, instead of bigger, and he's been half-heartedly looking for somewhere to rent on his own. He's all talk, though, can't see him moving out anytime soon. Decky is much too Decky for that.

I happen to adore my flat, have never appreciated a space more in my life, but I like seeing Decky outside, like listening to his stories about the tech shop, like hearing him complain lovingly about Dad, and I like the opportunity to stretch my legs.

'What about your shift, how was it?' Decky asks.

'Good,' I say, and I mean it.

I no longer come home smelling of chips and beer – I handed in my notice at The Rooster the day after the A-Level results, just like I said I would, with a text to Sasha that didn't even get a reply. Instead, there's a clinical, clean smell that clings to me twenty-four seven. For the last ten weeks, I have been driving around Vetobridge and the surrounding villages, tending to the personal care of disabled adults and the elderly. It was Decky's idea. He saw the advertisement online and sent it to me, and it made sense. It really made sense. Looking after other people was something I knew I was good at, something I knew I could do. I hadn't worked since mid-August, and my savings were completely gone. It came at exactly the right time, and it was exactly the right choice.

The Rooster is up for sale. Rumours say Norm is retiring, finally, and as I know all too well there is always some truth in a rumour.

'How's aul Dennis? Did you see him today?'

'Aul Dennis is great,' I grin. 'He was my last for the day. He was asking about you, actually. Wants to meet you to pick your brains. He wants to get himself a gaming laptop and needs to know what sort he should get.'

'Fuck off, he's ninety!'

'He's eighty-five,' I correct. 'And mentally he's entirely there. It's just his legs that aren't much cop. Can you write me down the name of a good one and I'll bring it to him next week?'

'Aye.' Decky is chuckling.

We come to what I have grown to think of as Our Bench, and we both collapse onto it and look towards the dark sea.

When we have been silent for a few minutes, Decky says, 'So, when are you going to tell me?'

I turn my head to him. 'What?'

He smiles ruefully. 'It's not the kind of thing you can hide forever. It's not the kind of thing you can hide at all, now, really.'

Ridiculously, I feel myself blush, and I'm glad it's dark.

I look down at my padded jacket. Fair enough, I won't be able to keep it under wraps much longer.

'How long have you known?' I ask finally.

'Like four months.'

'No, you haven't!'

'Yes, about four months. Three maybe. I could just tell. I can see it in your face.'

'Are you saying my face has got fat?'

'No,' Decky laughs and puts his arm around me. I've grown used to this as well. These tiny little affections that weren't there before. They're more comfort than I would ever admit. 'No, I'm not. I'm just saying... I know you, Abs. I know you better than anyone. I think for a while you got so caught up in us being your brothers, that you've kinda forgotten you're our sister, too.'

I think about that. There is a weird, twisted logic to it. I think it's true.

'When are you due?' Decky asks, more seriously.

'March,' I say. 'Middle of March. I was gonna tell you.' I put one hand on my stomach self-consciously. For months, this has been something that's just for me. The one thing I had for myself, my one secret. I knew I'd have to tell everyone eventually, but it was nice, for a while, to have time to get my head around having a baby without having to explain it to anyone else.

'Is it Max's?'

I nod.

'Does he know?'

I shake my head.

'Are you going to tell him?'

'Yes,' I say immediately. 'It's his kid, I have to tell him. We won't get back together, though.'

It's the first time I've said it out loud, but I know it's true. It feels good to say it out loud, I'm making it final, putting it into words. If I say it out loud, it's true.

'He can be as involved as he wants, but I definitely don't want to be with him.'

I've seen Max once since our fight. It was a week after Katie's funeral – a busy, heart-breaking funeral, attended by every resident of Vetobridge, it seemed – and I texted him asking him to meet me for a coffee so I could give him back the three solitary items he'd left in my flat.

I still hadn't realised – or rather, hadn't had time to think about or admit to myself – that I was pregnant, that I'd been pregnant since before the night of the attack, so ordered two Americanos for us when I arrived first. I finished mine, and was half-way through another when he finally got there, late. It struck me that maybe our coffee order was the only thing we had in common now.

We hugged when we met, and there was something missing. It was formal, where we'd once been so giddy, cold where we'd been so hot.

'How have you been?' Max asked. 'You look really good.'

'Fine, thanks,' I said, as an answer to both. I knew it was probably a polite lie. The last week of August I barely slept a wink. I asked him how he was, we talked about the weather. We were talking about the weather – that was how I knew it was over.

Then, before I could help myself I blurted out, 'Where are you going to live?'

'At home,' Max said, his brow furrowed. 'Where else?'

I wondered if us splitting up had put a stop to his plan of finding somewhere else to live. It was strange, uncomfortable, surely? Living with, sleeping next to someone that you didn't really like, didn't really know any more. Knowing what you'd done, how there was nothing you could ever do that would change that fact...

We chatted awkwardly for a few minutes and I handed him a plastic Lidl bag with a shirt, a tie and a toothbrush.

And then he left before I could tell him the truth about Jack.

Part of me had wanted to scream it.

Ha ha, I told you, I was right, he was innocent, you were wrong, wrong, wrong

But of course, Jack wasn't innocent by any means.

Everything that happened in the wake of Katie Waltz's death was rumours. Hastily whispered in the hairdressers', accompanied by knowing nods over coffees just like that... Everyone knew Jack had been arrested and charged, and everyone knew he'd been let go some hours later, after he'd finally, mercifully told the truth. Just in time to save himself and much, much too late to save Katie.

Ben Ringwall was charged with her rape and is awaiting trial. We're not sure where or when. There was talk of dropping it, given the circumstances, but Katie's death seems to have made her mum, Norm, the population of our island, more determined than ever to have someone pay for what happened. So still, nobody is listening to what Katie said she wanted.

One of my patients heard that Ben's older brother is also going to be charged for posting the pictures, for some of the comments he made on his anonymous Facebook account. Some people believe it was reading these comments that led Katie to do what she did. I'm not quite sure what the charge is, there's a legal team working on it, but I hope to God they get him for something. Someone had had a night out with Katie the year before and still had pictures on her phone, and she happily shared them with someone who shared them with Damien Ringwall. Who took to social media in the twisted hope of tarring Katie's name and getting his little brother out of the police station.

'I hope Max wants to be involved,' I say now to Decky, voicing another of the thoughts that have kept me awake on the nights when my bladder hasn't. 'I don't know if I... I don't know if I can do this on my own.'

'You're not on your own,' Decky says. 'And even if you were, it's not like you haven't done it before.'

Jack hangs in the air between us, mingling with our fogging breaths. Jack took his first steps on this beach, took his first swim in this sea. We walked home from school across this promenade, we got ice creams on Fridays from the Mellow Mallow kiosk just behind us. And then, on a warm night in June, Jack walked to the rockpools with Katie Waltz and some boys he thought were his friends and made the biggest mistake of his life. A mistake he and I will both spend the rest of our lives thinking about. What a privilege it is to live to regret something.

'Have you spoken to him?' I ask, my voice wavering.

'Once or twice,' Decky says. 'He isn't coming to Vetobridge for Christmas.'

'Okay,' I say, and it is.

'Have you?' Decky asks. 'Spoken to him?'

'No.'

Jack took his full scholarship at MUSE and the on-site, en-suite dorm room that came with it. He got a job in the library and he enjoys his course. He's doing well, I hear. He and Decky message sometimes when they're gaming together, Ciarán has been down to see him twice, and even Jordan has sent a few texts. I'm the only one who hasn't spoken to Jack, and nobody is more surprised about that than I.

I don't know how long it will take, if I will ever be able to look at him again without the teeth-gritting anger.

Maybe. Just maybe.

All he did was turn away, not say anything, tell one or two tiny lies. We all do that.

Just little mistakes.

We lie to kind nurses about the causes of injuries.

We let people take advantage of our naïvety, hurt us, and we say nothing because it's easier.

We confront victims and accuse them of lying.

We let crying girls flee from our homes and we don't ask any awkward questions.

We lie for the people we love.

We fish mobile phones out of drains for them in the middle of the night, remove SIM cards and chew them up, run the pieces over in our cars and throw the carnage into the sea.

Not before we've had a look at what's on them.

After work one night at the end of June, four nights after Katie Waltz was raped, I took a detour home. Not a detour, exactly. I drove to the Spar garage at the far side of Vetobridge, and I used my phone torch to look into the drain between it and a housing estate called Wits End. I think someone was murdered there once. An influencer or something?

The back cover of a phone shone back at me, stuck on a ledge just two feet below my hand. I'd taken the litter picker from The Rooster, the one we used to reach the high switches, and manoeuvred it down the drain, gently, gently, trying not to hit the phone at the wrong angle and send it tumbling into the depths below. It took a full, breath-held minute, but I got it out.

Jack's phone.

Or so I thought.

I put it in the pocket of my cardigan and walked quickly back to my car, not wanting to look up in case there were any cameras. I wasn't sure how I would, or could, explain that one.

When I had parked up at the back of the Vape Shop ten minutes later, I took it out from my pocket again.

I glanced up at the window of my flat. A light was on. Jack was awake.

I tapped the phone on my leg, feeling jittery, sick, confused.

What was on this phone? Why had Jack got rid of it?

And then I did the only thing I was ever really going to do in that situation. The thing I'd known I was going to do since before I took the litter picker from the bar. I turned the phone on.

Or I tried to. It was obviously dead, so I plugged it into my car charger and waited impatiently, glancing up at the window of the flat.

Then the Apple logo appeared, clear as day. While the screen was a little scratched and the handset itself felt wet and dirty, it seemed there was nothing wrong with the phone.

I frowned when the wallpaper appeared. It was a generic background picture – a black and orange design that came with the phone, I'd seen it before. Jack's wallpaper, for the last month or two, had been a picture of his year group, taken on a sunny day outside Seaview High. Not this generic thing… Had he taken the SIM card out?

But, no. Vodafone UK was showing at the top. Bars of signal. 4G, even.

I swiped up, ready to type in Jack's passcode, but the phone unlocked itself. There was no passcode.

I turned the phone over, confused. A standard iPhone, the same as mine. Black, same as Jack's. A plain black cover. But not Jack's background or his password. On instinct, I removed the phone cover and something fell into my lap.

I picked it up. A shiny student ID with a grainy photograph on it and the words Southern Regional College Vetobridge printed across the top. I held the photo up closer to my face. I was no clearer who I was looking at, but knew it certainly wasn't the blond curls of Jack. Then I noticed a signature.

JONATHAN FERGUSON was written in untidy capitals along the bottom.

This wasn't Jack's phone. It was Fergie's.

The Blindspot

So where the bloody hell was Jack's? Had he lied when he told me he'd dropped his phone down the drain? Why? Why would he even have Fergie's phone in the first place?

What was on this that was so important?

It was either going to be a message or...

I glanced up at the window again, then navigated to Fergie's gallery.

The most recently taken video was six minutes long, and I couldn't make out anything from the thumbnail that showed. It was totally black.

With a shaky thumb, I clicked on it.

It took a second to load, then played.

Shuffling, black, movement.

Then my brother's face.

It was dark when the video was taken, but the phone had done a good job of picking out Jack's pale features. Someone had handed him the phone with the camera rolling – this phone, the one in my lap, I thought, feeling a bit sick and not knowing quite why – and he was holding it, shakily, a little below his face. It was impossible to tell where he was, but I could see some trees. And I could have a good guess.

I watched for six minutes as Jack held the camera, and shook slightly, and breathed.

Every now and then he would give a small, closed-mouth gasp, but he didn't speak.

There were other voices, other calls, murmurs. Grunts.

But Jack didn't move.

I stared at the video, then watched it again.

Then again.

After the third time, I felt fairly sure of two things:

One, that Jack had had no idea the camera he was holding was recording him, and two, that he'd meant to film something else entirely. Clearly he thought, in the dark, that the camera was facing whatever was happening. But instead it was filming his reaction to it. Whatever it was.

To something that had finished recording at two-twenty on the morning of 21st June.

I turned the sound up fully and watched again, ears straining to pick up the exact words.

Jack was breathing too hard to catch anything concrete, but I felt certain I knew what he was watching, almost as if I was able to see it reflected in his eyes.

That's when I turned the phone off, removed the SIM card from the tiny slot using a slide from my hair – 'Sorry, Fergie' I murmured – and chewed it up.

The phone stayed in my car, then the next night after work I ran the handset over and I threw everything into the sea. Whatever happened at the rockpools, I thought as I drove home afterwards, whoever was responsible... Jack had been there. He must have thought he was getting rid of evidence when he threw Fergie's phone into the drain, but really the only thing the video proved was where exactly Jack was and at what exact time. He had told the police he couldn't remember his precise whereabouts on the night it had happened, but Fergie's phone could provide that missing link. Is that why he did it?

Katie Waltz lives behind my eyes rent-free and I can barely get through an hour without thinking of her face. Of her knitted crop top that day in her bedroom. That stupid knitted top.

Of the life that lay ahead of her in an unsure and winding trail, vanished, gone with a couple of swallows. Her mum was on some medication for an operation she'd had, and Katie took the lot with half a bottle of vodka. Like a tragedy you'd see on the screen, not like a young woman in a small town. I think of her lying in her bed, waiting for it to happen. Waiting for her life to be over, because she knew all of *this* would never be over. And she was right, in a way.

And that makes me think of my love for Jack, once whole and beautiful and unblemished, now scalded and scarred.

Even if I do start to forgive him, even if the love starts to heal... It won't ever be the same. We won't ever be able to unsee the scar.

Decky and I talk a while longer, then we stand and begin to walk back towards the town centre, our hands deep in our pockets. I enjoy the pinch of the wind on my face.

'Do you know what it is?' Decky asks. He doesn't have to explain what he means.

I smile then, and suddenly I feel warm everywhere. 'A girl.'

'Aw, nice one. When are you gonna tell the other blades?'

I know Dad will be thrilled about my pregnancy, and about the fact she's a girl. Ciarán likes kids, he'll be fine, acceptable as an uncle. Jordan isn't keen on kids, but I haven't been too keen on Jordan lately. Mostly because I'm starting to realise that maybe he has a better grasp of this family than I ever have.

Decky will be the most amazing uncle.

And Jack… Well, I'm not sure about Jack. I still don't have a handle on my baby brother.

'Soon,' I say, yawning. 'Before Christmas anyway. Reckon Dad will babysit for me if I take a trip after she's born?'

'What?' Decky frowns. 'Where to?'

'I don't know yet. Somewhere.'

'Like Portdawdle?'

I laugh. 'No, Decky. They have invented ways of getting off this island, you know.'

'So I hear.'

'I want to get on a plane.'

'Why?'

I laugh again. 'Why? Why *not*, Declan?'

My trip will come soon enough. Somewhere warm, some sun, a few drinks. Some time to myself, or with Decky if he wants to come.

For now though, I think of my flat, the view from the semi-circular window, the perfectly straight, strong shelf that I put up all by myself. I've got a frame, ready and waiting to go up there, once I get a photograph of me and my daughter. I think of my empty bed that, recently, feels warm and welcoming because I won't really be alone in it.

'You heading straight home?' I ask when we come to Murphy's Arcade, our natural separation point.

'Nah,' Decky says. 'I'll go for a few pints at The Clandy first, I think. See Ashley. See you tomorrow, Abi. See you *both* tomorrow.'

We grin at one another and Decky raises a hand in farewell as he turns and walks against the wind towards The Clandy. He's been going there a lot recently, most nights after work. He claims it's to talk to Ashley but…

I wonder idly, as I make my way towards my car, parked on the street just up a bit, if Decky is becoming an alcoholic.

Yes, I think the signs are there. I think he probably is.

It doesn't matter too much.

I'll forgive him either way.

EPILOGUE

He laughs and takes a sip of the beer, even though he didn't find the joke funny and he *hates hates hates* the taste of beer. But they were all watching him when he was selecting his first drink from the packed dining table, and it was easier to take a beer than to actually ask for what he wanted which, if he was being honest, would have been a Malibu and Coke. Boys don't drink Malibu, he knows that, but he likes the taste and wishes it was acceptable. He had to stay on beer all night, after that.

They've come down to the beach to get away from the party – it was shit. Shit music coming from a tiny iPod speaker in the living room, most people sitting on the sofas or the floor or the chaise lounge, nobody dancing or even standing. All of them posh twats from The Academy. Well, the others said it was shit and full of posh twats, he'd just nodded and scoffed. He hadn't minded it, really. He was happy to sit and sip his beer and listen to the reasonably stilted conversation around him. Exams over, an entire glorious summer stretching out ahead of him. And then university. He still got a little judder of excitement when he thought about the research grant. He just had to get his A stars and he was in, his tuition paid. And though he wouldn't admit it to anyone – okay, maybe to Abi – he was ninety-nine per cent sure he'd got the three A stars he needed. He thought he'd got all four, actually.

At the party, one of the boys he used to play football with had spilled a bit of Cactus Jack's on the sofa and Paul, the boy who was throwing the party, the boy whose house was twenty times bigger than Jack's own, and who studied physics so seriously that you'd think he was gearing up for a Hawking biopic, had shouted at him and become

259

stressed and red in the face and made everybody move to the kitchen where they sat crowded around the dining table and made more stilted conversation and couldn't hear the music any more.

Jack hadn't minded, then, when Ben suggested they leave and go to the beach.

There were five of them: Ben, Fergie, Fitzy, Jack and, for some reason he couldn't quite discern, Katie Waltz. When they'd announced they were leaving, she'd just sort of followed.

Ben and Fergie and Fitzy were still Jack's closest friends. Or, rather, they were the boys he hung around with more than anyone else. They'd all gone to primary school together and formed a kind of unbreakable bond. They didn't have any classes with Jack now – indeed, only Ben had stayed on to do his A-Levels, and he was doing Media and PE and History, so he was on completely the opposite side of the school most days. But they were his friends. They'd play games on the Xbox at night together, which was fun, and before Jack got his job at the petrol station, they'd all gone to the pub together on a Friday, Ben ordering all the drinks because he was the only one with a real ID. Not that it mattered too much. If they didn't get served, they could go to The Rooster where Abi was working and she'd serve them all there.

Thinking of Abi, he stops in his tracks and pulls out his phone. It's only eleven – he could still go to Abi's housewarming party! He'd have to make up an excuse, though. He doesn't want the boys to know he is leaving their company to see his sister. Worse than that, he doesn't want them to ask if they can come with him.

Abi does not like Ben.

Granted, she doesn't *know* him, but everything she knows about him she hates.

He thinks back to the one time he introduced the pair of them, almost exactly two years ago.

It was his sixteenth birthday. She'd thrown him an amazing party in The Rooster, invited all his friends, everyone from his year.

Katie hadn't come.

She'd known about the party, certainly, because she'd seen his Snapchat message, but she hadn't replied. He'd told himself it was fine, she was probably busy that day, or maybe she'd felt awkward coming to a party organised by him and his sister. They got on fine at school, Jack and Katie, but things hadn't ever really been the same since…

He'd told himself it didn't matter: she'd see the photographs on Instagram, the Snapchat stories, and she'd know she'd missed a good night.

'I'm just gonna have to…' Jack looks around the beach, now, for an excuse. Quite literally looks around him.

The beach is quiet at this time of night. They've been walking for fifteen minutes and can see Vetobridge town centre just up ahead. The row of cafes, busy and bustling and colourful during the day at this time of year, are all in darkness now, the arcade the only light up ahead, at the far side of the cobbled street.

'Gonna have to what?' asks Fergie. 'You off for a shag, Soupy? Make sure you get evidence this time. *I* believe you about Nicole but thousands wouldn't.'

The others laugh, even Katie who, Jack is fairly sure, has no idea what they're talking about.

He doesn't let himself blush, choosing instead to flash Fergie his most charming smile-wink-eyebrow-raise combo that usually works on boys and girls alike.

'Who is it this time?' says Ben. 'The ginger from the party?'

They all laugh again, and even Jack finds himself wrinkling his nose at the image of Niamh Lloyd.

'Nah, not her,' Jack says. 'Can't tell you.'

'Nobody will fuck you in those dopey shorts,' Fergie says, and he darts over and pretends to pull them down.

Jack pushes him away as the others whoop, but it stings. Why did he wear the shorts?

'Who is she, who?'

'Can't tell you,' Jack repeats.

'Fulla shit,' Fitzy mumbles, and Jack pretends not to hear him.

'Give us a text when you're finished.'

'Should be hearing your phone vibrate in about, three minutes?'

More laughter.

'You're on seven,' says Ben. 'Fitz is on two, Fergie is on five and I'm on eight, so tonight makes all the difference. Remember, it's whoever has the most by nine o'clock tomorrow morning.'

'That's not fair!' protests Fitzy, kicking the sand in front of him as he skips on ahead, hands in his pockets. His head ducks in his tic and Jack winces. Jack hates his tic. Jack hates anything that singles out weakness. 'It's not fucking fair!' Fitzy says again. 'He doesn't even have pictures for his, never mind videos!' He nods at Jack, but his tic means he's nodding at everyone.

'Calm down,' Ben says. 'It's not like you'd win anyway, Spazzy Magee.'

They all laugh again, nobody more so than Katie. She must be drunk, Jack realises: she isn't someone who usually laughs at cruelty. She must have had more to drink at the party than he thought.

He's been in love with Katie Waltz since first year, or thereabouts. Ever since Mr Murray – or Max as he's come to think of him in recent years, since he knows his sister is shagging him – sat them next to one another in his science class. And, in a pleasing irony, there was chemistry. There really was. From the minute she sat down.

He'd put her next to Jack because he knew that Jack knew his stuff and Katie was struggling with the chemistry modules. She was smart in other ways though, Jack knew. In worldly ways he couldn't have put into words at the time.

While the other girls were plastering orange makeup on their faces and leaving fake tan handprints on their exercise books, Katie was sitting at the back of the classroom daydreaming and doodling. Her drawings were good too. Great even. And it was this he plucked up the courage to speak to her about.

It was a Friday afternoon in December. Abi had a rare Friday night off, so he was going to meet her in Xtra Vision after school. The shop's DVD collection was tiny, now, and it seemed every month there were fewer and fewer titles available for rental and more and more types of coffee available to buy. He didn't care what they watched or what snacks they got. Science was his last class of the day, and he glanced over at Katie's notebook to see she'd drawn a Christmas tree with a bunch of wrapped presents underneath.

'You're really good,' he said, bravely. 'I love the details of the wee gifts there.'

Katie grinned. She had braces already, was one of the first in the class to get them, but Jack thought she suited them. The elastics on them were green. He still remembers that.

'Thank you,' she said. 'I like drawing boxes, it calms me down.'

He wanted to say something else, thought even about asking her what she needed calming down for, but he couldn't think of a way to ask that didn't sound nosy or stupid.

'You're really good too,' Katie said, which saved him from thinking of something to say. 'At chemistry, I mean. All the sciences. Well, and at art as well. Aren't you top in everything?'

Jack felt a blush of hot pride.

It was true – the class tables had been published on the school website just the day before. He'd pretended he wasn't bothered, scoffed at it with his boy friends, but when he got home and saw Abi refreshing the website, he'd felt a jolt in his stomach and knew that actually he cared very, very much. He was top in every subject except PE, and that he'd already known – they'd had a Bleep test to determine the ranks for that one, and he'd been sixth. It had stung at the time, but his other firsts made up for it. Abi had teared up as she read his first high school report, and he was glad, so very glad from the tips of his toes, that he'd made her proud.

'Yeah,' he said, trying to sound nonchalant. 'But the art exam was stupid. You're a much better drawer than I am. You should have been first.'

'Your use of texture is better,' Katie said immediately. Jack wasn't sure what that meant, but he had a feeling it might have been the best compliment he'd ever received.

Texture. Yes, he remembers that.

'I'll see yous tomorrow,' he says to his friends, now.

'Fuck off, Soupy, you'll come back when you're finished – wise up!'

Jack frowns, but doesn't say anything.

'We'll still be out,' Ben confirms. 'Gimme a text when you're done. We'll have a few more drinks, maybe see if my brother can get us a smoke.'

'Right,' Jack says, more sure now than ever that he will *not* be coming back.

'Ooh, will there be enough for me?' asks Katie.

Jack looks at her in surprise.

Katie left school after their GCSEs, and he hasn't really seen her much since then. They Snapchat the odd time, just pictures of nothing with tiny captions, she asking about Jack's A-Levels and he about Katie's art course in college. Sometimes – and Jack loves these times – they'll do half-face selfies with self-deprecating captions, and they send bolts of electricity up Jack's spine. She has beautiful teeth, really nice eyes. She's not stick thin like most of the girls in his year, she looks like... Well, she looks like a woman, he thinks. Not a girl. She's a woman.

He looks at her again, now.

She's definitely drunk.

She's smiling, giddy, but she's also stumbling just a little bit.

She's wearing heels tonight, so she's only an inch or two shorter than he is. Her heels keep getting stuck between stones and she lags behind them a bit, having to stop to free them. She's wearing a dress that comes to her knees. It's got a funny animal print pattern on it, but the colours are vivid blue and orange, so Jack's not sure what animal it's supposed to be.

She looks different.

Not like the Katie he sat next to for years, chatting and laughing. Not the Katie he showed his notes to, or prompted to give answers when she hadn't been listening. Not even like the Katie who came over to his house that time – that one, awful time he can't bear to think about, when she'd rejected his pathetic, juvenile advances. Of course she had. Who wanted to have sex on a raggedy old sofa in a tiny shitty house full of people? Not that it was sex he was after, but maybe a hand job? Still, it hadn't been the right time or place. He knows that.

He still blushes scarlet at the memory.

She doesn't look like that Katie.

She looks like... Well, like the rest of them.

He asked her earlier how her course was going and she gave a vague sort of answer, polite enough, and immediately turned away to talk to someone else.

He cursed himself, then. It wasn't cool to talk about school or college when you were at a party, and he *knew* that, he did. Why was he messing up so much? Why did she always make him mess up so much?

Because you're in love with her, he thinks to himself. *Because you love that she's different and she doesn't give a shit what anyone thinks. Unlike you.*

He was careful what he said after that, only joining in when the subject turned to football or girls.

He makes his excuses and leaves with his same smile-and-wink combo.

The boys raise their hands in farewell, wiggle their eyebrows.

Katie doesn't even look at him.

Decky is very drunk when Jack arrives at Abi's new flat.

He's been there loads this week, helping her carry boxes up the flight of stairs. It's really nice, and the stairwell smells like strawberries and vanilla, owing to the Vape Shop that shares the back entrance.

He's really happy for her, and she seems really happy too.

Decky is outside, smoking, and raises a silent hand to his brother when he sees him.

'You okay?' Jack asks.

Decky nods, his eyes unfocused. 'You didn't bring anythin'?'

'Bring what? What was I meant to bring?'

'It's a housewarming party, dickhead. You're meant to bring her something. Fucking wine or a fucking…' Decky looks around the car park, which is dangerously full. Jack has no idea how most of the cars are going to get out, unless these people have organised who is going when. 'A fucking houseplant,' Decky finishes.

'A houseplant?' Jack feels panic rise in his chest. He didn't know he had to get her something. He didn't think that was a rule when the person in question was your own sister, when you'd spent hours and hours this week talking to her about views and paint colours and room sizes. Surely that exempted you?

And, what? Was he meant to have brought a present with him to Paul Smith's house? Carried it about with him all night, looking like a dickhead?

'Twat,' Decky announces, taking a drag from his cigarette and throwing it to the ground.

'Pick that up,' Jack says quickly. 'I might not have got her a present but at least I'm not littering right at the door to her new house.'

Decky rolls his eyes, but he picks up the cigarette butt, stumbling only a little bit.

'Gwan,' he says, motioning to Jack. 'Gwan in. Say the champagne I got was from both of us.'

Jack sighs in relief, though really there was no way any of his brothers would let him embarrass himself like that. 'Thanks, Deck.'

Abi isn't drunk at all – she seems too intent on walking around and filling glasses, talking to people for a few minutes at a time before hurrying on to the next one. She is flushed, but looks happy. Jack's idea of a nightmare, but she's sociable enough.

She beams when she sees him, and pulls him into a hug.

'How was your party?' she asks, breathlessly.

'Bit lame,' he says. Then, in an echo of Fitzy, 'Posh twats from The Academy ruined it. How's it going here?'

She flaps her hand impatiently. 'Fine, fine. And today went well, you think?'

'Yeah!' He can smile properly at her now. If there's one thing he knows he can do properly, it's exams. He knows he aced today. He wouldn't be surprised if he got full marks. 'Yeah, it was great.'

'I can't believe that's you all done,' she says. She looks like she might get teary, the way she always does when she thinks about what comes next. 'No more school. A man now!'

'I dunno about that,' Jack says. 'Think I've done enough to get in, though.'

They never say the name MUSE, they just say 'get in' or 'go to uni'. There's only one option, as far as Jack is concerned. MUSE is his first choice, and he didn't bother putting down a second. If he doesn't get into MUSE, he just won't go. He refuses to go overseas, probably wouldn't even go much further down south. He refuses to be far away from Abi. She needs him. He needs her. So he has to get in. He will. He's done enough, he always has.

'Well done,' Abi says. She reaches to pull a full champagne flute from the kitchen countertop. 'Here you go.'

'That's from me and Deck,' he blurts. 'The champers.'

'Oh,' she says. 'Brilliant, thank you.'

He takes a polite sip. He doesn't really like champagne either.

'There's Malibu on the coffee table,' she says. 'Coke in the fridge. Go ahead! Do you know everyone?'

She knows him better than anyone. He doesn't mind pouring himself a glass of what he actually wants here. Nobody will sneer at him, and even if they wanted to, they won't when Abi is around. Not in her house. He can have Malibu and Coke all night if he wants to. His phone buzzes and he ignores it.

'I think so.' He looks around the tiny flat for the first time since he came in. She's fitted more people in here than he thought she'd be able to. Mostly girls and boys who went to Seaview High, none of whom have moved very far away. He knows one from the butcher's, two from Tesco, one from the arcade. Some of these people he thinks might be regulars at The Rooster. He couldn't name them all but, yes, of course he knows them. They're from Vetobridge and so is he.

'Thought you'd be out with your friends all night,' Abi says, and he knows it is a question because he knows her so well.

'Mm,' Jack says. 'So did I. They were being a bit...'

Abi raises her eyebrows, inviting him to go on.

She'd met Fitzy and Fergie before, at the same birthday she met Ben.

The three of them had showed up together late and – Jack was fairly certain – drunk. They were rude to Norm, not thanking him for their free beers, and immediately demanded to know which girls everyone was planning on sleeping with.

'It's not that kind of party,' Jack had reminded them. 'My family are here.'

'It's always that kind of party,' Fitzy said, curling his upper lip like Jack was being ridiculous.

'Where is Sexpot Campbell?' Ben asked, waggling his eyebrows. 'Or was she too busy giving blowies in the back car park to come?'

Jack had made the mistake – the horrible, unforgivable, stupid mistake – about a year before of admitting that Abi had a boyfriend. Ben had been asking after his chances with her, and Jack was keen to move the subject on, so he told them all she wasn't available. That she'd been with someone for a few years. When they probed with more questions, refusing to let it alone, he told them he wasn't sure who her boyfriend was, that he hadn't met him, but the mystery man picked her up in his car every now and then. That had made them all hoot with laughter, and Jack cursed himself every day for not realising how it sounded.

He didn't answer Ben's question. He didn't have to – Abi was behind the bar a minute later, her forehead glistening, a little out of breath.

At Ben's insistence, Jack introduced them.

She glanced at Ben, her smile no more than a straight line, and then Jack saw her do something he'd never seen before. Just a look – a split second, a fleeting thing. She looked him up and down.

Not in the way you might look someone up and down if you were attracted to them.

Like, the opposite of that.

With the tiniest move of her eyes, of her head, she managed to look at Ben Ringwall in a way that said, *I know what you think you are, and I'm here to tell you that you're fucking pathetic, mate.*

His sister, who was polite and thoughtful, selfless to a tee, had told Ben Ringwall, brother of Damien Ringwall, no less, that he was a prick. All without opening her mouth.

He had never been so impressed, by her or anyone else, and he actually snorted slightly into his drink.

She left a minute later to go and tend to the food, and he looked at his friends.

Fitzy was ticking, his head flinching to the side as he pointed at Ben.

'Ooooh, she give you some look!'

'She did and all,' Fergie agreed, his smile wide. 'Don't think she'll be taking you out to the car park anytime soon, mate.'

'What? You joking? She fancies me.'

Fitzy and Fergie hooted with laughter, and Jack heard himself joining in.

'She really doesn't,' Fergie said.

'She really, really doesn't,' Jack agreed. It felt strange to be on that side of the joke for once.

'She's a prick tease,' Ben said, shrugging, but Jack was pretty sure he was blushing. 'Just a slut.'

Jack didn't let this get to him – there was no point with Ben, or the others. They were just words, words couldn't hurt Abi and didn't matter at all. Plus as long as he knew it wasn't true, he could let it slide.

'She'll maybe take you out to the car park to beat the shite outta you,' Jack added.

The other two roared with laughter and he felt quite proud of himself, and quite proud of Abi, and full of a strange love of his town, his brothers, even of his dad.

Is this being drunk? He'd asked himself. He knew now, of course, that it was.

'Gotta mingle,' Abi says now. She pretends to roll her eyes, but Jack thinks she likes it.

He notices Max isn't there, and wonders, with an awful, cruel squeeze of hope, if maybe they've fallen out.

He likes Max, thinks he's a nice guy, a good teacher. He seems to make Abi happy, even if Abi has never officially told any of them about their affair. Although, he reasons, pouring himself a tumbler of Malibu and getting some ice from the freezer, you never really know what goes on in a relationship unless you're in it. Abi isn't stupid, though. She wouldn't be with him if he didn't treat her properly, so he must be a good... boyfriend? Lover? He shivers, not wanting to think of Abi as anyone's mistress, but what else was she, really, when everyone knows Mr Murray has a wife at home? A hot wife, as well. She'd come to a few assemblies to talk about mental health and the benefits of yoga, and the vast majority of boys in his year group had decided she was the ultimate wankbank material. Jack agreed eagerly, of course, even though personally he thought she was a bit too slim and her voice was annoying.

Thinking about Mrs Murray makes him think about Katie again. How different she is – or was. How much he fucked up, that day in the living room, almost exactly six years ago now.

How different things might have been if he'd just wised up.

Jordan and Abi had both been taking the piss out of him that day. Laughing at him because he was pathetic, because he was a naïve little frigid virgin. That's what all the boys in his class had said too, but that he could deal with. To hear it at *home*, from his own brother and sister... That was too much.

He'd just wanted to touch Katie. Maybe her boobs, just so he could say he could, see if she'd be interested in touching him...

Then he could tell his friends, could let it slip to his brothers and sister, and then they'd all know he wasn't frigid. He was anything but.

He'd just gone for it. One minute they'd been a foot apart, both sets of eyes on the TV, and the next he'd just reached over and put his hand on the boob closest to him.

She'd frozen, her eyes wide, then pushed his hand away.

It was the worst feeling. The humiliation that actually made him think his face was on fire – there was no getting away from that, no getting over it. There was no way to make it better... Unless...

He tried again, even more clumsily, moving towards her with the top half of his body, hoping a kiss would seal the deal – couples always seemed to kiss before they did any of the sexual stuff. In films, anyway. So maybe Katie was just annoyed because he hadn't kissed her first. This was a date, after all. They'd both called it that.

But that was worse, and she didn't like that either.

Jack talks to people, chats, sips. Speaks briefly to Abi before she is pulled away again. He listens to a long story that has an interesting and funny climax, and he marvels at how different this party is, how much easier it is when he can be Abi's Brother and doesn't have to be Jack.

His phone buzzes again, and this time he takes it out. Both texts are from Ben.

Were r u?

Then, sent an hour or so later:

Damo got us weeeeeeed!

He winces. He doesn't like his friends when they've been smoking. They're boring. More boring than they usually are. He'll leave them to it, see them tomorrow.

Then he remembers that Katie is with them.

Katie, who barely drinks – or so he'd thought – and who was already pretty drunk when he left her an hour ago. Will she smoke weed with them?

He thinks of her grandfather, Abi's boss, Norm. They're an eccentric family, sure, but he's certain they don't approve of drugs. Or is he being old-fashioned again? Jack has noticed he has a habit of taking his sister's opinions on things and passing them off as his own. Maybe drugs, especially these supposedly tame, easy ones, aren't bad. So many people do them... they can't be as dangerous as the Anti-Drug Roadshows in primary school made them out to be. Can they? And they're kind of... hippie-ish, Katie's family. So maybe she's used to it.

He's still not comfortable with the idea of Katie being with *them* when they're on that stuff.

Another text, this time from Fergie.

What number u on now? Proof this time, faggot

He sighs. That stupid bet. Why on earth had he agreed to it?

He knows why, he thinks, taking another swig of Malibu. Delicious. Because the rest of them did. Because he wasn't going to be the only one not participating. Because if he said, no, I don't want to try and have sex with as many girls as possible by the end of this school year, they'd have called him a faggot and actually meant it.

What was he supposed to do?

He glances around to make sure Abi isn't peering over his shoulder. She's in the corner, texting, her forehead creased.

So she *has* fallen out with Max.

He doesn't let himself feel the tiny pump of euphoria that threatens. He's not sure why he doesn't want them to be together, he just knows he'd feel better, more comfortable, if they weren't.

He texts Fergie back: *Eight now. Coming back, where are you?*

Fergie replies immediately: *Beach, near Murphys*

Katie still there?

Yea lol, y?

Jack doesn't reply. His phone is on one per cent battery anyway. He puts it in his pocket and sets down his glass.

The party seems to be winding down now; it's nearly one o'clock and more than half of the guests have made their excuses and left. The flat will need tidying tomorrow – to make up for forgetting to get her a present, he'll offer to come round and help clean up. She has a day off tomorrow, maybe they could go to the cinema or go for a drive somewhere. There's something appealing about any beach that isn't the Vetobridge beach. If they went early enough, they could beat the traffic to Portdawdle. They could clean after.

Abi's on the phone now, in the corner. He tries to motion to her, but she doesn't see him, so he leaves without saying goodbye to anyone.

It's a fair bit cooler now, but still fine for the long shorts he has on. These stupid long shorts. The comments he's been getting all night about them still make his cheeks burn.

He walks quickly, sees nobody, and is skipping down the stone promenade steps in half an hour. He's sweating from the walk, blots at his cheeks with the back of his hand. A text from Fergie appears, asking where he is, but before he can reply his phone vibrates and dies in his hand.

He hears them before he sees them. Just up ahead, a group of shadowy black figures, resting on the huge rocks that keep the tide from the promenade.

'... to take it so serious. It's just a wee friendly bet for the end of the school year.'

'Aye, even though Fitz hasn't been to school since he was about, ten!'

'All the important things you need to know in life, you won't learn them in a classroom, will ya?'

'Fuck me. That's the smartest thing he's ever said. Did you record that?'

Laughter.

Jack pastes a smile on his face – it sounds like Katie must have left, he can't hear her.

He squints as he gets nearer, trying to make out who is who. No glasses.

'Oi oi!' shouts Ben.

The smell of weed hits Jack in the face like a physical barrier and he tries not to wrinkle his nose.

'There he is!' Jack is close enough to see his friends now: Ben takes a swig from a huge plastic bottle of cider that has been picked up since he left. 'Casanova.'

'Cassie who?' Fergie asks. He is standing up on a rock, eyes on his phone screen, and he passes the joint to Ben without looking up.

'Never mind.' Ben rolls his eyes at Jack, and Jack feels that pull towards his friends again. He likes that, being included in a joke.

When the joke is on someone else, and he can just roll his eyes back, or grin, and that's the right thing to do. That's the right answer. Those moments, that's what makes it worth it. Being friends with them. Ben has relegated the cider bottle to the ground in favour of the weed. 'Get your dick sucked, Casanova?'

Jack pretends to take a bow. 'My lips are…' He stops, his lowered eyes spotting something.

He was wrong – Katie is still there. She's lying next to Fitzy, her back against the rocks, her head lolling to the side, resting on his shoulder. Fitzy has his arm around her, looks smug when he sees Jack looking. She's asleep. Or, maybe…

'She pass out?' Jack asks, trying to sound merely curious. He feels his heart beating fast under his T-shirt, and he can't quite put a finger on why.

'Aye,' says Ben, who is now smoking with his shoulders hunched, the way he always does when he's smoking weed instead of tobacco. Jack isn't sure why he does that, but he's copied the action himself more than once. He knows there is no scientific logic behind it, it's not like it'll get you stoned faster. Ben takes a puff and adds, 'Couldn't hack it. Or maybe Fitz is so boring she's just fallen asleep.'

They all laugh, including Jack.

'Goin' for a piss,' says Fergie, putting his phone away. 'Soupy, don't follow me, I know what you Campbells are like for cock munching.'

Jack grits his teeth and forces a smile as they all whoop with laughter.

'Number you on now?' Ben asks him.

'Eight,' Jack says coolly.

'Proof!' demands Fitzy, using his free arm to point accusingly at him. His eyes are wide and wild. 'I don't believe you!'

'Nobody cares what you believe,' Ben says. 'This game is between me and Soupy.' He is smiling at Jack as if they're sharing a secret, but if they are, Jack doesn't know what it is. 'I believe you, Soup.'

Jack nods and smiles, used to playing it cool, used to lying in front of his friends. He's been doing it his whole life.

'D'ya wanna smoke?' Ben holds the joint out to him.

'Sure.' He takes it and takes the smallest puff he can manage before handing it back. He tries to push it out of his mouth without inhaling, willing himself not to cough. He's imagined more than once how mortifying it would be to have an asthma attack in front of them. If that happened, he really would rather it just killed him.

Ben is still looking at him, a strange glint in his eyes.

'Are yous staying out much longer?' Jack asks, trying to sound casual.

'Why?' asks Fergie, strutting back towards them and zipping up his trousers. 'Your sister have a bedtime for you? Or are you just a bit chilly in them shorts?'

'Just wondering,' Jack says. His eyes keep flicking to Katie, who hasn't moved since he got here. She's really very drunk, and she must have had some of the weed, to be like this. He knows where she lives, walked her home a few times when they were eleven or twelve. Abi picked her up that day. How can he make it seem casual that he wants to walk her home? They'll take the piss out of him for months if he shows any concern for her. The only way they wouldn't would be if...

He hesitates. Ben sees him looking and follows his gaze.

'What are you thinking, Soupy, you dirty bastard?' He passes the joint back to Fergie and comes to put an arm around Jack's shoulders. 'Are you thinking we're tied?'

Jack snorts a laugh. 'No, no—'

'I was thinking the same thing,' Ben continues. 'Eight apiece. Who wins if we're tied? Only, it's not over yet, is it?' He leans into Jack's face and wiggles his eyebrows. 'You want to have a go, don't you?'

'Oi!' says Fitzy from the ground. 'That's not fair! If anyone's having a go, it's me!'

'Why, cuz you've had your arm round her for the last half hour?' Fergie asks. 'And that's the closest you've been to a woman from when you were suckin' on your ma's tits?'

Ben and Fergie laugh, high-pitched and cruel.

Over Fitzy's protests, Ben continues to purr in Jack's ear, 'You're thinkin' about it, aren't you? Dirty wee fucker.' He laughs right in

275

Jack's ear, so loud it hurts and he winces. Ben's breath is sweet with weed and sour with beer, and the deodorant he plasters himself in has worn off over the course of the long night.

'I was just—' Jack can't think of a way to say it that sounds right. 'I was – I'll maybe take her home.'

The others whoop.

'I'll bet you'd love that,' Ben says. 'I bet you would. But that's not fair. It's only fair if she picks you over me. And I don't think she will. She's been giving me *fuck me* eyes all night, I think she's gaggin' for it.'

Jack smiles, but his teeth are gritted again.

'Wise up,' he says, keeping his smile on, keeping his voice light. 'She's barely conscious. How could she *pick*—'

'Oh, she's heard yous,' says Fitzy.

They all turn to look at Katie, whose head has fallen to the other side. She twists her neck up and around until her gaze lands on Jack. Jack breathes a sigh of relief, but only for a second.

'Jack Campbell,' she slurs. She's had more to drink, Jack thinks. A lot more. She points at him, one eye closed as though to try and see him better. 'Jack... Cam. I know you. You're – you in your, in Pine Street. You know.' Suddenly she raises her voice. 'Jack knows what I mean! Jack Campbell knows what I mean!' She is properly shouting now. 'You ask him.'

Jack's heart beats quickly, but he shares Fergie's confused look as though he has no idea what she's on about.

Do not mention it please do not tell them I tried it on when we were kids and you rejected me so definitely please do not tell them how pathetic and frigid I was please don't tell them

Fitzy snorts. 'Daft bitch.'

Without looking at him, Katie pushes Fitzy's arm away from her and struggles to her feet.

'Got to get – going to get myself... Another drink. No more smokes, thank you.'

She isn't directing this at anyone in particular but holds her hands out to Jack in a somewhat defensive gesture.

She starts to stumble away, her heel catching yet again in the stones and making her trip. The boys laugh.

'Wait,' Jack hears himself saying. 'There's plenty of cider here, why don't you stay—'

'Fuck you, Jack Campbell!' Katie shouts, her voice high and loud, her eyes struggling to focus on him. 'Stop trying to get me – *drunk*. You and your tiny cock can fuck off.'

The uproar from the other three is deafening. As Katie stumbles down the stones towards the sea, Fitzy stands and joins Ben and Fergie, who have their arms around one another. Ben is crying of laughter, and Fergie is pointing at Jack, hardly able to breathe. Fitzy ticks, then again, then again, each time barking a laugh.

'His – his tiny cock!' Fergie manages. 'Fuck me, she's quality.'

'She fucking is, she's great,' Ben agrees. 'We should bring her out more often. What do you reckon, Soupy? Don't think she's picked you this time, mate.'

'She's wild when she's drunk,' adds Fergie. 'My sister had a night out with her once and took some photos, you wanna see the cut of her. Drunk mess.'

'Mess,' agrees Fitzy, as though he is contributing.

Jack is facing away from them, watching Katie in her slow manoeuvre down the beach, his cheeks blazing, and a strange feeling in his chest.

How dare she.

He was trying to help her, he was the only one thinking about her safety, and she goes and says that. In front of *them*. Why did she even say it? She's never seen his cock. She was just trying to hurt him, to get him back for… For what happened. Or what didn't happen, really.

Not for the first time, he wonders why she didn't tell anyone about it.

She didn't even ask to move seats in science or form class – they sat beside each other until she left school, making small talk and never looking at each other.

Maybe she was just as embarrassed as him. Maybe it was all a misunderstanding, and nowhere near as serious as he's come to think over the last few years. Maybe they were on the same page and she lost her nerve at the last minute. Yes, that's probably it. She wanted it too, all of the things he'd wanted – but they were very young, and she didn't know how to handle it.

Katie trips on a stone and falls forward, her arms trying – and failing, this time, to break her fall.

While the boys' laughter is renewed, Jack runs towards her, glad to get away from the scene of his greatest embarrassment. He'll never be able to look the boys in the face again.

'Did you hurt yourself?' he asks, coming to a stop next to her, crouching to put a hand on her back.

'DON'T!' Katie shouts, swatting blindly behind her, in his general direction. 'Leave me – leave me alone. I don't need… No more weed.'

'No more weed,' Jack agrees. 'Why don't you come and sit down over here, and when you get yourself together a bit we can walk you home. Yeah?'

'Fuck off,' Katie mumbles.

She brushes her face and hair with her hands, and examines the front of her dress. There is a long rip in the fabric, where she has landed and cut it on the sharp stones. Jack notices her makeup is running, her mascara pooling under her eyes, and he wonders if he should tell her.

'My fucking dress,' she whispers, trying in vain to pull the torn pieces together. 'I made it myself.'

Against his will, Jack is impressed. But he can't let on, the boys aren't too far behind him. Can't be impressed by anything girls do. Not out loud.

'You've ripped your tights as well,' he points out, and when Katie moves herself around, the white leg beneath the long ladder glints in the moonlight. Her leg is bleeding. Badly. 'Does it hurt? There are stones in it.'

Katie nods miserably, and lets herself sit down on her bum, like a child.

'It's the fucking weed,' she murmurs, and Jack knows exactly what she means. The first few times he smoked with the boys, his head felt like it was swimming alongside him, and he had the strongest, most overwhelming desire to sleep for a week. 'I feel...' She trails off, closing her eyes, and Jack notices her torso is swaying somewhat, as though she's dizzy even though she's sitting down.

He should take her home.

'Can you walk?' he whispers. 'Do you want me to—'

'Speak up!' calls Fergie. The boys have caught up to them and are circling them. 'No use whispering sweet nothings when you can shout them. It's all about proof, Soupy! We going up to the rockpools or not?'

'Rockpools?' Jack asks, frowning. He hasn't been there since he was a child. Abi used to take him after school sometimes, and they'd dip his net into the pools and see what fish they could find. He found the net in one of his drawers the other day and smiled at it fondly.

'Bit more private,' Ben says, as though this answers the question.

Katie has stood up and is teetering on one leg, trying to take off her tights.

'Sticking – to me,' she pants. Her heels have been removed and she holds them in one hand. She lurches forward, dangerously, and Jack flinches, but she manages to slide her tights off and ball them up in her fist. Ben, Fergie and Fitzy, of course, wolf whistle and jeer. Because that's what they do.

'Rockpools,' Katie announces, as though it had been her idea, and she starts to stride, barefoot, back up towards the sandy part of the beach.

The boys laugh and follow her.

'Here!' she says, as an afterthought, turning back to Jack. She thrusts the tights and shoes into his hands and he has no choice but to accept them. 'Take these.'

Fitzy makes a noise like a horse and the three boys pretend to gallop off ahead of them. Ben stops to pick up the cider from where he has set it, then turns to Jack and winks.

Jack looks miserably at the load he is being asked to carry and considers dropping them all onto the sand. But then, how would she walk home? He's not sure he could piggyback her the whole way. He sighs, wraps the thin tights around his scarred hand like a bandage and carries the shoes by the heels.

It takes only ten minutes to get to the rockpools. Up the beach, through the trees.

Jack watches from the back as Katie leads the way, veering to one side and then the other, twice almost lurching forward to fall, but they make it with no more injuries. He worries about her bare feet on the stony beach, then the dry grass and rocks, but Katie doesn't seem to notice.

Ben and Fergie are speaking quietly to one another, their heads pressed close together. Twice he hears them snort with laughter, once they turn in unison to glance at him. He wonders if it's about the shorts again. These fucking shorts.

Katie takes the cider from Ben's hand and goes to take a swig.

'Oh, no you don't.' Ben puts his hand over the top and leans towards her. 'What's the magic word?'

'Please,' Katie says.

'And do I get a kiss?'

She pecks him once on the mouth and pulls the bottle away to take a drink. It seems to give her a much-needed energy boost, and she makes for the first rockpool with renewed vigour.

'We skinny dipping?' Fitzy asks, trying to waggle his eyebrows and ticking dramatically.

'I think we should go a bit further,' Ben announces. 'To the hidden ones on the other side.'

He leads the way towards a dense thicket of trees. The hidden entrance is here somewhere.

They push their way through the tangles of stiff branches and emerge into the clearing Jack recognises from his childhood.

Two rockpools, side by side, both filled with seawater and all manner of little creatures.

Now, in the real, deep dark, the moonlight glints off Ben's head as he struts on in front. He shaves his head, which Jack has always thought was an unusual choice, but the others say it's because he's bald anyway, so maybe he doesn't have much of a choice. Better to choose what people will say about you than have them come up with their own ideas. Jack understands that.

Fitzy and Fergie are pushing one another now, pretending they're going to get the other into the pools. They're not like eighteen-year-olds at all, more like kids.

Jack can't see the cider anywhere and worries someone has thrown the empty plastic bottle to the ground.

Katie, with her new burst of energy, is close behind them, striding quickly as though she's got somewhere to go. Jack has a feeling maybe she thinks she's going home. Her eyes are unfocused.

He should have stayed at Abi's party, he thinks miserably. Should have waited and gone home with Decky. Then he'd be in bed, asleep, instead of trekking aimlessly about the town at this time of night with a girl who hates him and says horrible things about him and a group of lads he's starting to lose patience with. It'll be different when he gets into MUSE. He can make new friends there. He can be anyone he wants to be. He can start wearing fingerless gloves to hide his scar, and then nobody will think him any different. Abi says university will be different anyway, that nobody will comment on his hand because nobody will care, even if they do notice. He's not so sure about that. He notices the flaws in people, and he considers himself a fairly nice guy, so if *he* notices…

But if he hadn't come, Katie would be alone with the boys. She might never get home.

He's doing a good deed, really.

'How much further? My feet are so sore.' Jack turns to face Katie. For the first time, she doesn't sound hysterically drunk. She sounds like a child, fed up and tired and complaining. 'I'm so tired, if we'll be much more – much longer – I have to have a sleep.'

'You can't have a sleep here,' Jack says uncomfortably. 'There's nowhere to—'

'Jack Campbell,' Katie says, shaking her head as if it's the most ridiculous thing she's uttered in her life. 'Fucking Jack Campbell.'

She pushes past him, using a finger to stab at his shoulder as if he is nothing. As if he is a tiny insignificance, not even worth the bother of looking at.

He's done trying to help her.

Fuck her.

Katie leans against one of the huge boulders surrounding the rockpools, and lets her head fall back against it.

'No skinny dipping,' she says, waggling a finger at no one in particular. 'It's too cold.'

Jack looks at her feet, at the toenails that have each been painted a different colour. He realises he's still holding her shoes, so he makes a point of throwing them towards her, trying to show how little he cares for her stuff. One falls into the pool, the other scuffs along the ground and comes to rest at Fitzy's feet. Once again, Fitzy has taken his position at her side, one arm around her.

'You got another smoke, Benny?' asks Fergie.

'Nah.' Ben isn't looking at his friend, he's watching Katie the way you might watch a trail of clever ants carrying food away from a picnic. With great interest and the slightest hint of disgust.

'Damo being a scobe, is he?'

'Shut up, Fergie.'

Fergie tuts. 'I'm bored now. She was good craic earlier, you all were, but now—'

'Now, she's gonna be number nine,' Ben says with a grin.

Jack catches Fergie's eye for the briefest moment.

Katie's head has lolled forward, so her chin rests on her chest. Fitzy has a hand on her cheek, and is saying her name.

'Nah, sorry mate,' Fitzy says. 'She's gone.'

Katie's is out cold, her eyes rolling.

Nobody will be able to get her home now.

'I know what'll wake her up,' Ben says. 'Jack, get your phone out.'

He registers both the proper use of his first name and the strange request. He doesn't try to hide his confusion. 'What do you need it for?'

'Get your phone out, Jacky.'

Jack stares at Ben, his heart beating quickly, feeling a slow trickle of unease in his stomach. 'It's dead,' he answers finally.

Ben tuts. 'Same. Who's got a phone? Fergie, get your phone out.'

Fergie looks just as confused, but he obediently takes his iPhone – the same colour and model as Jack's – from his pocket.

'Set it to record,' Ben instructs. 'No question about proof when it comes to me.'

And Jack starts to understand, on some level, in some deep, dark part of his brain, what is about to happen. Maybe what was inevitable when someone – who even was it? – had suggested the rockpools, on a warm, dark night, with a very drunk woman in tow.

'Give Soupy your phone.'

And then Ben is undoing his belt, and Jack feels sick, but he cannot look away.

Fitzy is giggling, as if it all might be a joke.

Fergie is pushing his phone at Jack, and Jack takes it, numbly, seeing it is set to record. He can't see anything else on the screen, it is too dark.

Why me why have you given me this phone

He wants to ask it out loud but the time for talking seems to have passed. Nobody else is.

He looks at Katie, in the animal print dress she made herself. The torn dress, the bloody leg. She has no shoes on. Her toenails each a different colour. Where are her tights? They're no longer in his hand; he's dropped them. Useless Jack.

It's Fergie's phone why not him why am I holding Fergie's phone why me

He thinks of her doodles on the margins of her homework pages. Of the way drawing boxes calmed her down.

Why did you ask for my phone first why is it always me why do you all torture me

Then he thinks of the way she didn't come to his sixteenth birthday, even though he'd invited her. Even though he'd crossed his fingers every single day in the week leading up to it, hoping and praying that she would come, that he could apologise and make it right.

Because I always do whatever you say, that's why

Of the fact she didn't even text to say happy birthday, didn't ask him afterwards how it was or apologise that she couldn't make it.

Because I do anything you dare me to do because that is who I am because that is how desperate I am to fit in with you and not be the butt of your jokes

Of the wish he'd made as he'd blown out his sixteen candles, that she would realise what a prick tease she'd been and pay for standing him up.

He thinks of her saying 'tiny cock' to him in front of his friends.

And he lets it happen.

It is only after – and it can't have taken more than four, five minutes – that he thinks about what this means. What the word is for it. Giving it a word makes it real. He glances down at the phone in his hand and stops the recording.

Ben is saying something.

The other two, who had looked uncomfortable at the start, seem to have accepted this turn of events. Seem to have, in a way, been enjoying themselves.

Jack starts moving backwards, his eyes still on Katie.

His body feels empty.

'Soupy, what's up?'

He doesn't answer, just keeps moving away from them. He has to get away.

What would Abi say, if she knew?

Oh my God, Jack thinks. *Abi.*

'Soupy, where are you going? Come here!'

'At least give me my phone?' Fergie calls. 'Soups, wait a minute!'

Fergie moves as if he is going to give chase, but Ben stops him with a hand.

'He won't say anything,' Ben says. Jack knows his friend – his friend? really? – is looking at him, but he won't look back. He can't. 'He won't say a word. He knows what'll happen if he does.'

The Blindspot

'That's great, but I need my phone. Oi! SOUPY!'

But Jack is still stumbling, picking up speed, unable to look at Katie any more, unable to look at any of them. He trips on a stone but he barely notices.

'Say nothing!' Ben calls. For the first time, a hint of panic in his voice. 'Say FUCKING NOTHING!'

Jack says nothing.

He stumbles until he is at the secret entrance, pushes his way through the opening in the hedge, his heart hammering in his ears, his blood pumping as if he's run a marathon—

He stops, turns off Fergie's phone with a shaking finger.

He isn't sure why, he just knows he doesn't want it turned on. It feels warm in his hand, then warm in his pocket, hot against his leg like it's on fire. Like what's on it will surely burn through him.

He doesn't want to talk to them, doesn't want to see them ever again. None of them. Wants to get rid of this stupid tarnished phone – maybe he'll even toss his own, what's the point in having it? – and forget it ever happened and never even think about them again.

None of them.

Fuck them.

Fuck them all.

And then he starts running.

ACKNOWLEDGEMENTS

My first thank you is to my agent, Charlotte Seymour, who is a complete professional, is always quick to answer my questions and set me right, and who is just generally a joy.

A huge thank you also to my extremely talented friend and mentor, Kira-Anne Pelican, whose invaluable advice and feedback in the early stages of drafting and planning for *The Blindspot* saved me a lot of time and a lot of rewriting. I am in awe of your skill.

I received some extremely helpful technical advice from Stuart Gibbon of Gib Consultancy on the policing aspects of *The Blindspot*, for which I am so grateful. Any errors or unlikelihoods in this respect are entirely my own. Or perhaps they just made for a better story.

Thank you of course to my best friend and first reader always, KP. I hope you are my first reader for the next 60 years. Likewise, thank you to my mum and dad who, while not my first readers, are perhaps the most enthusiastic ones.

Finally, I am incredibly grateful for the enthusiasm, support, and skill that Carolyn and the team at Bedford Square Publishers have shown in making *The Blindspot* into a reality.

Oh, and John – you're welcome.

ABOUT THE AUTHOR

Photo credit © Karen Proctor

Hannah King is a writer from County Down, Northern Ireland, where she lives with her partner and their dogs. *The Blindspot* is her second novel, after the critically acclaimed *She and I*.

 @_hankingauthor